Possessed...

There she was. Susan Mitchell. Standing by the bottom of my son's bed with a luminescent smile on her face. As I watched, a shadow rose up behind her, and I caught the merest whiff of jackal bites and crocodile smiles. Susan turned, pulling back when she saw what was there. I decided that if she was making tracks, so would we. I started to back up, pushing Kip behind me, but the apparition was growing larger, amorphous and swirling like a whirlpool of energy, and I found myself mesmerized. I couldn't look away.

"Mom? Mom!" Kip's tentative voice shook me out of my paralysis. As I broke free from the trance, I thought I caught a glimpse of cold steel teeth in the heart of the shadow. I broke into a sweat—this couldn't be good. Couldn't be safe. I had to get Kip out of the room *now,* but before I could move the creature lunged, dissipating Susan's image as it shot right through her misty body on a beeline for . . . me!

Chintz 'n China Mysteries by Yasmine Galenorn

GHOST OF A CHANCE
LEGEND OF THE JADE DRAGON
MURDER UNDER A MYSTIC MOON
A HARVEST OF BONES
ONE HEX OF A WEDDING

Ghost of a Chance

Yasmine Galenorn

BERKLEY PRIME CRIME, NEW YORK

GHOST OF A CHANCE

A Berkley Prime Crime Book / published by arrangement with the author

PRINTING HISTORY
Berkley Prime Crime mass-market edition / August 2003

Copyright © 2003 by Yasmine Galenorn.
Cover art by Stephanie Thompson Henderson.
Cover design by Jill Boltin.
Text design by Kristin del Rosario.

For information address: The Berkley Publishing Group, a division of Penguin Group (USA) Inc., 375 Hudson Street, New York, New York 10014.

ISBN: 0-425-19128-1

Berkley Prime Crime Books are published by The Berkley Publishing Group, a division of Penguin Group (USA) Inc., 375 Hudson Street, New York, New York 10014. The name BERKLEY PRIME CRIME and the BERKLEY PRIME CRIME design are trademarks belonging to Penguin Group (USA) Inc.

PRINTED IN THE UNITED STATES OF AMERICA

10 9 8 7 6 5

To the memory of my mother, Helen,
who has visited me from "the other side"
I miss you
1927—2000

ACKNOWLEDGMENTS

"Thank you's" are due to many people: Samwise, my wonderful husband; Carolyn Agosta, my brilliant critique partner; Jeff Kleinman—for his support, advice, and encouragement.

To my agent, Meredith Bernstein, and my editor at Berkley, Christine Zika—so many thanks to both of you for taking a chance on me and for helping me shape the book into its final form.

Huge hugs are due to friends, both online and offline: Alexandra, Aaron, Siduri, Sue, my sister Wanda, and all the wonderful members of Writers Will Be Warped. Also a heartfelt thank you to Ukko, Rauni, Mielikki, and Tapio.

And last, to all of my readers, both old and new. Without you, all of our stories would languish in the corner, dust-covered and forgotten.

Bright Blessings and thank you!
~the Painted Panther~
~Yasmine Galenorn~

Writing is nothing more than a guided dream.

—JORGE LUIS BORGES (1899–1986)
Doctor Brodie's Report

One

❧

MY NAME IS Emerald O'Brien and I never set out to be a detective, but when Susan Mitchell's ghost appeared in my bedroom and told me that she'd been murdered, my life took a U-turn and I've never looked back.

Oh, sure, most people would have been scared out of their wits, but I'm used to dealing with the supernatural, so spirits and spooks don't bother me unless I figure out that my shadowy guests intend some sort of nasty surprise. My Nanna taught me how to work with my psychic abilities early on, and when the ghosts come calling, I don't freak out or hide under the covers or scream for help. I fully admit to being a coward when it comes to ill-tempered brutes and eight-legged beasties, and I have an unnatural hesitation about eating mushy bread. But show me a ghost and I can usually hold my own.

I'm not a professional ghost-hunter, though. I own the Chintz 'n China Tea Room. Not Tea *Shoppe,* spelled with the cutesy extra *pe,* but *Room.* We sell fine china, go hunting for rare pieces customers ask for, serve tea and cookies all day long, and soup for lunch during the week. I also offer my services as a tarot reader.

Chiqetaw may be a small town, but I get my fair share of clients coming in. Mainly wonderful older women who want to know how the coming holidays are going to be, or if it's the right time to make that investment they were planning on. I don't answer health questions, I don't lie and tell them what they want to hear, I just read the cards as they fall, and most of my customers come back for more. They seem to find my candor refreshing, a relief to me since I'm not always as diplomatic as I probably should be.

Considering that I'm the only professional tarot reader in town, and considering my handiwork with folk magic, it's not surprising that I got labeled the "witch of the village." At least they didn't stick "old" in there—I don't quite fit any of the clichés in the movies, you know—the scary old hag out on the edge of the woods, or the lovely wise woman always ready to heal the sick. I'm thirty-six, divorced, and as far from a domestic goddess as you can get. I wouldn't know my way around a health food store if you paid me, and I have two brilliant, quirky children.

Anyway, that's where Susan Mitchell comes in. Or her ghost, rather. Given my reputation, it didn't really surprise me when she showed up at my bedside. I just wish she'd picked a better night. I was lying under the covers, fighting my usual insomnia, with a sinus headache so bad that it felt like somebody was using my face as a punching bag. I had on my sleep mask, trying to doze off in that desperate "please, oh, please, let me go to sleep" way all insomniacs have, when I heard a rustle in the corner. Samantha yowled and bounded off the bed. Somebody else was in the room.

Great. My eight-year-old wanted to get up to play Ninja Fighters or some equally violent video game and had startled the cat. Or my daughter was sneaking in from a late night's star gazing and wanted to talk over her latest discovery. I never knew when I'd find her sprawled on the roof in the middle of the night, using the telescope to spy on both Mars and the neighbors. More than once she held me breathless as she filled me in on some pretty kinky goings-on next door before I'd snapped out of it and warned her about the dangers of becoming a teenaged voyeur.

Prepared for anything—or so I thought—I sat up and pulled off the mask and there she was. Susan Mitchell. Or rather, the ghostly remains of Susan Mitchell. Of course, at the time, I didn't know that was her name. All I knew was that a short, translucent blonde was hovering about three inches above the edge of my bed. With a groan, I rolled over and closed my eyes, willing her to go away. After a moment the hairs on my arms stood at attention and I knew she was still there. Sigh. I was going to have to take care of this.

I swung my feet over the edge of the bed and felt for my slippers, all the while keeping track of the now-alert and rather excited-looking spirit. The gleam in her eye made me nervous, and I wondered if I'd have to resort to my handy-dandy middle-of-the-night exorcise-those-beasties ritual, but she pulled back as I poked my arms through the sleeves of my flannel robe. Then she folded her hands together, prayerlike. Maybe it was this gesture that warmed my heart, maybe it was the grateful look on her face. Whatever the reason, I felt a little kindlier toward her and, sinus headache or not, decided to find out what she wanted.

I tucked my hands in the crook of my underarms. It was so cold I could see my breath. *The Sixth Sense* had it right—it did get colder when ghosts were around, but it wasn't because they were angry. I'd dealt with enough spirits to know that they seemed to coast in off the astral breeze and bring the wake of it with them.

The ghost hovered there, about two feet taller than me thanks to the fact that she was floating in midair. She seemed to be waiting for me to speak. I wasn't sure what to say. Most spirits I'd dealt with in the past hadn't been interested in the humans who shared their space. I rather preferred it that way.

After a few minutes of this standoff, I decided that she was either shy or didn't know how to speak to me. If I ever wanted to get back to sleep, I'd have to be the one to make the first move. I took a deep breath and planted myself on the foot of the bed, near enough to seem friendly, but not enough to be a target should she decide to get nasty. "Hi, I'm Emerald. You can call me Em. Who are you, and what do you want?" Not very original, but blunt and to the point.

She cocked her head, beaming. I hoped she wasn't one of those spirits who could manipulate physical objects. The last thing I needed was a hug from beyond the grave. Granted, my grandmother had done just that, after Roy blackened my eye and stomped out to go live with his bimbo. But right now I didn't feel like being the recipient of any ghostly embrace.

She seemed to be trying to speak—her mouth moved but I couldn't hear anything. I shook my head and she tried again. Finally, her eyes flashed with frustration and she glided over to my desk, which sat below the Monticello window overlooking the backyard. A pen began to vibrate and went scribbling across the stationery scattered on the top of the desk.

In scrawls that were almost illegible, the name "Susan Mitchell" covered the page. The name seemed familiar, but I couldn't place it. I looked at the ghost. "You? You're Susan Mitchell?"

She nodded. As soon as she filled another page, the pen fell to the floor. I gingerly picked up the paper and looked at the letters that danced across the paper. What I saw made my blood run cold. I glanced up, and Susan looked at me wistfully. She pointed to the note, then to me, and vanished in a puff of icy air.

I looked at the note again. The words were damning. In looping letters she had written: *"I was murdered by my husband but nobody knows. Help me."*

What did she expect me to do? True, I was considered the town witch, but I owned a *china shop,* for cripes' sake—I didn't run a detective agency. Now I was supposed to go to the police and say that Susan Mitchell's ghost had appeared by the foot of my bed, begging me to prove that her husband had killed her? I didn't know who she was or where she had lived. I didn't even know if she was telling the truth—ghosts could lie, too. And I wasn't sure why she'd shown up in my bedroom, except for the fact that I was a pretty good medium and happened to be Chiqetaw's only professional tarot reader when I wasn't busy selling Earl Grey tea and Royal Winton china. But somehow, the paper in my hand seemed to have captured the spirit's mood. Sorrow echoed through her words . . . sorrow and resignation. How could I ignore the plea for help? Just because she was dead didn't mean Susan Mitchell was at peace. But what could I do? And where would I start?

Feeling more awake than ever, I trundled downstairs. Nothing beat a good pot of Moroccan Mint served up in a chintzware teacup at three in the morning when you were trying to figure out how to help a ghost prove she was murdered.

MORNING CAME FAR too early. I squinted, aware in some faint corner of my mind that I had fallen asleep in the rocking chair, and found myself staring into my son's bewildered face. My eyelashes were stuck together, and there was a ball of fuzz on my lap—Nebula, one of Samantha's kittens, had curled up for a good, long snooze. I gently shooed the cat down. I had the feeling that standing up was only going to lead to pain, so I avoided it for as long as possible. In the end, I gave Kip a blurry-eyed grin as I pushed myself to my feet.

"You okay, Mom?"

I leaned down and planted a kiss on his head. "I'm fine, bud. My insomnia's been acting up, but it's nothing to worry about. Have you had breakfast yet?"

He shrugged. "Leftover pie."

"Healthy, huh?" Nature called and I made a stiff-legged dash upstairs to my bathroom.

Sun slanted through the rose window that I had the carpenter install when I bought the house a little over a year ago. The light cast a rosy hue over the pale canary of the walls, and the result always startled me as a blush of tangerine filled the room. I leaned against the vanity as I washed my face, savoring the few moments alone, not thinking of last night, not thinking of the day—just enjoying my own company. My mother had sent me a bar of jasmine-scented soap from her last trip to Hawaii, and I worked up a good lather because I loved the smell and because it felt like soft cream.

After a quick shower, I slapped on some moisturizer and braided my hair so it would dry into a mass of waves. I had stopped dyeing it when we moved to Chiqetaw and only now was getting used to seeing the long, silver strands interweave through the brunette. I tucked a bandanna around my head to keep from catching cold. Utilitarian, if not pretty.

Still blurry-eyed, I pulled on a pair of jeans and a sweater. As much as I'd rather spend the morning figuring out just what had happened last night, Saturday was cleaning day down at my shop. We opened at noon, after waging war on all the cobwebs and dust bunnies that had collected under the counters and tables throughout the week.

Kip pounded on the door. "Mom, are you sure you're okay? I grabbed a Pop-Tart, too."

I smiled. Eight years old and he didn't know how to work a cereal box yet. My little slacker. But he helped around the house and finished his chores without complaining too loudly, so I wasn't going to bitch about his lack of motor skills in the cornflakes department. I blinked at myself once, twice, then opened the door and shuffled out. My mind was beginning to race, but my body definitely lagged behind.

Kip leaned against the wall with the remains of the toaster pastry. He had a wary look in his eyes and crumbs on his face. I immediately knew something was up. I reached out and tousled his head. "Whatchyu doing, kiddo?"

He gave me one of his long looks. He was so good at them that he could reduce an adult to gibberish within five minutes. I was proud of him for it. Not every woman's son had the ability to disconcert his elders, and it seemed more useful than anything the Boy Scouts could have taught him.

"Waiting for you. Why did you stay up all night?"

Did I detect a hint of concern in his voice? Could Kip have possibly seen the ghost, too? My son was far too psychic for his own good at such a young age. I'd been trying to help him learn how to control and cope with it for the past year. Though his talent had been apparent from birth, it had blossomed out since Roy left us. A lot of things had blossomed since then.

He took a deep breath and plunged ahead with what I was afraid I was going to hear. "Mom, I thought I felt something in the house last night. I had a nightmare."

Nightmare? Kip hadn't had nightmares for over a year. "What was it about, kiddo?"

"Some lady, I guess. I dunno. I woke up in the middle of the night and was worried about you. I thought maybe something was going to hurt you." He swallowed the last of the Pop-Tart and wiped his hands on his jeans.

Normally, when Kip was upset in the middle of the night he would come tapping gently on my door and creep under the covers next to me. That he hadn't done so this time told me that he'd been too frightened to leave the security of his own bed. I didn't want him to worry, didn't want to talk about the ghost until I'd figured out what was going on. "Well, I look all right this morning, don't I? It was probably a dream, my Kipling."

He gave me a penetrating glance, and I knew he knew I was hiding something, but I also knew he knew I wasn't going to tell him until and unless I was good and ready. He nodded and bolted for the stairs, stopping long enough to turn at the railing. "Okay. Can I go over to Sly's?"

Sly was his current best friend and a little con artist, but Kip had enough brains to keep from getting involved in whatever trouble that kid had cooked up. I waved him away. "Wear your jacket—it's cold out. And don't forget that I want you at the store in an hour. Be there." One of the kids' chores was to help out on Saturday mornings. He took the stairs two at a time and vanished out the front door with a slam.

On the way to the kitchen, I stopped by the rocker and picked up the sheets of paper on which my ghostly visitor had written. The moment I touched them, I felt a wave of sadness overwhelm me. I looked at the writing. No, it hadn't been a dream. Susan's presence had been real enough. *"I was murdered by my husband but nobody knows. Help me."* How the hell was I supposed to deal with this? I didn't even know who she was.

I cracked eggs into the skillet and started toasting the bread, while Miranda grabbed the paper from the front porch. She gave me a quick peck on the cheek as I slid our breakfast onto the ruby crystal dishes I had so coveted for years. Roy had thought them too old-fashioned. After he left, I didn't care what he thought. In fact, I had decided to find a set of Cranberry Spode to go with them. The contrast would be startling and eye-catching.

Miranda poured the juice. With a bite of runny yolk on toast, I opened the paper and glanced through the news. There, down at the bottom of the page, an article caught my attention. The headline read, "Local Romance Writer Found Dead in Home."

> Susan Walker Mitchell died Thursday evening after slipping into a diabetic coma. Mae Tailor, the Mitchells' housekeeper, found Ms. Mitchell unconscious upon returning to the residence at about 4:00 P.M. on Thursday afternoon. Blood tests confirmed the presence of both alcohol and Valium in Ms. Mitchell's system, a dangerous combination. However, doctors attribute her death to hypoglycemic coma, brought on by a failure to eat after taking her morning insulin.
>
> "The levels of Valium and alcohol were high, but not within life-threatening ranges," Dr. Johansen, the Mitchells' family physician, stated. "Mrs. Mitchell has been admitted to the hospital four times in the past year for low-blood-sugar seizures . . . unfortunately, no one was with her this time to prevent her from slipping into a coma." Ms. Mitchell died without regaining consciousness.

Ms. Mitchell was well loved for her work in the community theater, but she was best known for her career as a romance novelist. She produced twenty-nine books over the past fifteen years, including the best-selling *Love on Clancy Lane*. Her books are read worldwide.

Survived by her husband, Walter Mitchell, Chiqetaw, and a daughter, Diana Mitchell, Seattle, Ms. Mitchell will be greatly missed.

I stopped reading. *Of course. Susan Mitchell. The romance novelist.* I remembered seeing her mentioned in the paper before, though I'd never met her. The photograph beside the obituary was most definitely that of my ghostly visitor.

"Is everything okay, Mom?" Oh no, not her, too. It was bad enough that Kip had sensed something, but Miranda spooked too easily, and I didn't want her involved in any part of this yet.

I squelched the urge to blurt out the truth. "No . . . no . . . nothing wrong. Go ahead and run along. Remember to be at the store by ten."

She grabbed her pack and raced out the door to catch the bus. Grabbing a pen and a steno book I always keep handy near the phone, I ripped the article out of the paper and tucked everything in my purse.

So my ghost was real, or had been. Diabetic coma? Murder? With a dozen thoughts reeling through my head, I made my way out to the car and pulled out of the driveway. I had a lot to do before opening the shop. The only trouble was, I didn't know where to begin.

Two

✦

CHIQETAW IS AN easy town to navigate—the streets are fairly straight, and the traffic, sparse. It was spitting snow as I guided my car down Main Street. The town council had decided to put up the Christmas decorations early this year, starting the day before Thanksgiving. Now, two weeks before Christmas, strands of colored lights sparkled around the lampposts and bare-branched trees that lined the main drag. I took a deep breath of the chill air that flowed in through the open crack of the window. God, how I loved this time of year.

Forty-five minutes before I was supposed to meet the kids at the store—enough to do a little digging. I pulled into the parking lot of Harlow's Gym. Harlow Rainmark was my best friend in this little burg, and without her I think I'd have gone bananas when I first moved here. Named after Jean Harlow by her starstruck mother, she had valiantly tried to live up to the legend, slipping into dangerous territory as she forced the envelope farther and farther in her youth.

I slammed the door of my Grand Cherokee—one of the few real luxuries I allowed myself—and pushed through the double doors of Chiqetaw's only spa.

Harlow was behind the desk. Her face brightened and she wrinkled her nose. "I was hoping you'd show up. It's dead in here. If it gets any slower I'm going to have to turn this place into a morgue." Her windblown tangle of hair never failed to amaze me. It was as if someone had taken a curling iron and crimped the shoulder-length strands into ribbons of shimmering, coiled gold. It came as no surprise to anyone when they found out that she'd been a professional model until she gave up her career and moved back to Chiqetaw to marry her childhood sweetheart.

"Cleaning day at C 'n C. I'm not due at the store for close to an hour. It's snowing, by the way."

"Ugh." Harlow hated both cleaning and snow. I agreed with her on housework, but the cold—I loved winter. She was much more of a sun bunny than I.

I dropped into one of the chairs that faced the customer service desk. "Sure is dead in here."

She shrugged. "Yeah, I know. What's up?"

I dug into my purse and pulled out my notebook and the clipping. "I need some info if you've got it."

She leaned forward, always curious. The woman had a nose for gossip like no one else I'd ever met, and if I needed to know anything about anybody in this little burg, she was the place to start.

I handed her the obituary and flipped open my notebook. "Susan—did you know her?"

She read the clipping. "Yeah, I knew her. She was in the Chiqetaw Players."

"That's why I asked you." I knew that Harlow was one of the primary sponsors of the little theater group. If anybody knew anything about the members, she would.

Harlow tapped a polished fingernail against the paper. "Susan had talent. Lots of it. I've read all of her books. It's hard to believe that she'd let this happen. I always assumed she was careful about her diabetes. I guess the condition is harder to keep track of than I thought." She handed me back the article. "What do you want to know?"

"What about her husband? Did they have a good marriage?"

She raised one eyebrow. "You aren't looking for a sugar daddy, are you?" When I glared at her, she winked. "Just kidding. I'm going to assume you have a good reason for asking, since I've never known you to go muckraking before." She glanced around. The gym was bare. Luckily, she didn't really need the income. She'd been one of the few smart ones with her money, investing for the days when she would be too old to play the cover girl.

She took a deep breath and slowly let it out. "Susan used to think her marriage was perfect, but I hear she filed for divorce recently. Walt's a scum. Rich and powerful, but a scum. He tried to seduce me last spring, and when I told him to fuck off, he spread a few well-placed rumors that I was a dyke who just married James for his money. Nobody believed him, but nobody would confirm that he was the one who was spreading the gossip, either. I never told Susan though. I didn't want to hurt her."

I knew Harlow well enough to know she wouldn't lie about something like this. "So, Walter's a scuzbag. I wonder why she married him."

Harlow shrugged. "I dunno. We weren't really close. I wanted to be friends and there were times when she opened up, but when I think about it, she never let anybody get too near. You know what I mean? It was almost like she was afraid to let people into her life." A puzzled expression crossed her face. "I wonder what happens to her estate now."

"Won't Walter get it? They were still married."

Harl frowned. "I don't know. They've got a daughter, though I gather she never comes home. Apparently the girl isn't very stable." Leaning forward even though the gym was empty, she whispered, "You know, Susan ran away when she was a teenager. Rumor mill had it that she went chasing after a boy, but I have no idea what happened. She ran off before she graduated. About a year and a half later, she returned to Chiqetaw, pregnant. She married Walter and would never talk about the time she was gone."

I jotted everything down, making brief, terse notes and underlining the words. It made me feel a little bit like a detective, and I bit my lip to keep back a silly grin. I probably wouldn't be able to read my own writing tomorrow, but what I could decipher should jog my memory.

"Interesting." I sat back and contemplated the huge sculpture that took up almost a third of the lobby. Harlow loved being a benefactor; the spa was liberally peppered with local artists' attempts to break into the spotlight.

She rested her legs on the desk, full of old *Shape* and *Muscle & Fitness* magazines, her feet encased in a pair of Sketchers. Chic. Everything about her was trendy, always a few months ahead of everybody else. When I hung out with her too much, I began to feel like a blimp next to that sleek, too-thin, too-toned body of hers.

"Can I ask why you want to know all this?" Harl was used to me talking about all sorts of *ooo*-spooky things, but I wasn't sure how she'd take my latest revelation.

"Susan showed up in my bedroom last night. I think she has some unfinished business she needs to take care of."

She stared at me. "*Susan* was hanging out in your room? You mean her ghost?"

"Well, she's dead. She couldn't be there any other way, now, could she?" I feigned a sudden interest in my fingernails, glancing at Harl through my lowered lashes.

"I see." Her voice was so even it scared me. One of these days, she'd break down and have them cart me away to the funny farm. "And did she tell you what she wanted?" A mixture of laughter and fear danced in her oh-so-blue eyes.

"Kind of."

"Awfully cryptic, aren't we? I have *got* to hear the full story, but I have the feeling you're not going to spill it right now, are you?"

I gave her a rueful grin and stood up. "Not now, babe, but I promise to tell you everything as soon as I've got more time." I was on my way out when another thought struck me. "Hey, I'd love to 'casually' meet a few people who might have been close friends of hers. Is there going to be a reception following the service?"

Harlow tossed her magazine back on the pile. "I have no idea, but I'll try to find out. Meanwhile, why don't you come with James and me to the opening of *Obsidian*? Starts at eight sharp, tonight. It's a play by a local writer. His name is Andrew Martinez, and he was in Susan's writing group." She grinned. "You won't believe what else he writes. Anyway, James and I are taking him out afterward to celebrate the new show. Tag along?"

"Are you sure that I won't be intruding?" I hated being a fifth wheel and chances were Andrew already had a girlfriend. Celebrations like sit-down dinners always felt awkward now that I was divorced.

She got that all-too-hopeful look that always spelled trouble for me. "He's unattached and won't be bringing a date. I'll say that you and I want to play catch up. The autumn's been so hectic that it's really true, you know— we need to spend an afternoon gossiping. And who knows? Maybe something will come of the meeting."

I narrowed my eyes. "It never works out, Harl. Don't even go there. But yeah, I'll come with you. I can use an evening out, and the kids can grab something from McDonald's."

She told me that the play would be at the local high school gymnasium. I gave her a hug and headed out, wondering what she would think when I told her the whole story. Unlike most of the residents of Chiqetaw, Harl accepted my quirkiness without comment, but when I started talking about ghosts, she got spooked. I think she must have been scared by some mutant pervert on a bad Halloween.

BY NOON, WE'D polished every inch of the Chintz 'n China. I excused Kip and Miranda after handing them each a five-dollar bill. "Be home by six at the latest. If you want, stop and pick up some take-out for dinner. I've got to go out for a while tonight and won't have time to fix anything."

They pocketed the money and took off, Miranda for the library and Kip for Sly's. In Seattle, I'd never have been so carefree. Too many things could happen to kids if we didn't keep tabs on them. But in Chiqetaw it seemed as though the outer world hadn't quite caught up. At least not on an everyday basis. Here, it was still safe to leave the car unlocked when I ran into a shop. Kids in Chiqetaw didn't disappear on their way to Mickey D's.

Once Cinnamon and I were alone, I snapped up the "Open" sign and smiled wearily at her. "Well, the place looks better. Thanks for coming in this morning. We needed the help. Starting Monday, I'll need you here all day, six days a week, through the Christmas rush. Can you manage that?"

She nodded, eyes wide. This was her first real job. She was twenty-two and took her responsibility so seriously that sometimes it made me want to laugh, but I didn't, because you just couldn't buy loyalty like that in an employee anymore. The girl had three kids. Her boyfriend had been thrown in jail a little over six months ago. "I can use the extra money." She fiddled with the linen napkins she was folding. "Christmas is going to be tight this year." Tight was right—Cinnamon didn't get any child support, and she lived with her mother.

She put the water on to boil. We served tea and a few baked goods that I ordered from the local bakery every day. On weekdays, we dished up homemade soup and biscuits during the lunch hour. Most of my business, however, came from people buying china and imported teas, jellies, jams, crackers, real anglophile stock and wares.

As she filled three giant thermoses I saw that she had chosen Misty Lemon, Orange Spice, and, of course, the ever-present Earl Grey. With sudden inspiration, I chalked "Citrus Surprise Afternoon" on the menuboard and broke open a couple of jars of marmalade and lemon curd to go with the sliced pound cake and muffins we were selling. The scent of lemon curd made me hungry. Remembering my uneaten breakfast, I slathered a spoonful on a piece of the cake, grinning at Cinnamon as I wiped crumbs off my shirt.

"Is good," I mumbled. She snorted, but within a moment she joined me in the impromptu lunch. We pushed aside the newspapers on one of the little tea tables that set in the alcove by the window and sat down with our tea and cake to wait for the first customers of the day.

Within moments, Nancy Reynolds pushed through the door, looking for her special order. A flurry of snow followed her in—winter had arrived strong and early this year. I popped the last of the cake in my mouth, gulped down my tea, and dove into the afternoon.

BETWEEN CLEANING THE shop and getting ready for the play, I had no time to follow up on any of the information I'd gotten from Harlow. I raced home, made sure the kids were okay, then shuffled through my closet. Someday soon I was going to have to break down and go shopping, like it or not.

Jeans and sweatshirt wouldn't do. I'd always preferred long skirts and warm turtlenecks. I finally decided on a calf-length black rayon skirt, a royal purple turtleneck, and a gold necklace. Dressy, but not so dressy that I'd stand out. I didn't want to admit that I might end up on a blind date. Harl's fix-ups never worked. I perfunctorily sprayed my wrists and neck with Opium and brushed out my hair. The braids had left it with a gentle cascade of waves. It had been a long time since I had a chance to dress up.

Kip meandered into the foyer as I clattered down the stairs. He stopped cold at the sight of me. "Mom, you look great! Where are you going again? I forgot."

"To the opening of a play. One of Harlow's friends wrote it." I fastened a pair of gold hoops on my ears and transferred everything over to my good purse.

Kip pursed his lips in a grin. "Yeah, I bet. She fixing you up again? You sure look ready for a date."

"You're eight going on eighteen, know that?" I pointed to the clock. "I'm not going to be out late, so your homework better be finished by the time I get back. Miranda's in charge, and if something goes wrong, you have my cell number, and Mrs. Trask is right down the street. I called her, she knows I'm going to be out for a couple hours, so she'll be home if you need her."

He snickered—a habit he picked up from me. "Yeah, yeah. My homework's already done." I gave him a hug, and he hugged me back. "You smell good." Softly, he added, "Mom, are you ever going to get married again?"

The question stunned me. Was he worried about me, or worried that I would replace his father? I sat down on the bench in the hall and pulled him over to sit next to me. "What makes you ask that?"

"You seem lonely." With a twinkle in his eye, he poked me in the ribs. "I wouldn't mind, as long as he's nice! It'd be cool to have another guy around again." He jumped up and, waving his bagged sandwich, disappeared into the living room.

Lonely? I grabbed my keys and slid behind the wheel. I suppose, after my reaction to Roy's defection, that it was obvious to the kids that I didn't relish being single, though I'd come a long ways since those days. Granted, I did wander around the house till 3:00 A.M. on the nights when I couldn't sleep, but I thought of myself as happy. Miranda and Kip were good kids, they weren't in trouble, and they were healthy and thriving. My business was doing pretty well, and I lived in a town that, for the most part, accepted my eccentricities. I had friends and a social life of sorts. I could take care of myself.

So was I unhappy being single? As I pulled out of the driveway, I realized that as much as I'd like to, I couldn't answer the question.

Three

❖

DESPITE THE LACK of traffic, I was late getting to the theater and ended up tiptoeing up and down the aisles until I spotted Harlow. I slid into my seat and settled back to watch the show. The play itself was good, but the Chiqetaw Players butchered it. During the performance, I kept stealing glances at the man I assumed was Andrew. He winced every time somebody onstage tripped over a line.

After the show, Harlow introduced us as we trooped backstage to congratulate the cast. Andrew shook my hand. His grip was firm, cool. "May I ask what you thought of the show?"

I mulled over my options. What could I say? I glanced around, no actors in sight. "Uh . . . to be honest, the play itself was wonderful. The production stank. You're not working with the Seattle Rep here."

"You frequent the theater?" He lowered his voice. "I don't think most of the mighty Chiqetaw Players know anything about what they're trying to do."

"I majored in drama." I gave him a sidelong smile. He relaxed, and his eyes lit up in a way that made me think of the minister from Sunday school when I was a little girl, except my minister hadn't had a long, sleek, ink-black ponytail.

Harlow and James were deep in conversation with the lead actress. The flurry of tech talk really didn't interest me. Andrew glared at them. "I don't think it wise for me to go over there right now. I'm not as judicious with my praise as Harlow. Then again, it's not her play." He shrugged with an exaggerated "What can you do?" gesture.

"Must be rough, seeing your work mangled like that." I leaned against one of the dressing tables. I'd worn my high-heeled boots, and they were pinching my toes. They made me feel sexy every time I put them on. Until I had to walk in them, that is.

He took my arm and motioned to the Green Room, where the actors were mingling with other guests. There were two empty places on the sofa and, grateful, I sat down. He sat down next to me, and I moved my knee so it wasn't touching his.

"So tell me, why did you leave the theater?"

"A husband and two children." Simple but true. Yes, officer, I am guilty—I got married, got pregnant, and gave up a golden career as an usher, no doubt.

"You're married?" Andrew glanced at my hand. I thought I saw a glimmer of disappointment in his eyes.

I held up my naked fingers and wiggled them. "Not anymore. Ex as in x-ed out of my life. We split two years ago. I got the kids and he got his mistress." Time to turn the conversation toward my own ends. "Do you work with the Chiqetaw Players a lot?"

There was a loud swell of singing from the crowd—apparently it was someone's birthday—and the noise died down. He glanced around the room. "No, but a woman who was in my writers group convinced me to let her theater troupe produce my new play. Unfortunately, she wasn't . . . couldn't . . . make it to the opening. After that performance, I'm sorry *I* came."

I knew he was talking about Susan; I could feel her energy in his words. Perfect. Now how to continue this thread? "I hear a woman from the Chiqetaw Players died the other day. A real tragedy. She took too much medication or something." There. If he wanted, he could walk right into the snare.

He nodded. "Susan Mitchell. She and I were in the same writing group. She was a good friend. I still can't believe she's dead."

The look on his face made me feel like I'd punched him in the gut. I gave him a sympathetic nod and bit my lip. Sometimes I could be a real bitch and not even realize it, and for once, I didn't like that part of me. "I'm sorry. I didn't realize that we were talking about the same woman." A lie, but I wanted to save face and I didn't want him thinking I was deliberately trying to hurt him.

He gave me a tight smile. "No problem. Susan and I were talking about becoming critique partners, but it never would have worked."

Critique partners? What could he write that would mesh with Susan's work? "Not to pry, but what do you write? I mean, besides plays?"

His teeth flashed white against his naturally tanned skin. "I'm a romance writer, too, though I'm not nearly as well known as Susan was. I write under the name of Andrea Martin."

Romances? The man wrote romance novels? Intrigued, I almost forgot why I was there but what he said next brought me back into focus.

"I think Walter would have objected to our partnership. He didn't appreciate the work she put into her books."

I stared at the floor. He had given me the perfect opening, but I didn't know quite how to proceed. I didn't want to come off like some yellow journalist, scrounging for dirty laundry. But I needed to know. I searched his face. "You were close to her, weren't you?"

He paused for a moment, and when he spoke, it sounded as if he had chosen each word precisely. "She was a good friend. I'm going to miss her."

"I'm sorry." I sat there for another moment, feeling like I should say more. Here he was, hurting over the death of his friend, and all I could manage was vague sentiment. Finally I blurted out, "I'm no good at sympathy—I never know what to say. My ex used to complain about how blunt I was, and I guess he had a point."

Andrew relaxed. He leaned closer as the noise from the crowd got louder. He said something I couldn't hear and I shook my head, so he leaned over, his lips near my ear. "Do you really want to go to dinner with Harl and James?"

I gave him a half-cocked grin and shook my head. His eyes lit up again, and I realized how much they sparkled. "Not really," I confessed. "I want to get out of this crowd, out of these boots, and I'd prefer a bowl of soup instead of a fancy dinner."

"C'mon!" He jumped up, grabbed my hand, and headed for the door. I barely had time to grab my coat and purse as I struggled to keep up. Harlow turned in time to laugh and wave us on. I could have killed her for the knowing wink she sent my way as Andrew dragged me out into the cold.

The streets were beginning to freeze when we stumbled out into the frosty night. I loved the squeak of new snow under my boots—it made me think of northern nights and the aurora borealis—a clean, clear feeling. We only had a few inches of snow so far, but my breath left puffs of ice crystals in front of my face, and I glanced at the sky. The clouds had parted, and a shimmering expanse of stars twinkled overhead. The temperature was going to plummet.

"So, where do you want to go for that bowl of soup? Forest's End is still open, it's a good diner." Andrew let go of my hand and fumbled in his pockets for his gloves. I pulled mine out of my purse and slid them on, holding one hand over my nose and mouth so the chill air didn't bite into my lungs.

A glance at my watch told me that it was almost nine. "Not to be forward, but what about my place? I have turkey soup in the refrigerator. I also have two children who I need to get home to. Otherwise, I'm going to have to take a rain check."

"Sounds good to me. I'll follow you in my car." He waited until I was safely in my Cherokee. We crept out of the parking lot onto roads glistening with black ice.

Once home, I slammed the car door and motioned for Andrew to follow me up the stairs to the front porch. The light in Miranda's room was on, but the window was closed. For once, it was too cold for her to perch on the roof. Andrew followed my gaze and looked curiously at the railing. I could see the question in his eyes.

"My daughter is studying astronomy; she likes to sit on the roof, so I built her a guardrail." I waited for the usual reaction that I got when people realized I let my daughter hide out on the roof at night with a telescope, but he grinned.

"Better than having her roaming the streets. Now, you said something about turkey soup?"

One of Kip's video games echoed from the living room—a series of *ughs* and *crashes* and *oofs*. Mario Brothers maybe, or whatever he was playing nowadays. I couldn't keep up with all of them.

The scent of the rose-cinnamon potpourri drifted through the air. I loved my home. Comfort—we were all comfortable here. Flooded with a deep sense of satisfaction, I shook off my coat and hung it in the closet. Andrew handed me his, and we sat on the bench that stretched along the wall of the foyer to take off our boots.

Miranda came galloping down the stairs. She stopped short at the sight of the strange man in our hallway. I introduced them. Andrew waited for her to extend her hand first. I liked that—I would never bring a man into my home whom I felt might disturb my children in any way. She gave him the once-over, then turned to me. "What show did you see?"

I planted a quick kiss on her forehead. "We were at a play, not the movies. In fact, Andrew wrote the show—it's called *Obsidian*."

"Jenny's mom is in that . . . Mrs. Dillon." She led the way into the living room, where Kip gave us a dazed nod. He got so caught up in his games that I could probably waltz around naked and he'd never notice. But at Andrew's appearance, he let go of the mouse and asked, "Who's this?"

Andrew leaned over to look at the computer game that Kip was involved in. "Andrew Martinez is the name. Hope you guys don't mind, but your mother invited me over for a bowl of soup, and frankly, I'm starved. What are you playing?" I watched them interact, joking around at the computer. Kip missed having a man around the house, and I always kept an eye on him with male friends so he wouldn't get too attached.

"Who wants soup?" Everybody did, and so I stabbed my thumb toward the kitchen. They dutifully trooped in, and I put Miranda to work making toast while Kip set the table. Andrew got stuck with making hot cocoa. He wrinkled his nose at the Swiss Mix box.

"I don't think so. Do you have sugar, milk, and cocoa powder?"

I grinned. "Why? Don't you like my easy-does-it short-cut?"

He laughed and tossed the box of cocoa mix back on the counter. "Homemade soup deserves real hot cocoa. Kip, why don't you show me where to find a heavy pan and we'll make it up right."

Miranda poked me in the ribs and I decided to interpret her jab as approval. Andrew whisked cocoa and sugar together, and added milk he steamed using my espresso machine. He finished with a drop of peppermint extract and set Kip to searching for the bag of marshmallows I had tucked away from Thanksgiving. The soup was hot, the toast was brown and crunchy, and we all sat down at the table.

I tasted the chocolate and took a deep breath, letting it out slowly. "Heavenly. I have to make this for the shop sometime. Can I have the recipe?"

"Recipe? It's simple enough, but sure, I'll write it out for you. The trick is in getting the proportions right. As for the soup, this is the best meal I've had in days."

"You're joking." I bit into the toast. While the others dipped their bread in their soup, I preferred mine with a crunch—I never crumbled crackers into soup, either.

Kip spoke up. "Mom is a really good cook when she's got the time. She's teaching me. She wanted to teach

Randa, but Ran didn't want to learn." Miranda reached over and flicked Kip on the nose, but instead of hitting her back, he snorted. "It's true! You told Mom you'd rather eat out all the time than have to learn to cook."

"At least I'm doing something important with my time instead of playing stupid games." Miranda sniffed and went back to her soup. "You're such a baby."

Kip grinned. "I like being a kid, I get away with more. Sly gets away with everything."

I sighed. "We're really going to have to have a talk about that kid one of these days. I hope you know that what works on his folks is not going to work with me."

My son scooped another spoonful of carrots and turkey and noodles into his mouth. "I know."

"Don't talk with your mouth full," I said automatically. I turned to Andrew. His bowl was almost empty. "More?"

He pushed back his chair. "Yes, but I'll get it." He brought the pan back to the table and served both of us.

The kids were full. Either that, or their curiosity had worn thin. I excused them and they ran off into the other room, Miranda stopping to slap a paper in front of me. "You need to sign this and drop it off at the school."

"What is it?" I glanced over the slip.

"It says you give me permission to take the scholarship test. Remember, for Space Camp? Without your signature, they won't let me in the door."

And if she didn't win that scholarship, we couldn't afford to send Randa to Space Camp. "Take this and put it on my desk, please. I'll sign it later." I handed her the slip and she sighed, grabbed it back, and ran off with a half wave. Chiqetaw Middle School insisted on knowing that all permission slips were actually signed by the parents, not by enterprising young forgers.

Andrew watched as she darted out of the room. "Great kids. Do they ever give you any trouble?"

I almost choked on my soup. "That's a good one. Smart and funny do not preclude annoying and downright sneaky." Chuckling, I shook my head. "You should see them when they aren't on their best for company. Actually, though, they are good kids, and I'm proud of both of them. It hasn't been easy the past couple years, raising them alone, but I think we've done okay."

Andrew leaned back in his chair and contemplated me with a soft look. His eyes were gentle, and as he held my gaze, butterflies tickled my stomach. "I enjoyed tonight, Emerald. I'd like to see you again. I'm not seeing anyone right now, and if you aren't. . . ."

He wanted to date me? I hadn't expected this. "Andrew," I said slowly, "I would love to see you again, but I have to be honest about something first."

A worried look crossed his face, and he leaned forward. "Did I say something wrong? Don't be afraid to be blunt. My ego isn't that fragile." He was joking, but I could tell that like most men, he didn't want me to turn him down.

"No, no. You didn't say anything wrong."

"It's the fact that I write romance novels, isn't it? You think it's unmanly?" He gave me a cornball look. "If you agree to go out with me, I promise that I won't show up in a ruffled shirt open to my waist."

I laughed. The man was not only gorgeous, but he also had a sense of humor. I took a deep breath. If nothing else, I owed him the truth. "When Harlow invited me to your play tonight, it was as a favor to me. I'm trying to gather some information, and she said you might be able to help. I didn't expect you'd end up asking me out. You need to know this because I don't want you thinking I'd go out with you just to pick your brain. I really would like to see you again."

What was he going to think when I tried to explain why I wanted information on Susan? I had enough skeletons in my closet to qualify for a first-class ticket to La-La Land. This ghost business was a whole 'nother category of weird.

He looked at me with those dark eyes, and I could sense both curiosity and a certain wariness hiding behind his stare. "Information? I see. Well, why don't you tell me what you want to know?"

"To do that, I'm going to have to tell you why, and I guarantee you'll think I'm nuts." Okay. Here went nothing. "I need to know some things about Susan Mitchell."

"Susan?" He shifted in his chair. I had the feeling he hadn't been totally honest with me about their relationship but couldn't put my finger on what he'd left out.

"Did Harlow by chance tell you I'm a tarot reader? A lot of folks also consider me the town witch."

He coughed but covered it up as quickly as he could. "Well, no. That didn't come up. Are you? The town witch, I mean."

"Not exactly. Well, close enough so—yeah, I guess I am. So anyway. Does that bother you?"

His lips spread out in a big smile. "Bother me? I grew up Catholic but left the church years ago. So long as you don't go all *Blair Witch* on me, I don't care what you believe. Is that all? How does this relate to Susan?"

So far, so good. Here came the hard part. "You see, over the years I've dealt with more than my share of spirits."

His smile began to fade. "Spirits? As in ghosts?"

"Yes, as in ghosts." I could tell that he was pulling back. Most people were fine with the idea of alternative beliefs until we tossed actual magic and mysticism in their face. Once faced with the reality, they backtracked fast. Like the first black family on the block or a new Jewish neighbor, everything seemed safe enough as long as it was theoretical. The old "not in my neighborhood" attitude still prevailed.

I decided to spill it. "Last night, the spirit of Susan Mitchell appeared in my bedroom. There has to be some reason why she approached me, so I'm trying to find out more about her." Might as well keep it general; the last thing I needed was for her husband to slap a lawsuit for slander on me, should Andrew decide I was deranged and go blabbing about what I told him.

He edged out of his chair. "Let me get this straight. Susan's ghost appeared in your bedroom last night?"

I nodded.

"How do you know it was her?" There was an odd inflection in his voice, and I knew that I'd hit a nerve.

"She told me," I said. Not quite a lie. He didn't need

to see the papers with the spirit writing on them yet.

He cocked his head and frowned. "Susan's spirit not only appeared in your room, but she talked to you? What did she have to say?"

I sighed. This was going just about like I'd expected. He wouldn't believe me, and I'd never get him to talk about her. And after this, I sincerely doubted if he'd want to date me, either. "She has some unfinished business, and I wanted to help her out. Is this bothering you? Should I just drop the subject?"

He carried the dishes over to the sink. "I just don't know what to believe. I mean, a good friend of mine dies, and then some stranger tells me that she saw my friend's ghost—it's a lot to take in. I'm not sure what I think." He seemed antsy, and I waited for him to make a mad dash for the door, but after pouring himself a glass of water, he sat down at the table again. "Have you always seen spirits?"

Had I? When I thought about it, the answer was yes— ever since I was a little girl. It had gotten so bad that I developed a pattern of insomnia that never quite left. "Yeah, actually. It used to scare the hell out of me; when I saw *The Sixth Sense,* the movie struck home so much it freaked me out. When my Nanna came to live with us, she taught me to handle having the sight. She taught me a lot of things."

He played with the salt and pepper shakers. After a moment he asked, "How often does this happen? I mean, do you hear voices in your head? Do you talk with spirit guides? I guess what I'm asking . . ."

I exhaled slowly. "What you're asking is if I'm nuts. No, I'm not. I don't hear voices in my head. I usually rely on common sense more than spirit guides, though I do pay attention to my intuition. Spirits show up in my house once in a while, but not on a regular basis."

"You're sure it was Susan?" He pressed his lips together. I had the feeling that if it had been any other spirit, he wouldn't be so freaked.

"When I saw the article in the paper this morning, I recognized her right away. I'm sorry, I shouldn't have brought this up." It had been a long day, and all I wanted to do was to snuggle up in my bathrobe and crash out on the sofa with the kids.

He must have sensed my mood, because he glanced at the clock. It was ten-thirty. "It's late and I'd better go home. I'll call you tomorrow, okay?"

There wasn't much left to say, so I escorted him to the door, where he slipped on his boots and coat and headed down the sidewalk. He turned back briefly, as if he were going to say something, then shook his head and waved a tight little wave and continued to his car. I shut the door and locked it behind me.

Great, another guy who thought I was nuts. Life sucked sometimes.

F̶our
⁂

TAP, TAP, TAP. Tap, tap, tap. The noises
started around midnight, waking me out of a nightmare. Worn out from the roller-coaster day, I lurched out
of bed as a knock ricocheted across the ceiling. Did it
come from my dream, or was it real? I listened, squinting
into the darkness. No, there it was, and another, deep, as
if embedded within the wooden beams overhead. The only
thing above the ceiling was crawl space and roof. Squir-
rels, maybe? They were all over the trees, the little bug-
gers. Remembering Nanna's advice, I searched for the
obvious. *Play the skeptic,* I could hear my grandmother
saying, *until you can no longer dismiss what you've seen.*

My door flew open, and Kip came running in. "S-s-s-
s-omething's in my room!" Something must have scared
him—he was stuttering, an old problem that surfaced only
when he was afraid.

My son had never suffered from "monster under the
bed" syndrome; if he said something was in his room,
something was. I'd chased away more than one creepy-
crawly that decided to hang out in his closet. Lost souls
flocked to bright young spirits like moths to a flame. I
managed to keep the house warded, but once in awhile,

things still got past my guard. He crawled into my arms and leaned against my chest as I sat down on the bed and stroked his hair. The sounds on the ceiling continued, though fainter. I asked him what he had seen.

"A lady. I woke up because I thought I heard you crying. She was leaning over my bed and she seemed pretty upset. She was trying to tell me something. Her mouth moved, but no words came out. I saw something big and bad in back of her, like a shadow. When I turned on my light, they both disappeared." He shivered. "Was she the reason you couldn't sleep last night?"

He knew, he always knew. I tried to avoid lying to my children. I wanted them to trust me. "I saw her for the first time last night. She asked me to help her. I guess I'm not acting fast enough to make her happy."

"Is she lost?" He knew all about wandering spirits. I trained him young, so he wouldn't be frightened of his abilities as he grew up. "I think she might be."

"Lost? No. I don't think so. But she has a problem that wasn't cleared up before she died, and she wants my help. Trouble is, I don't know if I *can* help her. That's all you need to know for now, kiddo. But we'll do something to keep her out of your room."

He hesitated as if there was something more he wanted to say.

"What is it? Is there something else I should know?" I waited, but after a few seconds he shook his head. The poor kid was probably scared out of his wits but didn't want to admit it. I grabbed my robe and, Kip's hand safely tucked into mine, we went to inspect his room.

Like all boys his age, his room existed in a perpetual state of disarray. I ignored the mess. Later I'd remind him that clutter attracted chaos. He let go of my hand and sat on the foot of the bed as I took three deep breaths and lowered myself into a trance, searching with the vague feelers and wisps that were my antennae.

My mind began to drift—lighter and lighter, until it felt like I was standing at the top of a cliff. Then—one long dive, down past the blur of lost sleep, through the confusion with Andrew, through worry and stress, deep into the corners of my mind—which at this point felt like the pit of my stomach. After a few minutes, a swirl of mist surrounded me that indicated I had managed to find a doorway into the energy, a kaleidoscope vortex into which I plunged and soared upward—Icarus rising like mercury on a dog day and then . . . I opened my eyes.

B-I-N-G-O.

There she was. Susan Mitchell. Standing by the bottom of my son's bed with a luminescent smile on her face. As I watched, a shadow rose up behind her, and I caught the merest whiff of jackal bites and crocodile smiles. Susan turned, pulling back when she saw what was there. I decided that if she was making tracks, so would we. I started to back up, pushing Kip behind me, but the apparition was growing larger, amorphous and swirling like a whirlpool of energy, and I found myself mesmerized. I couldn't look away.

"Mom? Mom!" Kip's tentative voice shook me out of my paralysis. As I broke free from the trance, I thought I caught a glimpse of cold steel teeth in the heart of the shadow. I broke into a sweat—this couldn't be good. Couldn't be safe. I had to get Kip out of the room *now,* but before I could move, the creature lunged, dissipating Susan's image as it shot right through her misty body on a beeline for me. Both Kip and I screamed as the thing plowed through me like a freight train.

Kip gasped and lurched forward, bumping against my back. "Mom!"

I whirled around as his scream cut short, just in time to catch him in my arms as he sprawled to the floor. "Kip? Kip?" What was happening to my son? His eyes rolled back in his head, and he began to convulse. A seizure? Could he be having some sort of epileptic fit? That glazed stare was too close to a death mask. But the convulsions stopped and, with a look that told me that Kip wasn't anywhere behind those gleaming eyes, he lifted his head and began to laugh. "Kip! Can you hear me?"

Miranda came racing into the room. She stopped cold at the sight of her brother. "What's wrong?"

"Don't underestimate me, bitch. I'm here to stay." The

voice emanating from my son's mouth was dark and masculine. Miranda let out a little shriek. By now the shadow had separated enough from Kip that we could see mist rising out of his body.

Thick, like a haze of smog, the energy from everything going on threatened to overwhelm me. Kip fighting against the possession, anger fueling the spirit, Miranda's confusion and panic over her baby brother; together, these emotions formed a vortex, an undertow in a psychic whirlpool, and I was battling the current, trying to pull my son out of the maelstrom.

"In my room—get the bottle of amethyst water and my ward rune!" I yelled at Miranda, willing her to move, to break free of her fear. Her eyes darted first to Kip, then back at me. With a choked cry, she turned and raced out of the door.

I leaned over my son, forcing myself to quit shaking as I focused on the spirit that was using him as a megaphone. "Get out of my son, now!" Miranda rushed back in, clutching the bottle and my copper warding rune. She held them out to me, shaking so hard that I could barely grab hold of them.

I slapped the copper plate down over his heart, where the sigil would help me concentrate the energy. The etched rune on the copper began to glow. Using my teeth, I pulled the cork out of the bottle and splashed his face with the water. I took a guess that the spirit had entered his body through his third eye—the psychic portal on the forehead—so that seemed the most logical place from which to try and evict the bastard.

"Kneel on his other side." I glanced up to make sure she heard me. Miranda obediently dropped to the floor, but looked about ready to lose it. As if the spirit sensed what I was planning, Kip began to convulse, his body burning with fever. I pushed him flat against the floor, straddling him in order to pin him down with my knees.

I cupped my hands over the ward rune. The copper felt hot beneath my fingers. "Put your hands on top of mine. I know you're scared, but I need you to help."

"Okay. . . ." Miranda was slow, the fear making her sluggish.

"Get your hands over mine. Damn it, move when I tell you!" She gave me a wounded look but obeyed. I inhaled deeply as I anchored into the feel of the wood floor, to the stability of the soil beneath. The tendrils of earth mana began to flow through my body, calming my raging mind. No room for doubt. No room for anger. This had to work. Kip's life depended on it.

I began to whisper, letting the words grow louder with each round. "Be gone, be gone, be gone, be gone!"

Like a bonfire sputtering at first, then catching hold and roaring to life, the force of the chant expanded, growing deeper as if it were no longer coming from my breath but out of the mouth of a wind tunnel, like some giant street cleaner sweeping away the chaos that had claimed my son. I nodded to Miranda. Trembling at first, she settled into the rhythm. Lilting and celestial, her voice darted over the words like a hummingbird hovering over a bird feeder.

I increased the urgency of the chant. Kip began to thrash, jerking wildly as a loud *whoosh* reverberated through the room. A rush of mist swirled up from his body and vanished out the window. Miranda burst into tears. I smoothed back Kip's hair and felt for his pulse. It was steady, and he was breathing softly, with a good rhythm. The fever had broken. As I slumped against the foot of his bed, the copper rune dropped to the floor.

When I managed to muster up enough energy, I tipped his chin. "Kip? Kip? Kipling, speak to me." His eyes fluttered, and he struggled to yawn. Miranda, weeping silently, crept over to snuggle next to us.

I kissed her forehead. "You did real good helping me, Randa. He's okay. Everything is going to be okay." I wished I felt as confident as I sounded.

KIP DOVE INTO his sandwich. I cautioned him to slow down so he wouldn't choke. Being possessed wasn't a walk in the park, especially for an eight-year-old boy, but I had the sneaking suspicion that he was a little too excited about the whole situation.

I handed Randa her sandwich and fixed one for myself. "After tonight, Susan can kiss my ass if she thinks I'm going to help her. I'll blow her ghostly butt to hell before I let her and her friend near this house again."

Miranda picked at her food.

Kip swallowed and took a sip of his milk. "Why can't you help her? I don't think that thing is her friend." He was recovering too quickly for my comfort. For once, I would have rather seen him scared witless, but I also knew that adrenaline worked wonders to overpower fear. I hoped the excitement would wear off after he had calmed down and gotten some food into him.

"Do you remember anything? Did the spirit leave any impressions in your mind?" One thing was certain: If that creature was foolhardy enough to commandeer my son's body, he wasn't the brightest bulb in the socket. But then again, what did he have to lose? Mr. Big & Ugly was already dead, if—indeed—he had ever been alive. I couldn't do anything worse to him than banish him from my home. Susan wanted vengeance, justice. That I could understand. The part of me that still smarted from Roy's betrayal empathized with the dead woman. But what did this other creature want? What frightened me most was his comment about being here to stay.

Kip gulped down the rest of his milk. Normally I'd object, but tonight wasn't the time to complain about table manners. He wiped his mouth with the back of his hand and squinted, one eye closed tight. "I dunno . . . it's fuzzy, like a dream. He did get pretty mad when you chased him out." He grinned at me. "You can sure kick butt, Mom."

I looked into the eyes of my son, blood of my blood, soul of my soul. "Watch your mouth, kiddo." I contemplated his nonchalance. He was doing his best to convince me he was unscathed. "You want me to help Susan, even after everything that happened, don't you?" He nodded. "It would mean that she'd be hanging out here more. Can you guys handle having a ghost around if I can prevent the other spirit from coming back?"

Miranda shoved her chair back. "No! I don't want her here. I don't like ghosts!"

"You're just jealous because I'm like Mom!" Kip leaped up, and they were at it again. "Knock it off!" I dragged them into the living room, where I shoved them unceremoniously onto the sofa. "No more. Do you hear me?" They quieted down. "I have had it with these petty squabbles! One moment you two are fine and the next you're at each other's throats."

Miranda shuffled her feet on the carpet and mumbled. "I'm trying to study for the scholarship test. I have to be at the top to win. I can't handle this kind of stuff."

My daughter was determined to attend Space Camp for teens. It was an extra that we couldn't afford, but she had managed to dig up a scholarship fund for tuition and was studying like crazy so she could ace the test and "go live like the astronauts" for a week.

"I won't let this become a nightly affair." I slid onto the sofa next to her and stroked her long, raven hair back from her face. "Is there something else you aren't telling me?"

She coughed, trying not to cry, but I could see the tears peeking out from her lashes. "Nothing's wrong. Just . . . you and Kip do all this stuff together and I'm left out because I like other stuff! I'm tired of being the third wheel around here!" She started to flounce out of the room, but I grabbed her arm and drew her back.

Third wheel? That clarified a lot of things that had been going on around here, but now was not the time to push.

Kip smacked the arm of the sofa, pouting. He had to have an ulterior motive. The euphoric afterglow of possession couldn't account for his desire to let Susan Mitchell wander freely around our house only an hour after some psycho nightmare had taken control of his body.

After a few moments I made my decision. "Here is what we are going to do. You are both going to sleep on the sofa the rest of the night, and I'll sleep in the rocking chair and keep watch. Tomorrow I'll decide what to do once I've had time to think the situation through." Both camps set up an immediate protest, but I put a stop to it with a raised hand. "I don't want to hear it. End of discussion. Now help me open the sofa."

When they were safely tucked under the comforter, I settled myself into the rocker, threw an afghan over my legs, and turned out the light. Tomorrow promised to be a long day. I needed advice, and that meant a trip to Murray's.

Five

⁜

I HADN'T SEEN Murray since the annual summer fish-fry festival that her tribe sponsored every year. The kids and I always joined them over in Quinault as family guests. She had moved off the reservation when she was a teenager but maintained close contact with the elders there. She was the niece of a medicine woman, fully versed in both native traditions and my own more European beliefs. She accepted the supernatural and yet was dedicated to her calling as a cop. Like the Amazons of old, she was tall and muscled, with curving breasts and streaming black hair that she always wore in a long French braid. Her wide nose and deep-set eyes reflected her heritage. She reminded me of part Indian princess, part warrior woman.

Her house hadn't changed much, even though she'd been talking about renovating every time we got together during the spring. She had gotten around to a new coat of paint—the two-story monstrosity now sported a pale pink color instead of weathered gray—and what looked like a rose garden bordered the driveway. But instead of taming the sense of wildness that always surrounded her life, these changes seemed to have magnified the fecundity of the yard, and it felt more feral than ever, even under the layers of snow. Thick clumps of fern and ivy forced their way through the blanket of white, and I had the feeling that, come spring, the yard would be filled with wildflowers and berry thickets.

She must have heard my car pull up because before I set one foot on the bottom step, she threw open the door and flew down the steps to give me a big hug. "Hey, babe! It's been too long. How are the kids? How's the shop doing? Come *on,* girl, get your butt in the house—it's freezing out here!" With Murray, there was always a flurry of words, then sudden, abrupt silence while she waited for you to digest what she said.

Her name was actually Anna, but the day she joined the police force, way back in Seattle when we were younger and more naive, the guys had started calling her by her last name, and the nickname wormed its way into her civilian life. She would always be Murray to me. She was my best friend from my old life, Harl from my new one. Together they kept me in tune with myself.

The inside of her house was as vibrant as the outside. Plants filled every inch of available space in the room. Murray had always loved exotic animals, and two floor-to-ceiling glass-enclosed cages took up an entire wall. Each built-in section had its own door, heat lamp, wooden branches, water tub, and hiding places for the tenants. Both cages were empty at the moment. I looked around the room.

Bingo! Sid, a seven-foot-long red-tailed boa, coiled on one of the recliners. After a moment I spotted Nancy, another boa, three feet long and brilliant green, curled around the banister of the staircase railing. Nancy had a nasty temper, as did many emerald tree boas, but Sid and I got along.

"Park your butt." Murray pointed to the coffee table where an espresso pot, a creamer full of half-and-half, and a bottle of chocolate syrup waited. I parked it right in her grandmother's rocking chair. After we chatted and downed a couple of double espressos, I was ready to fill her in on the reason for my visit. I drained the last of my chocolate-laced caffeine fix, trying to figure out how to ease into the subject.

"I met a guy, Murray. I'm not sure if it will go anywhere, but—"

She whooped. "It's about time! I've been waiting for you to get out in the dating arena again. Who is he? What's his name? Do I know him?"

"Andrew Martinez. He's a local writer, and I'm not sure if we're going to make it past the first date, which we already had. Kinda."

She poured more espresso. "Andrew Martinez, huh? So what's he like? Where did you meet, and why do you sound so pessimistic?"

"He wrote a play that the Chiqetaw Players are producing—*Obsidian*. He's gorgeous, single, seems nice." I took a deep breath. "Murray, did you read the paper yesterday? About that writer's death?"

Murray gave me a long, studied look. "Writer? The insulin OD case? What's that got to do with your new guy?"

I paused a beat. "Some weird things have been going on; both Andrew and Susan Mitchell—the woman who died—are involved."

"Weird? How weird?"

"Weird as in I saw Susan's ghost the other night. Recognized her the next day when I read the article in the paper about her death. Weird as in Andrew was one of her closest friends and, thanks to my snooping, he asked me out."

Murray narrowed her eyes and stared at me over the top of her cup. "What does she want, and why did she show herself to you?" She leaned against the back of the sofa and crossed her legs yoga-style. Even though she was a big woman, Murray was incredibly limber and graceful. She could outrun the fastest man on the force. "I've got goose bumps. Speak of the dead and they listen." She lifted her arm. The skin was raised and puckered with little bumps. Energy crackled off her hands.

"Susan told me that her husband murdered her."

"Did she tell you how or why?"

I shook my head. "No, in fact she wants me to prove it. She says nobody knows about it. She's upset, Murray."

Murray pushed her hair back from her eyes. "Before you go any farther, I'm going to tell you something. The department looked into Susan's death already. She was supposed to have given up alcohol, and yet they found wine in her system; half of a bottle was spilled on the floor next to her. Her maid picked up a new prescription of Valium for her because Susan said she was out, yet she had Valium in her system, so she had to have some stashed around the house."

"What else did you find out?"

"Walter, her husband, was in a meeting during the time she slid into a coma. Twelve people can account for his whereabouts—we did a quiet background check, since the case was so unusual. She had filed divorce papers, and he knew about it. His friends say he was relieved because he had been wanting to file for divorce himself. We questioned everybody in her writing and theater groups. I think I may have even spoken to this Martinez guy—tall with dark hair, right? Nothing to indicate that her husband killed her. Nothing out of the ordinary was reported; the maid said no one was expected over that day. I'm afraid that you're off base on this one."

"What if she had been having an affair? Is there any chance that Walter could have hired somebody—"

She broke in. "Was she having an affair? Or is that speculation?"

"Speculation. I have no idea what was going on in her personal life. She told me that her husband murdered her, and I was trying to think up possible reasons."

Murray tossed me her television remote. "You have a serious problem with the TV, Em. You've been watching too many episodes of *Justice Files*. Most 'jealous rage' murderers usually leave lots of blood and gore around. Consider these facts: One, Susan Mitchell was well known for screwing up with her diabetes. Two, she was alone all morning; nobody noticed anything out of the ordinary. Three, Walter's time is accounted for. And four, Susan Mitchell was popping Valium and booze, and the two are a dangerous combo even for a nondiabetic." She ticked off her points on her fingers.

"So the doctors think—"

"She gave herself a shot of insulin, swallowed a couple of Valium and a glass or two of wine, forgot to eat, and fell asleep. Bingo . . . coma. We know she went into convulsions; they found bite marks—her own—on her tongue. Accidental insulin overdose. Possible suicide, but don't you let that slip out or we'd have the Mitchells breathing down our neck. There's no way we'll ever know whether she meant to kill herself. She was dead by the time the medics transported her to the hospital."

"And nobody else was in the house?"

"Seems that way. Cars come and go all the time on that street. Nobody notices when neighbors have company unless there's something fishy about them, and that ever-so-helpful nosy old lady of mystery stories must either have been out of town or she moved to a different neighborhood. The truth is that Susan was well known for screwing up her insulin dosages. She'd been in the hospital four times over the past year because she forgot to eat and went into seizure. This time nobody was there to help her."

I made a series of mental notes, hoping I could remember everything. "She took Valium on a regular basis?"

"Yep. Walt said she'd been trying to cut down on the booze, but it looks like she had a relapse. Susan knew she couldn't drink; diabetics really shouldn't ever touch alcohol, but her discipline sucked."

"So you think the ghost is lying to me?"

"I think that Susan is confused. Maybe it's her way of holding on to this world. Not all spirits are ready to let go. She came to you because you're good at hearing the dead. End of case. Now tell me about Andy. He *is* pretty cute."

"It's Andrew, thank you, and I dunno if we're going to be doing much dating. He kind of freaked when I told him I saw her ghost. They were close friends."

"And you told him all that? Jeez, woman, what are

you, nuts? That sort of revelation you leave for the second date. Maybe the third." She waited for a moment. "There's something more. You're upset. What's wrong?"

I scrunched my nose and sighed. "Bad stuff, Murray. I think an astral nasty has tagged along on Susan's heels. I call him Mr. Big & Ugly—Mr. B & U for short. There's no other way to describe the thing. It took possession of Kip last night, and I didn't think I was going to pull him out of it."

"Not good. Do you think Susan and Mr. B & U are related? Or maybe the thing is piggybacking in on her wake?"

"I don't know; it blew right through her, vaporized her manifestation, then charged right through *me*. I'm thinking these two aren't exactly buddies."

"Have you done a reading on this situation yet?"

"No." I shook my head. "I'm too close to the subject. I was wondering if you would lay out a spread for me."

She opened the top of her handcarved rolltop desk that rested against a wall covered with a tapestry. She had woven the canvas in her teen years; it described the life of her Quinault ancestors. I had encouraged her to show it in a gallery, but she said it was personal and that she didn't need to show it off to be happy.

"Which deck?" Murray was one of my few friends who could read tarot and do a good job of it. I went to her for *my* readings when I needed advice.

"Oh, the forest one—you know the one I mean. Woodburn's deck?"

She withdrew a small deck of cards from the desk. I cleared off the coffee table. As I piled the books onto the floor, there was a flicker of color, and Sid popped his head out from beneath the table. He slithered over to my leg and made his way onto the rocking chair, where he coiled into a ball behind my butt. I let him rest there—Sid was gentle; perhaps more gentle than any snake had a right to be. Nancy, on the other hand, would bite if she was feeling frisky, and though not venomous, those teeth had a sting to them.

Murray shuffled the cards a few times and handed the deck to me. "You know the drill."

I focused on the situation and began to shuffle. The cards were a comforting weight in my hands, familiar and tingling. Nanna had taught me how to read when I was barely into my teens, and I, in turn, had taught Murray. She was good; not as good as I was, but good enough for me to trust.

She laid out a five-card spread. I glanced over them briefly. The Tower—I'd expected that, though the actual sight of it left me sweating. The five of swords, the High Priestess, the Devil. The ten of swords—confusion.

Murray straightened her shoulders as she contemplated the layout. "I don't like this, Em. You have some serious big-time power cards here mixed with clear danger signals. Let's see . . . watch out for half-truths and betrayals. Whether deliberate or not, they are woven into this matter like the threads in a spider's web. Put your hand on a single strand and you send shock waves through the whole situation. A dark force behind the scenes is working to upset the balance. Masculine power unchecked . . . much is still hidden from view, and you may make wrong assumptions if you base them solely on what you see on the surface. Be cautious about misreading things. Listen to your intuition or you could topple your world."

As she spoke, a knot formed in my stomach, and I knew her reading was right on target. It wasn't what I wanted to hear. "Great. A well of trouble. Is there any way I can walk away from all this and not get involved?"

"I don't think so." She turned over two more cards. Death and the Fool. "Em, you can't avoid this. We're talking fate here—destiny—and if you don't take control of the situation, it will run over you. Grab the reins, and you might be able to use it to your advantage. Either way, a new cycle is opening up that you can't avoid." She tapped the Death card. "Transformation . . . but I also get a queasy feeling on this one. Be careful the next few weeks, okay? You don't want to transform yourself out of this world."

I had the same queasy feeling and thought quickly

about my will and whether or not everything was in order. "Yeah, I'll be careful. So, what's the outcome?"

She flipped another card. The Moon. "I don't know. Not enough has manifested to predict what's going to happen. Whatever is going on in your life has some heavy ramifications. Keep your eyes open."

As she folded the cards back into the deck, I excused myself and went to the kitchen for a drink of water. A psychic earthquake was rumbling, and I was right at the epicenter. She followed me. "C'mon. Help me get my Christmas tree into the living room. I could use an extra set of muscles."

We pushed our way out onto the enclosed back porch, which was crowded with craft supplies. "How many projects do you have going?"

She pointed to a loom on which she was weaving what looked like a shawl. "That's going to be a tribal shawl for my aunt. And that"—she pointed to a pile of stained wood pieces—"will be my mother's new bird feeder. I should be able to finish them both by next weekend."

"I don't know how you can keep so many projects straight. It would drive me nuts." I took a deep breath and looked at the sky. The clouds had vaporized, and the sun was actually making an appearance. The snow covering the yard glistened and scrunched under our feet as we traipsed down the back steps and over to the woodshed, where a huge conifer stood propped against the wall. Leaving a trail of branches and needles, we wrestled the eight-foot fir into the house. Murray loved celebrations, and even though she lived alone, she never failed to decorate. We got the tree set up in the corner and stood back to stare at the hulking evergreen.

She reached out and lightly ran her fingers over the needles. "Here's to the holidays. So what else is new? How's your business going? The kids?"

I picked up one of the stray branches and inhaled. The woodland scent was calming. "Business is good. I'm in your debt for convincing me to move here. I still can't get over how well my china shop is doing out here in the boonies. I'm getting customers from Bellingham coming in, and from across the Canadian border, too."

"In Chiqetaw you don't have much competition. There are scores of china shops in Seattle. Here you have the entire town at your feet."

"Well, whatever the reason, I'm starting to make a lot more money this year than last. I think I'll ask Cinnamon to stay on full-time after the holidays. She could use the hours."

"She's a good girl."

"Stupid about her choices, but yeah, a good girl. Those three kids of hers are better behaved than half of the wealthy brats around here. Speaking of kids, Kip's been hanging out with that Sly kid. They're best friends, and it's starting to show. Miranda worries me, as usual. Too bookish. It's not normal to be thirteen and be so bookish."

"Don't sweat it. She's got a good head on her shoulders. Let her use it. Hear from Roy lately?"

I snorted. "The scumbag? Are you kidding? Oh, yeah, he's bucking for Father of the Year. No word about Christmas presents. Remember how he forgot Miranda's birthday in August? I went out and bought her a gift and told her it was from her dad, but she knew better. I can't lie to those kids. Never have been any good at it."

Murray considered the problem, then tilted her head to the left and shrugged. "Nothing you can do. They are going to figure out that he's a dirtbag pretty soon. You have to be there to pick up the pieces. Help me put Sid and Nancy to bed?"

"What is this? 'Work the guest' day?" I winked at her and lifted Sid off the sofa, where he was curled in a tight ball, and let him coil around my waist. She went in search of Nancy as I carried the boa over to the cages lining the wall. He weighed a good seventy-five pounds. As he slid a curious head up to tongue the air near my face, I could swear he remembered me. I opened the door and let him slither back into his home. Murray did the same with Nancy.

"They're looking gorgeous. Happy campers all?" Ever since we'd been roommates, Murray had talked about reptiles and amphibians and arachnids with all the passion of a biologist. I sometimes wondered why she'd taken up law enforcement instead, but whenever I asked, she shrugged off the question. I had a feeling it was something to do with her brother, an alcoholic, but never pried.

"I thought Nancy had mouth rot, but lucky for us, it was a false alarm. The vet gave them both a clean bill of health last visit." She sounded just like a proud mama.

"That's good to hear. I tell you, I'm so glad I gave in and picked up the cats. Kip and Miranda have calmed down a lot since we brought them home. They missed Fluto so much, and so did I."

"You got new cats? Last time we talked, you were headed to Seattle to bring Fluto home. What happened?"

"Roy decided that his little rich bitch couldn't live without her. Damned idiot, I was so mad I almost took a baseball bat to his head."

"Oh, yeah, Emerald the slugger. I can see it now. Score one home run for Em, one strike for the Scuz! When was this?"

"When I went to shake him up about missing several child support payments. He makes enough money; there's no way on earth I'll let him out of supporting his children. Anyway, I picked up a mother and three babies from the animal shelter a few weeks ago. They've wormed their way right into our hearts."

"I still think a snake would have taught them more about the cycles of life. You get the whole thing . . . life—death—the food chain. Feed a live mouse to a hungry snake and you understand the hunt." She pulled out a roll of paper towels and a spray bottle from the cabinet next to the cages.

"Delightful. Cats hunt mice, too, you know. I'm hoping the kittens give the kids a stronger sense of stability. I don't know why I didn't agree last year when they asked."

Murray sprayed her hands with a mixture of bleach and water, then wiped them on a paper towel. She handed me the bottle. "Wash. You don't want to take any chances after you handle a snake or lizard." She waited till I dried my hands. "I can tell you why you waited so long to go out and pick out a new pet. You can't go back now. By cementing the bond with a new cat, you redefined your family. And this time, that definition of family doesn't include Roy."

I thought about it for a moment. She was right. "Those sociology classes you took really stayed with you, didn't they? You make everything sound so clear."

Murray gave me a big hug. "Actually, I get my insight from my aunt, White Deer. She reads situations like they were made of glass and has been teaching me how to look below the surface. I think you're ready for change, and you're scared. But you'll pull through; you've got too much going for you to sit withering in that big old bed, all alone."

She walked me out to the Cherokee. I glanced up at the clouds banking the sky. "Think we'll get much more snow this year?"

"The onions from my garden say so—thick skin. And the caterpillars had unusually hairy coats this year. Oh!" She pressed my arm. "Wait a moment, I almost forgot." She ran back inside, and a moment later reappeared with a shopping bag. I peeked inside. Presents. Three gifts wrapped in shiny silver paper with blue bows.

"For the kids? I still have to do my shopping."

"Well, I am their godmother, aren't I? There's one in there for you, too. What are you doing for Christmas?"

"I don't know. Truth is, I've ignored the holidays as much as possible the past couple of years. Haven't even bought a real tree—just little tabletop ones that were pre-decorated." Ashamed, I hung my head. "I've been really lax, Murray. Lazy and self-absorbed and selfish."

She frowned. "No, you've been mourning the death of your marriage. Listen, I'm not going home this year—I have to work Christmas Eve, but I've got Christmas Day free. I don't go on duty until 8:00 P.M. How about if I come over during the morning and we'll cook up a big Christmas dinner and play games and sit around and gossip? I can be moral support. Call me motivation, if you like."

It was the best offer I'd had in months. The kids would

be thrilled, they adored Murray. "You know I'd love that. So will the kids."

She tucked the shopping bag into the backseat. "Drive safe—we're gearing up for a freeze tonight."

"I hope that the spooks don't ruin the holidays for us. Miranda was so freaked last night. It was bad, Murray. Real bad."

She closed her eyes and leaned against the door, her head resting on the windowframe, a pensive look on her face. "Be careful, Em. There's so much chaos swirling around your home, but . . . Susan stands separate from it. Unrelated energies caught up in a whirlwind together. Watch Kip—he's at the center of the vortex."

I didn't like the sound of that. "Any advice about how to keep my babies safe?"

She shook her head. "That's it. That's all I got."

That was enough. I needed to get rid of Susan as fast as I could, whether it meant exorcising her or finding her murderer. And for either choice, I needed people who had been close to her, who might be able to help persuade her and her ghoulish retinue to leave us alone. It was time to tell Harlow the rest of the story.

Six

✦

AFTER I LEFT Murray's, I swung by the shop. I gave Harlow a call and asked her if she could come by later in the evening. She agreed if I'd promise to fill her in on everything that had happened. Since James was going to be working all evening, she agreed to stop over at about nine-thirty.

The Chintz 'n China Tea Room was open on Sundays from noon until four, and usually I had Cinnamon come in and work the counter while I took the day off. But this week I'd agreed to a private shopping trip at the request of a group of tea lovers from Surrey, British Columbia, who had come down on a bus tour of china shops. My store was the first stop on their itinerary. They would head back to Bellingham, then down to Everett for dinner and to spend the night. Delightfully mannered, they bought a bit of this and a bit of that, had a cup of tea, and stocked up on some of the delicacies I carried from local vendors who sold only in the Northwest. By the time I managed to close the doors, it was almost suppertime.

I was surprised to find Miranda in the living room. She seldom waited around on her astronomy club nights. "I saw Murray today, and why aren't you at your meeting?"

"I wanted to show you my jacket before I left." She held up her parka. "I need a new one. I can barely zip this one up."

Sigh. Another expense. The mail from Saturday was sitting on the foyer table. I thumbed through the letters—bills mainly. A letter from Roy. I ripped it open. Finally—the child support payments he owed for the past three months. Apparently my strong-armed tactics had worked. I motioned for Randa to wait a minute and read the scribbled note that instructed me to buy some sort of Christmas gifts for the kids and stick his name on them. He'd *pay me back* later. Oh, how lovely. Wasn't he a peach?

As much as I wanted to lash out, I decided to grit my teeth as usual. At least I *got* my child support, late or not. The courts and my threats to expose him as a deadbeat to his friends saw to that. I sighed and tucked the check and letter in my purse. Lucky for us, with Chiqetaw's low cost of living, we managed on a lot less than we had in the city. The refrigerator was always full, we paid our bills on time and sometimes had enough left over for a luxury or two.

"Hand me your jacket." I inspected the coat. It was still in good enough condition to give to a secondhand shop. "Would you mind if we looked at Value Village first? If we can't find something nice, we'll drive over to the mall and pick out a new one."

She shrugged. "As long as it's gray or black. Just don't buy me used underwear. How was Murray? How are Sid and Nancy?"

I planted a light kiss on the top of her head, and for once she didn't squirm away. "Sid and Nancy are good. Murray's thinking of spending Christmas dinner with us. Would you like that?"

Her face lit up with a glow I hadn't seen for quite a while. "That would be great! Are we going to have a real tree this year? I miss decorating."

Yet another reminder that I'd been slacking big-time as a parent. "I know you do, honey, and yes, we will get a tree this year. I promise. So, what's on your agenda at the meeting tonight?"

"We're debating an argument sparked off by a post on one of the forums at astronomy.com about solar flare activity and their effects on satellites and hi-tech communications. I hope Mr. Gardner's wife doesn't serve spaghetti again—we've had it the last two times. I need three bucks for my donation for the meal."

I handed her a five. She stuffed a couple of notebooks in her pack along with a book on NASA and wiggled into her coat. The fabric strained across her breasts, the zipper barely managing its trip up her chest. Thirteen and she was almost a B-cup, like I'd been at that age. It took all I could do to get her into a bra, but finally, after one day of me wearing a T-shirt and no bra, she was convinced of gravity's effects on big boobs and conceded the argument.

"You *do* need a new coat."

She flashed me an impish grin. "Yeah. I do." With a quick peck on my cheek, she slung her pack over her shoulder and headed for the back door. "I'm meeting Liam at the library after the meeting. For an hour, okay? He's tutoring me for the English quiz. I'll be home by ten."

"Randa . . ." I hesitated, unsure as to whether to voice my concerns now or save them for later. She waited patiently. "I know you aren't dating, and I know that you're careful, but don't you think you should find a girl for a best friend?"

"Best friend? What makes you think Liam is my best friend?"

I shrugged. "He's been hanging around a lot the past few weeks. I think that you might be seeing too much of him."

She leaned up on her toes and gave me a peck on the cheek. "Don't worry, Mom. Liam's a jerk, like all boys. I only hang around him because he's good in English and I need help. When I've gotten past the hard part of the class, I'll dump him and you won't have anything to worry about."

Oh boy, so I wasn't dealing with Little-Miss-Wanna-Date and they weren't doing anything I had to worry about. I was facing the Men-Are-Scum Monster. I wasn't sure which one was worse. "You know, honey, boys are human beings, too. They do have feelings," I cautioned her. "Some are going to be jerks and some are going to be nice."

"Whatever. Hey, I gotta go. See you later." She headed for the door. I sighed. She would have to learn the hard way that using people the way she did would only buy loneliness. In some ways, Randa was very much her father's daughter. The thought scared me.

"Come ten o'clock, you'd better be walking through the front door. Now get out of here and have a good time."

She disappeared down the sidewalk into the blustery evening. A light dusting of snow had started to fall, and I breathed a prayer of gratitude that I lived here in Chiqetaw instead of frantic, dollar-driven Seattle. Ghosts or not, our house felt like a haven against the assaults of the world, and watching my daughter walk off into the gloom, I realized I was much more relaxed as a parent now than I had been in the city. Even though the suspicion of a murder here in Chiqetaw now hovered in my thoughts, it still offered a safe place to bring up my chicks.

Kip bounced in about ten minutes later and headed straight for the refrigerator.

"Whoa, buster. Too near dinner. What shall we have tonight? It's Miranda's astronomy club night. Do you want Greek? Moroccan? Maybe Japanese?"

He cocked his head, thought for a moment, and gave me a sheepish grin. "Can we eat American and have macaroni and cheese with hotdogs? And chocolate cake?"

Yep, he'd been over at Sly's. Every time he saw what they were having for dinner, he always asked to have the same thing. Sly's mother was the only one I knew who still cooked boxed mac 'n' cheese casseroles with sliced wieners. I shuddered; the one shop I really missed in this town was Trader Joe's. Finding decent frankfurters was going to be a chore, and the butcher was closed. "Okay, kiddo, but we're using kielbasa instead of hotdogs, and real cheddar instead of Velveeta." I grabbed my keys and purse and shooed him out to the car.

The trip to QFC didn't take long—ten minutes to locate the Polish sausage and pick out a chocolate cake that caught Kip's fancy. I tossed a brick of sharp cheddar into the cart and added a bottle of Talking Rain.

On the ride home, Kip turned off his handheld video game. "Mom, have you decided what to do about Mrs. Mitchell?"

"Yes, I think so. I'll talk to you and your sister about it later." Apparently satisfied, he went back to playing with his Game Boy.

We got home in time to hear the phone ringing. By the time I unlocked the door and grabbed the receiver, whoever it was had hung up. After I put the groceries away, I dialed voice messaging. To my surprise, Andrew's voice spilled into my ear.

"I need to talk to you. Can I come over? I'm sorry I left so abruptly last night. I'd like a chance to apologize. Please call, it's important." I wrote down his number. What had happened? Once again, I had the feeling of being inexorably drawn into a spider's web. He must have been sitting on the phone, because it barely managed one ring before he yanked up the receiver. Another apology tumbled out. I invited him for dinner, and he said he'd be over in fifteen minutes.

Kip's eyes lit up when he found out Andrew was joining us. Kip pitched in, carefully setting the table and filling the water goblets with milk. I had to restrain my laughter when I saw him dig out the candlesticks and ceremoniously place them on the table. So Kip wasn't above playing matchmaker.

As the kielbasa sizzled in the pan, I tossed in a scant handful of diced shallots and minced garlic, along with some paprika and parsley. A pungent cloud of steam roiled up in my eyes; as I wiped away the stinging tears, an earthy smell filled the kitchen, and my mouth began to water. Kip's idea hadn't been a bad one, at that. Elbow noodles bubbled along cheerfully while I grated the cheese in the food processor, then stirred the sausage and cheese into the macaroni. The doorbell rang. Kip raced to get it.

Andrew was carrying a bouquet of red carnations. He peeked around the corner. "These are yet another way of saying I'm sorry." He handed me the flowers, and I took a deep breath of the faint but spicy scent. "Something smells good," he added, lifting the lid off the noodles.

I slapped his hand away. "No tasting before dinner. Go wash up, both of you. Kip will show you where."

They ducked out of the kitchen while I poured the mac 'n' cheese into one serving dish and the broccoli into another. I slid the cake onto a crystal stand and set it on the end of the table, then removed the candles and tucked them back in the sideboard. The carnations brightened up a copper milk jug, cheering up the kitchen. By the time they returned, dinner was ready.

After eating, Kip disappeared up the stairs to finish his homework, taking another slice of cake with him. Andrew handed me the dishes while I rinsed and stacked. As the dishwasher churned, I made espresso and asked Andrew to grate some bittersweet chocolate. I'd already had way too much caffeine, but who was counting?

He rested his elbows on the table. "I feel like I was very rude last night. I'd like a chance to explain. You really spooked me when you said you saw Susan's ghost."

I cleaned the table and took my seat opposite his. "Don't apologize. I shouldn't have sprung all that on you like I did. Was it just the fact that she was your friend or something else that bothered you?"

He hemmed and hawed for a few minutes, then finally blurted out, "The truth is . . . I saw her, too. I tried to tell myself it was just a dream, but after what you told me, I had to admit to myself that it was real. Thursday night I went to bed early. Right after I started to drift off, I had the feeling there was something in the room with me. I looked up, and there she was. I didn't handle it as well as you did."

"What did you do?" That Susan had shown up at his place before coming to me for help told me that there must be a strong connection between them. She had only approached me after her attempt to communicate with Andrew failed.

He turned a little green. "Remember—these things don't usually happen to me. I was startled and . . . well, I threw the alarm clock at her and hid my head under the covers. When I looked out again, she was gone."

Threw the alarm clock? Hid under the covers? Really brave reactions for such a strong man. I stifled a snort. "Let me get this straight: The ghost of one of your best friends shows up, and you throw a clock at her and then duck under the covers?"

He shrugged. "I said I didn't cope with it very well. Anyway, she vanished, and that was it. I didn't know she was dead at that time, and I wrote it off as being just a weird dream until Friday morning, when I found out what happened."

The look on his face stopped me from laughing. Some people simply weren't cut out to answer the door when the paranormal came knocking. I leaned back in my chair, thinking about the situation. Andrew seemed serious about what he was saying. "Why are you telling me this now?"

He inhaled deeply and let it out with a slow whistle. "I've been thinking a lot about it since last night. Now I believe that she was there, trying to tell me something, and I was too afraid to listen. So she found you. She must trust you if she came to you for help. I want to know what's going on, and if I can, I want to help, too. Susan was a good friend; I don't want to let her down."

"You'll have to be honest with me. You'll have to tell me about your friendship with her. If you want me to help, I need to know everything that was going on. And . . . I'll have to tell you everything she said to me. Some of it may be hard for you to believe." I tried to feel out his energy, but he was hard to read. "Just a sec." I held up my hand before he answered and told him I'd be right back.

I slipped into the living room and pulled out a deck of tarot cards from the desk. After a quick shuffle, I concentrated on whether he was trustworthy and drew a card. The three of wands. Virtue. Honesty. Truthfulness. I could trust what he told me. I just hoped he could fill in some of the missing pieces.

When I returned to the kitchen, I gave him the go-ahead and instructed him to tell me everything. He got himself a glass of water and, with a haunted look, began to talk. "The truth is that Susan was in love with me. That was our biggest problem. We had a fight the night before she died—the last time we ever spoke. She died thinking I was angry with her."

I had thought there was some sort of romantic attachment involved, though I had been thinking more along the lines of an affair. I could still be right; he might still be holding back. "Go on," I said in what I hoped was a reassuring voice.

He continued. "Walter had been having affairs since they first got married, she told me. She finally hired a PI this year, and he got pictures. Once she had the proof in hand, something snapped. She freaked. Maybe this has something to do with why she can't rest."

I leaned across the table and gently touched his arm. I could hear the question in his voice. He was looking for answers to whether Susan killed herself, like the police had first suggested. "You said that she was in love with you? Were you in love with her? Did you . . . did you have an affair with Susan Mitchell?"

"No." He shook his head. "I swear, I never even kissed her. I loved her as a friend, but she grew really attached. She tried to get me to have an affair, and I told her no, I didn't sleep with married women. We laughed it off, to save the friendship, but the shadow was always there. I couldn't understand why she stayed with Walter, since she didn't love him. Especially when I found out he'd been hitting her."

Whoa! Walter had beat up Susan? "Wait a minute. You knew that he hit her and didn't ever bother to call the police?" What kind of man was Andrew?

"Yes, I knew," he said in a strangled voice. "I've known for months. I tried to talk her into leaving but she always brushed me off; she said she wasn't leaving Walter unless she had someone waiting in the wings. Well, it wasn't going to be me. When I threatened to call the cops on Walter, she said she'd deny everything; she was afraid that it would tarnish her image if her readers found out she was in an abusive marriage for so long. I told her they'd just buy her books faster—that they'd understand because some of them had probably already been in similar circumstances."

I began to see his quandary, and I understood Susan's reluctance. I knew from experience the shame of being in an abusive relationship; even though that shame wasn't warranted, it still controlled your life. I nodded for him to continue.

"Wednesday night, we had our writers meeting at her house, and after everyone left, she got nasty. She got into the booze and I begged her to stop, to think of her health. We fought. She grew hysterical and told me that if I didn't run off with her, she knew someone who would. I figured it was best to leave, but when I got to my car, I realized that I had forgotten my briefcase. I ran back into the house without knocking—I didn't want to start another round— hoping that she would be out of the living room."

"Go on."

Andrew thrust his hands into his pockets and began to pace by the sink, his voice shaking as he finished his story. "Walter must have come in through the back door while we were fighting and heard us. They were in the kitchen and couldn't see me. He was screaming at her, obscenities I would never use on a woman . . . or anyone, for that matter. I heard a thud and headed for the kitchen door when Susan came bursting out, crying. She said Walter had stormed out to the club."

I closed my eyes, feeling the energy swirl around him as he talked. Walter had been furious, and Andrew knew about it. Had he told the cops about this? Would it make any difference, since Walter had an alibi?

"Once again, Susan begged me to run away with her. I don't break up marriages. She said I wasn't man enough to help her, that she'd deal with Walter in her own way. So I left. What else could I do?" He buried his face in his hands.

His revelation would take some thinking through. The fact that Walter beat up his wife on a regular basis put a new spin on the matter as far as I was concerned. If he could beat her, why couldn't he take it a step farther and kill her?

Folding his hands, Andrew slumped back down in his chair and stared at the floor. "Last night I had a dream after I left you and went home. I was sitting by Susan's grave. The snowdrifts were piling up. Susan walked up and led me over to a car, and you were in it. When I got in the passenger's side, you turned to me and held out your hand. I reached out, but at the last minute I panicked and pulled away. You got out of the car and walked off into the storm. I knew I couldn't let you go. I shouted, but you didn't hear me. You just kept walking."

The air in the room felt charged. I didn't know what to say. I leaned across the table and lifted his chin so that we were staring eye to eye. "Andrew, I believe in things that, if I were very poor and very loud, would get me locked up faster than you can say 'crazy woman.' Can you handle that I not only talk about these things, but that I totally, absolutely believe they are real?"

My words seemed to hang in the air forever. He searched my face, looking for something he might never find there. Then, slowly, he reached over to press his lips against mine. I melted into his kiss, tasting the lingering flavor of chocolate. He quizzed me with his touch, asking questions to which I didn't know the answer. After a moment, I pulled away. He reached for my hand. I hesitated before resting my fingertips on his palm.

It was time to reveal what Susan had said. "I've got something to tell you. Are you ready to hear what Susan had to say to me?" I paused but he didn't say anything, and I realized that he was waiting for me to continue. "Susan showed up at the foot of my bed Friday night. According to her, she was murdered. She said that Walter did it."

He tensed. I told him everything. Kip. The shadow. Susan and the automatic writing—the whole works. I couldn't look at him as I spilled out the story, couldn't chance seeing disbelief in his eyes. But he had to know, had to be able to handle my world if he wanted to be part of my life in any way.

Did I dare ask if he believed me? I didn't have the courage. He answered, though, without being prodded. "Last week I would have laughed you off." He wiped his chin where his five-o'clock stubble from the day before had deepened into a light beard. "Now you tell me that her spirit says she was murdered by that bastard. If he *did* kill her, I'll always feel that I had a part in it. Maybe I could have stopped him."

I asked the question to which I wasn't sure I wanted an answer. "Are you sure you weren't in love with her? Even a little bit?"

He settled back down in his chair. When he spoke, resignation filled his voice. "I don't know. I don't know much of anything. If she was murdered, I'll always feel guilty that I didn't stop Walter. And if Susan killed herself, I'll always believe my rejection drove her to it. Either way, I'm doomed."

Doomed.

He tugged on my hand. "Em?" There was a plea in his voice.

I felt as if I were teetering on a high wire. He reached up to trace the length of my chin and I closed my eyes, feeling the blood rush through my body on an all-points bulletin. I let him pull me onto his lap, where he pressed me to his chest, kissing me lightly. How could I get involved? How could I let myself trust? But it had been so long. As his lips nuzzled my hair, I gave in and melted into the heat of the kiss.

Seven

❖

I GLANCED AT the clock and disentangled myself from Andrew's embrace. Harlow should be on her way over. With Kip upstairs and Miranda due home soon, I didn't want them to come racing into the room to find me sitting on Andrew's lap. "I need something to drink."

He winked. "Whatever the lady wants. Scotch? Rum? What do you have?"

"I was thinking more along the lines of tea." I fished through the drawer in the sideboard and pulled out a box of black currant. The act of heating the water, of waiting till right before it boiled, then pouring it over the bags in a thin stream, always calmed me down. I filled the tea-kettle and set it on the burner, then selected a Woodland Spode pot from my collection. Andrew watched me in silence as I chose teacups and saucers and set the creamer and sugar bowl on the table. As I sliced a lemon and arranged the segments on a plate, I found myself hoping that he had been joking. I couldn't afford to be with some-one who liked to booze it up. Most people I knew drank socially, but I had stopped hanging out with the ones who couldn't handle their liquor.

I carved a thin wedge of the fudge cake and handed it

to him before I cut my own piece. The steam from the kettle billowed up, whistling a cheerful tune. I let the water stream into the teapot as I inhaled the gentle peppery scent and then set the pot on the table to steep.

"It's a ritual for you, isn't it? The act of tea, the selection of the china . . . what I would call pretension in others is part of your nature, and so it becomes an unrehearsed and totally natural performance. I like that." He mashed cake crumbs with his fork, then lifted his fork in salute to me.

Not knowing quite what to say, I gave him a smile and bit into the creamy fudge. QFC had it right—sugar. Lots of sugar. Chocolate frosting melted in my mouth, and I closed my eyes as the butter cream trickled down my throat. I prayed that no one would ever ask me to relinquish my sweet tooth. As I licked the back of the fork, it occurred to me that Susan couldn't have eaten this piece of cake, but I didn't really understand why.

"I don't know much about diabetes. Could Susan's death really have been an accident? The police think so. The hospital thinks so. Walter has an alibi."

"I'm not exactly a medical encyclopedia, but I can tell you that food like this is off-limits unless the patient is having a low-blood-sugar attack." Andrew dug into his cake. "My aunt has diabetes. She's never been in the hospital since the original diagnosis, but it has affected her in a number of smaller ways. She has some neurological problems due to the condition." He laid down his fork. "But why would a ghost lie? Aren't we supposed to know everything once we die? I got the impression that—what do you call them—spirit guides? That spirit guides are here for our best interests."

"Susan Mitchell isn't a spirit guide. Spirit guides come to you with advice, not with a bunch of problems. If there's one thing you find out damn quick when you work with the other side, it's that ghosts can and do lie, as much as the living. There's no rule book saying they have to play fair."

I started to pour tea for him, but Andrew covered his cup, so I filled my own and let it go at that. He must have

seen my disappointment because he said, "Thank you anyway—it smells wonderful, but I'm not much of a tea
drinker. So, if ghosts don't have to tell the truth, then
what's to say that Susan isn't lying?"

"Nothing, I guess. If Susan was carrying a grudge
against Walter it wouldn't be out of the question for her
to try to orchestrate a nasty surprise from beyond the
grave. Of course, she could haunt *him* if she wanted to
scare him. Seems much more effective to me. I know I'd
pick that route if I was her."

Andrew flashed me an incredulous look.

"What?" I swallowed my tea too fast and blistered my
tongue and the inside of my lip. Sputtering, I fished an
ice cube out of the freezer and popped it my mouth until
the pain receded to a dull ache.

Andrew leaned against the back of his chair, tipping
his head so he was staring at the ceiling. "Emerald, I have
to tell you this is one of the strangest evenings I've spent.
You're the most peculiar woman I've ever met, and I've
met plenty of quirky folks. Our discussion has to take the
cake. And it's a good cake, I might add." He dipped his
finger in the frosting and licked it. "Betty Crocker?"

I smacked him over the head with a dishtowel. "No.
QFC Bakery. Quick. Easy. Sweet. What more can I say?
You want homemade, you bring the cake next time."

"I might do that. Okay, I'll take the plunge. Give me
some of that tea." He pulled out a notebook as I filled his
cup. "Let's get serious. The fact is that accidents do happen. I know enough about diabetes to know that when
Susan had low-blood-sugar attacks, she got confused.
Low enough, and she might very well have taken more
insulin, forgetting that she had already given herself her
shot. That could lead to seizures and a coma. Or, if she
gave herself a shot but forgot to eat, same end. And when
diabetics go into comas with no one there to help, they
can die. Add alcohol and sedatives to the mixture and
you've got a disaster waiting to happen."

"How long was Susan diabetic? Isn't there an oral
medication she could have taken?"

He shook his head. "Nope. She was a type 1 diabetic—

she had the disease from an early age. I think she told me she first developed it when she was thirteen. Type 1's don't produce any insulin, so they're dependent on their shots to live. Type 2 diabetics can get by with oral meds—like my aunt. Her body still makes insulin, but not enough. The oral medication helps her utilize what she makes."

So if Susan didn't get her insulin, she would have died. If she got too much, same fate. "Not much room for error, is there? You'd think she would have been meticulous about her diet and shots."

He jotted down a couple of notes and looked at me with a sad smile. "Susan was careless, Em. She was in denial. She hated the shots, hated having the disease. She tried to pretend that everything was okay, that she could eat anything she wanted. However, I also know that she had a lot to live for and that she was working with a therapist about the problem. I think she was making progress—she didn't talk about it much, even to me. But over the past few months, at least during our writing group, she monitored her sugars constantly."

I rested my elbows on the table and gave him a piercing look. "So, bring it down to the wire. Do you believe that she committed suicide?"

Andrew sighed and stared at his notes. "Honestly? I don't know, but no, I can't believe it. Maybe it's denial on my part. If the cops found signs of a struggle, they wouldn't have closed the case, and the death certificate wouldn't read 'accident.' And as you said, Walter has an alibi."

"Yeah, he was in transit. Has anybody *ever* used insulin to kill?" The thought of someone taking what was essentially a lifesaving medication and using it as a weapon creeped me out.

"Good question. Maybe we can find a few answers. Can we use your computer?"

I led him into the living room and plugged in the password, then let him take the chair. "Too bad I can't tell Miranda about this—she's a computer whiz. That girl knows every trick in the book."

Andrew laughed, a full belly laugh. "I'll bet you ten bucks that my younger brother knows a few more than she does. The kid is fifteen and has been offered a summer internship at Microsoft next year. If he does well, he'll go back every summer until he graduates, at which time he'll apply for a permanent position. Here we go. . . ." He opened up a browser and typed in a URL. His fingers flew—he knew his way around the keyboard, that was for sure. Within seconds the search engine was spewing out web page after web page.

I read over his shoulder as he clicked through the different sites. It seemed that insulin had been the weapon of choice for a number of murderers. As we searched through article after article, I felt a knot grow in my stomach. "My God, people are cruel."

"Yes, they are. Well, this woman certainly didn't want to be burdened, did she?" A wife in England had killed her wheelchairbound husband and tried to make it look like a natural death.

"This is even more scary—look, a nurse in Illinois murdered twelve patients before the cops caught on and figured out that she was their serial killer. What makes someone do things like that?" I felt dazed; I knew bad things happen—they'd happened to me and to others I loved, but each time, it never failed to amaze me that there could be so many angry people out there aching to hurt someone else.

"I don't know, Em, but I've read enough true crime stories that I don't always sleep well at night. Some of the things I've learned in the research for my books has been horrifying. Oh, look—do you remember Claus von Bulow? He was acquitted on appeal, but there will always be speculation about the case."

I thought back. Von Bulow was the wealthy man whose wife died of what they conjectured to be an overdose of insulin. "I forgot about that case. So, this has happened before, but since a lot of the victims were already ill, or diabetic, there were no red flags waving to alert the investigators. But Susan was healthy and supposedly alone. Of course they are going to think she either had an accident or committed suicide." I thought about what Andrew had told me. "What do you think would happen if we told them that Walter had a history of beating his wife?"

"I think it's highly unlikely that they would break down his door and haul him off in handcuffs. For one thing, we haven't got any proof. I never actually saw him do it. Susan told me he did, but never showed me any bruises. Now, if Walter was the one who was dead, then Susan had motive to kill him, but what possible motive could he have since he was the one having the affairs?"

I speculated. "My sources tell me he wasn't fighting the divorce."

"We have to be careful." He clicked the browser closed and shoved himself back from the desk. "I'm not up for a promotion to the head of Walter's shit list. Who gave a huge donation to the policemen's ball last year? Walter. Who funded the initial start-up costs for the Big Brother program here? Walter. His shoes are so squeaky clean that he could stomp across your best tablecloth and leave it white as virgin snow."

I didn't know Walter had so much money. I had gotten the impression that Susan was the wealthy one in the family. "Are you sure the money for those donations came from Walter and not Susan?"

"He inherited money, trust me. First from his own father and then from his stepfather when the old geezer kicked off. Remember Bernard Addison? You might not—the old man died a couple of years back, probably right about the time you moved here. He was a prominent lawyer, well known for fixing cases with his wallet. Walter inherited both his own share of Bernard's money as well as his stepbrother Joshua's share."

Bernard had left blue-blood money to his stepson rather than his own son? "That sounds odd. I bet that didn't go over very well."

Andrew shrugged. "I don't really know. Joshua didn't stick around very long after Bernard's funeral, and he kept to himself a lot."

"Odd. Okay, back to the matter at hand. Harlow should be here any minute, and we'll have to go through the whole story again. She knows a little about what happened but not much. She also knows more about Walter than either you or I do." Come to think of it, Harlow had the dish on the entire town. I wanted her on my team.

He grinned. I took it as a sign of submission. "Okay, but don't you think she might get spooked?"

I snorted. "She's used to me and my 'witchy' ways." Andrew came around behind me and planted a light kiss on the top of my head. I leaned back against his chest. I could get way too used to this.

While we waited, he shuffled through my CD collection. He raised an eyebrow as he held up a couple of the disks. "Everlast? Nirvana? Beck? Dead Can Dance? The Beastie Boys? What are you, thirty going on eighteen? Are you sure these belong to you and not to Miranda?"

"Very funny. I'm thirty-six, thank you, and Miranda thinks about as much of my musical tastes as you seem to. I happen to like alternative music, and I refuse to let myself get stuck in the past like so many people I know." I slipped a disk into the stereo and turned up the bass, swaying to the heady beat.

The doorbell rang, and a moment later Harlow blew in, a flurry of snow behind her. She took one look at the two of us and grinned. "A party? I thought so. What did I tell you?"

I shushed her as she stripped off her coat and boots. I turned off the stereo and pointed toward the kitchen. "March your butt in there, woman. You'd better get your 'that's freaky' speech ready for me."

"Oh, goody! I could use a dose of freaky. Life's been too quiet lately." She gave Andrew a quick hug and an air kiss in that way that only beautiful people can get away with. "James sends his love. Well, he would have if he'd come out of that darkroom." I pushed the teapot over to her. She shook her head at the cake. "So, tell me everything. Did you really see Susan's ghost in your bedroom?" I nodded. She leaned forward. "What did she want? Spill it."

I sighed. "There's no good way to start, so I'll dive in. She says she was murdered. By Walter, no less."

Harl's eyes grew wide. "Oh, boy," she said. "I can tell this is going to be a doozy."

I QUICKLY BROUGHT Harlow up to speed, cautioning her not to mention the murder part when the kids were around. By the look on her face, I knew that she believed me, though all she said was, "Uh-huh." Andrew added in his own story, and her eyes grew even wider.

Miranda trailed in a short while later and waved hello, then headed upstairs to her bedroom. I called her back. "Honey, get Kip from his room, and both of you come down here."

Kip and Miranda trundled down the stairs. Randa proceeded to lecture us all about her dinner meeting. "The debate was okay, even though they're just like all adults, they never want to listen to anybody under twenty. And they had clam linguine tonight, even after I told them two months ago that I couldn't eat shellfish. They ignored me and took my three dollars anyway. I ate a little salad and the Jell-O."

About what I'd expect; the nerd patrol always ignored Miranda's shellfish allergy; it seemed like they had something with seafood in it every time. "Want me to make you a sandwich, honey?" I pulled the bread and ham and cheese out of the fridge, slapped together a thick sandwich, and grilled it in the toaster oven. Miranda poured herself a glass of juice and scooted in next to Harlow. I hoped Randa would behave tonight. Sometimes she treated Harl like an idiot, and I knew it was because Harl had been a model.

"Andrew and Harlow know about Susan, kids. We're going to try to help her." They reacted in unison, Miranda groaning and rolling her eyes while Kip perked up.

"I'm so sick of all this ghost business!" Miranda's voice took on her signature whine, kind of like a droning mosquito. "It's not fair. I'm trying to study for something that really matters, and you let Kip get his way with all this stupid stuff."

"Knock it off." I tapped her arm. "I told you I'll do

everything I can to keep you out of it, so you'd better change your tone pretty darned quick."

"She doesn't even care. Mrs. Mitchell could be in trouble and Randa wouldn't lift a finger to help." Kip threw a snide look at his sister.

I tapped *him,* on the head. "My temper's reaching flash point." They were well acquainted with my warning, and suddenly both got very busy—Miranda with her sandwich, while Kip examined his nails.

I sat down beside Randa and turned her by the shoulders to face me. "Honey, listen to me. I made a promise to keep you out of this as much as I can. Now, you are welcome to stay and listen if you keep quiet. Otherwise, maybe you should take your sandwich and go on up to your room?"

She hesitated. As much as she wanted to be left untouched by this ghost business, I knew she still wanted to be kept in the loop. Miranda was learning the hard facts about compromise. With a little huff, she stuffed an apple in her pocket, grabbed her plate, and stomped off to her room.

"Will she be okay?" Harlow watched her go.

"Welcome to Teen-Angstville. Check your manners at the door. She'll be fine. She's so focused on that scholarship test that she's been rude to everyone the past few weeks." I turned to Kip. "As for you, Officer Obnoxious—yes, I know what Susan wants. No, I am not going to tell you right now. No arguments. You can help, though. Would you like that?"

He eagerly agreed. I wondered how excited he'd be after I told him what I wanted him to do. "You need to help me clean house so that I can ward it against whatever that other spirit is trying to do. Can you get up an hour early and clean up your room? And I mean really clean—not this 'shove it in the closet' dodge you pull on me."

"Will do, Mom." If he was disappointed, he didn't show it. He plastered a quick kiss on my cheek, and I hugged him back.

"Okay. Scoot. You've got fifteen minutes left before bed, and I don't want to hear you firing up that Nintendo."

I had no doubt that an hour after he jumped out of bed in the morning, his room would be in better shape than it had been in months. He always left his regular chores until the last minute, but if I couched them as magical necessities, they became number-one top priority.

I turned back to Harl and Andrew, both of whom looked lost. There was so much to explain, and I had no idea how much either one of them wanted to hear. I could see that a snap course of Witchcraft & Folklore 101 was in order, but I didn't feel like playing teacher. Instead, I tossed the research that we had printed out onto the table.

"Any ideas? Harl, you haven't said much."

"It's freaky." She grinned.

"Yeah, freaky, all right. To be honest, I'd rather not deal with freaky this time."

Andrew stood up, looking exhausted. It had taken a lot of courage to come to me, I thought, especially after everything he'd divulged. He stretched, popping his back. "I never expected to get caught up into all of this when I asked you out to soup. But I'm willing to give it a shot."

Harl nodded thoughtfully. "Me too. We have to be careful, though. If Walter finds out what we're up to, we're in trouble. He could have us tossed in jail for slander so fast that we'd be singing Christmas carols from there." I had the sinking feeling that Harl might see this as the perfect outlet for revenge against his unwelcome advances.

Another pause and Andrew voiced the questions we were all thinking: "So, what's our next step? How do we try to investigate this?"

I'd been thinking about that. "Harl, what about the daughter? Maybe she knows something. Could you try to dig up whatever info you can?"

"I don't know if she'll help us," Andrew interrupted. "Susan had only recently reunited with Diana. She had also told me that the relationship was tenuous at best. Walter won't give the girl the time of day, I guess." His voice was so low that I barely caught his words. "They've been estranged for years, and Susan had once told me that he won't even allow her name to be spoken in the house."

"Sounds serious. Do you know where she is? I wonder if Walter even let her know her mother died. Maybe I can ask Murray whether the cops notified Diana."

Andrew shook his head. "I think she lives in Seattle, but I don't know exactly where. So, what should I do?"

I thought for a moment. "See if you can find out more about Walter and Susan's marriage. She was very rich. Even if he has money on his own, that's a powerful incentive. Also, you said Susan mentioned she had somebody who wanted her, 'even if you didn't.' Do you know who that was?"

He frowned, thinking it over. "I assumed she was lying, but I'll see if I can find out anything."

"What are you going to do?" Harl snapped her gum. She had the whitest teeth of anyone I knew. They practically glowed in the dark.

"I'm going to clean house and ward it—before you ask, that means I'm going to psychically protect it. Then we're going to have ourselves an old-fashioned séance and ask Susan to manifest. I think it's time we had a long talk with the first client of our little Spooks-R-Us agency."

Silence flooded the room. Andrew gave me a gentle kiss as he left. I leaned against the sill and waved, wondering what the hell was going to happen next. Murray said I was ready for change, and it looked like change had come calling whether or not I wanted to open the door.

Eight

✢

BEFORE I WENT to sleep, I pulled a thick album out of my nightstand and crawled under the handstitched quilt that Nanna had made me so many years ago. The black construction paper pages were frayed at the edges, but inside, the photos were carefully preserved in little plastic holders. I thumbed through the pictures of my childhood until I found what I was looking for. There she was—Nanna, in a tidy dress with a big apron tied over her abundant tummy.

"I sure wish you were here, Nanna," I whispered to her image. "You'd know how to deal with this." It had been Nanna who taught me how to clear out ghosts and tangle up trouble with a thread bottle. When I was seven, she taught me to charm gingerbread men for good luck at Christmas. By fourteen I could call home a wayward family member using a candle and a handful of dirt. I sniffed back a few tears. "I miss you." Could she hear me?

The door creaked, and I jerked my head up. Relieved to see that the intruder was Randa rather than some ghostly stalker, I waved her over. I had expected that she'd pop in sooner or later. She always seemed to make an appearance in my bedroom on the nights that we argued, as if she couldn't sleep until we sorted things out.

"What's up, chickie?" I started to put away the album but she jumped on the bed and reached for it. I handed it to her, surprised. She seldom took an interest in family matters. Sometimes I wondered if she'd gotten some notion that she was adopted.

"What are you looking at? Is that Nanna?" She fingered the picture, pulling the album closer.

"Yes, that's my Nanna. I wish you could have met her, pumpkin. She was an incredible woman. So why are you out of bed? It's almost one in the morning."

Randa yawned. "I couldn't seem to get to sleep." She leaned her head against my shoulder and looked up at me. "Sorry, Mom."

"Don't sweat it. We all get tense. You just have to learn to respect other people's feelings more than you do." I slid my arm around her shoulders and we leaned back against the headboard.

"Yeah, I guess so." She arranged the photo album so we could both look at it. "Why didn't I ever get to meet Nanna? She didn't die until I was four or five, did she?"

I sighed. She'd have to find out the truth someday. "Your daddy didn't like my family, honey. He didn't get along with my parents, and he especially didn't like Nanna. There was always a big fight whenever they ended up in the same room. I didn't go home much after I got married. I'm sorry, though. I think you would have liked my grandmother. You like your grandma and grandpa, don't you . . . my folks?"

She shrugged. "They seem nice. We don't get to see them much either. Nanna lived with you when you were little, didn't she?"

"She took care of Rose and me."

"Tell me about her. Maybe I'll be able to go to sleep." Randa yawned again and slid down under the covers, turning to me with earnest eyes. Moments like these were fewer now, and I treasured every one of them because I knew in a couple of years, they'd stop for good and my little girl would vanish in a cloud of teen angst like the one that had reared its head tonight.

"Okay. Ready?" She adjusted the covers and murmured a little "Yes." "Nanna came to live with us when I was about three. I was always her favorite, you know." I grinned. "Rose was barely out of diapers and Mother wanted to take a job as a secretary, helping Dad in the store. She hated housework. I think that's hereditary, because both you and I hate it, too. Anyway, Nanna came to live with us."

"Did Grandpa like her?"

"Well, your grandpa had mixed feelings about her. With Nanna there, Mother was happy because she could go back to work. Dad could save money by not having to pay either a baby-sitter or a secretary, which meant more money for the family."

"But the house smelled . . ." Randa prompted. I don't know how many times I had told her this story, but for some reason, she liked to hear it over and over again.

I nodded. "The house *reeked*. Nanna loved to cook, but she cooked a lot of cabbage and rye bread and she liked beer and strong cheeses. Well, this started what Rose and I later called the "War of the Grandmothers." Nappa had died years earlier—I never knew him—he died in the old country before Nanna came to the United States. But Dad's parents were alive and well. They didn't like Nanna. They were certain that her cooking was going to ruin us all, with the heavy breads and meats she served. They were very Irish white-lace-and-linens. And they were Catholic and Nanna was . . . well, whatever Nanna was, there wasn't a church built for her."

Miranda laughed. "I could say the same for you."

"Yeah, well, be glad your mother is so liberal. As long as you and Kip grow up to be good people, I won't care what you believe or how dirty your house is."

"That's not true. You may not like housework, but you hate dirty houses."

"Uh-huh. That's because Nanna pounded it into my head that dirt in the home breeds trouble. So I keep our home as clean as I do because I really believe she was right. When the cobwebs and dust pile up, all the musty thoughts and forgotten emotions get caught in their webs and attract spirits and all sorts of chaotic energy."

Miranda shifted. I thought she might be uncomfortable with the direction of the conversation, but she asked, "Is that why some houses give me the creeps when I first walk in? Joni's house is like that. She's asked me to stay overnight before, but I always feel like I'm being watched, so I tell her thanks, but I'm busy."

"Yep, that's why. And now, young woman, it's time for you to go to sleep. You can stay in here, if you like." The kids seldom came crawling into my bed, but once in a while they'd seek comfort in my room, looking for safety from the odd nightmare or noise in the night.

Randa yawned and stretched. "Thanks, but I think I can sleep now." She gave me a peck on the cheek and padded out of the room. I blew a silent kiss toward the door.

I ROSE EARLY to that dusky gray sky that accompanies predawn snowfalls, and scrubbed and dusted all corners of the house, especially the étagère, which held my most precious collectibles, including the Waterford crystal globe that Roy had bought for me when he found out I was pregnant with Randa. Of everything he'd given me, that was the most precious, and I'd kept it regardless of the bad blood between us.

Randa was still asleep when Kip joined me in the living room. "My room's clean. Should I unload the dishwasher?"

"Yep. I'll finish up in the living room here." I vacuumed and, as the sky began to lighten, straightened the last pile of magazines. After we finished, I brought out Nanna's little trunk of charms that she'd left to me and sorted through them till I found what I was looking for—a silver rune, Algiz, the Norse symbol of protection. It was hanging from a gold chain. Nanna had charmed it long ago.

I poked around until I found a cobalt blue jar that had been sealed with an airtight stopper. Nanna's homemade incense. I wasn't sure what it was made of—the recipe was in her diary underneath all of her jewelry and charm bags—but the only thing that mattered was that it still worked. Nanna had used it whenever she wanted to clear a house. There were a few rough cones left in the bottom of the jar. I'd have to make some more cones before long.

"The rune is supposed to be hung up over the front door. Get me the stepstool, would you?" As Kip headed for the kitchen, I called out, "Also bring me the hammer and a nail from the junk drawer." He lugged back in everything that I asked for and I set up the stepstool and climbed to the top step. After I'd pounded the nail in far enough to hold the weight of the pendant, but not so far that the chain would slip off, I hung the rune over the door. As I jumped down and looked at it critically, I flashed back to the time I was seven, when Nanna first hung this same rune over our door.

Grandma McGrady had had a fit and said Lucifer himself would come knocking. Nanna called her an old biddy in German. Apparently Grams knew enough of the language to understand the insult, and she set to squawking in a way that would have made any old hen proud. She never mentioned the rune again, but after that she refused to enter the house through the front door, blustering her way in through the kitchen and never failing to mention what a hassle it was to go around to the back of the house. Yet another battle in the War of the Grandmothers.

"What next?" Kip's eyes were shining. He looked so excited that I hated to break it to him that we had very little left to do.

"Why don't you help me light the incense?" I fumbled with one of the homemade cones, finally getting the sticky thing set into the conch shell I used for an incense burner. While Kip held the seashell, I struck a match to the top of the cone. A puff of smoke rose up, and the room took on the aroma of a herb garden—lavender and lemon, sage and cedar and black pepper. The smoke was pungent but not unpleasant. Nanna knew her stuff; the intervening years hadn't destroyed the potency.

I waved some of the smoke up to circle around the rune and motioned for Kip to set the shell on the coffee table, where the cone would burn itself out.

"What was it Nanna said when she used to do this? Oh . . . yeah, I remember . . . give me a minute here." I took a deep breath and let it out slowly, trying to focus as clearly on the words as she had always done. "All things unholy, all things profane, be expelled from this house, to never return again."

Kip waited expectantly. "That's it?" He looked disappointed.

"That's it. You expected more, didn't you?"

"I guess. Nothing happened."

"Didn't it? Feel the air—can you tell the difference?" I wasn't pulling one over on him; the air did feel cleaner, a little more settled.

He closed his eyes. "It felt all mixed up before. Now the house feels brighter."

"Good. You're learning. Remember, not every spell will end in special effects like on *Buffy* and *Charmed*. Actually, most won't." I started to put the rest of Nanna's stuff back in her trunk. It was then that I noticed that the ribbon I kept tied around her diary had come loose. "What's this? Someone's been reading Nanna's journal."

She had kept the silk ribbon tied with a triple knot; I always retied it the same way when I was done reading. But when I picked up the journal, it was bound with a sloppy double bow, much like a shoelace. Miranda wouldn't have had any interest in the book. I looked over at Kip. He was shuffling, staring at the floor. "Kip . . . have you been into Nanna's trunk? I want the truth."

He squirmed. "I'm sorry. I wanted to see what she had . . . what she wrote in her book." The look on his face told me that he knew how wrong he'd been to disobey me. He was never allowed to get into the trunk without my permission. When Kip first expressed an interest in learning Nanna's folkways, I agreed because it was safer than having him explore his psychic gifts on his own, but I warned him never to read or try anything pertaining to magic without my supervision. He had given me his promise—his oath on his honor. Apparently Kip's ego had decided to declare independence day.

"You realize how disappointed I am with you?"

"Yes, ma'am."

"What do you think I should do?"

He fidgeted with the tail of his shirt, shifting from one foot to another. I waited in silence, letting him imagine all sorts of terrible punishments—the power of suggestion was a wonderful tool. After a few minutes, tears began to roll down his cheeks and he blubbered a soggy, "I'm sorry."

As pathetic as he sounded, I knew that he was more sorry he had gotten caught than for what he'd done in the first place. "Oh, I think you are going to be sorry. You're grounded for two weeks. You come directly home or to the shop, whichever I tell you to do. No talking to Sly on the phone or any of your other buddies. No Nintendo for two weeks. The only places you will be going are to school, the shop, and with me when I tell you to come along. Do you understand?"

He sputtered but quickly backtracked when he took one look at my face. I was in no mood for negotiations. "Yes, ma'am. I'm really sorry, Mom."

"Umm-hmm. Okay, go wash your face. It's time for breakfast."

He wiped his nose with his sleeve. I'd have to remember to wash that shirt tonight. As he ran off to the bathroom, I carefully retied the knots on the diary. Charms, folklore, old spells, all required respect, and the only way to learn that respect was right from the beginning. Too many chances for spells to backfire, otherwise.

Kip would remember this day and thank me for being tough with him. Maybe not today or tomorrow or next week . . . but someday. Meanwhile, I would buy a padlock for Nanna's trunk. I hated the fact that I couldn't trust him, but he was too enchanted by anything that had to do with magic. If he wasn't careful, one of these days he'd land himself in hot water.

Miranda straggled in, rubbing her eyes. After our late-night talk she looked remarkably refreshed, if a little grungy. Her hands were stained with blue ink. If there was one leaky pen in the house, she would manage to find it.

"You haven't had a shower this morning, have you?" There was a vaguely ripe odor drifting off her pj's. I glanced at the clock and pulled out the bacon and eggs from the fridge. For once, I had a little time on my hands, and I intended to make us a breakfast that wasn't dripping with sugar.

She squinted. "I'll take one in gym. It's first period." With a sniff, her face lit up. "No cereal today? Yay! I'm hungry. Can we have scrambled eggs, please?"

I broke half a dozen eggs into a bowl and whipped them together with some minced shallots, red pepper chunks, cheddar cheese, and a sprinkling of parsley and lemon pepper. While they bubbled in the skillet, I slid two more slices of bread in the toaster. Miranda pulled out the juice and poured it into glasses, then set the table. "Thank you . . . you're a good girl."

She shrugged, but gave me a quick smile and I decided that would do—it was better than the grouch she usually was in the morning. I divided the eggs onto the plates while she buttered the toast. As we were setting the table, she reached out and put her hand on my arm. "Thanks for last night, Mom. I love those stories . . . can we go visit Grandma and Grandpa soon?" Her father's parents, the O'Briens, seldom asked about the children. I was grateful that my folks loved the kids and enjoyed showering them with attention whenever possible.

I kissed the top of her head. "They went to Arizona for Christmas. After they come back, we'll take a trip over to Aberdeen and stay for a few days. Will that work?" Happy, she sat down, unfolding her napkin into her lap.

Kip silently entered the kitchen and took his seat. He picked at his food while I finished making their lunches and joined them at the table with a demitasse. I fished a couple of slices of bacon onto my plate and snagged a slice of toast before everything disappeared. "Are we do-ing anything tonight?" Kip polished off his eggs and grabbed his milk. I rested a hand on his arm, and he slowed down.

"Actually, I've got plans with Harlow and Andrew.

Since you're grounded, I'm taking you to Mrs. Trask's for the night. I'm sure she'll be happy to take you."

Kip immediately put up a fuss. "Mom! It's about Susan, isn't it? What are you going to do? I want to help."

"Sorry, buster. You blew your chance." It was just as well that he'd disobeyed me. He'd be desperate to join us once he knew we were holding a séance, but there wasn't enough chintzware in England to convince me to let him be here, not when Susan came complete with her own private nightmare. "We're holding a séance. Don't bother whining. My word's final—no arguments. And," I added, knowing all too well how his mind worked, "if you expect to sneak out from Mrs. Trask's and go over to Sly's, think again. She's going to know you're grounded and will keep a close eye on you."

His lower lip quivered enough for me to tell that he was debating the politics of crying. I caught his eye and shook my head. He sighed and pulled on his coat. "Okay. Jeez, I want to help, Mom."

"You got grounded? What did you do this time?" Miranda snickered, and I gave her my *don't-even-go-there* look. She bent her head and studied her eggs again.

"I know you want to help." I hugged him as he zipped up the windbreaker. "But you aren't going to this time. Now, off to school and have a good day."

He shoved an armload of textbooks into his backpack, swung the pack over one shoulder, and grabbed his lunch as he raced out the door. Lincoln Elementary was only a few blocks away, and I made him walk the distance. Miranda usually rode her bike along the ten-block trip to the Chiqetaw Ridge Middle School, but the snow had put a stop to that. During the winter, she had to hoof it.

Miranda watched him go, her mouth full of egg and toast. She swallowed, raising an eyebrow. "Last time Mrs. Trask watched us overnight, she made Kip mop the bathroom floor because he left it in such a wreck after his bath. He told me he was going to try to do a binding so you wouldn't call her again."

So the little fox was up to tricks, was he? That was

probably what he was looking up in Nanna's diary. After all these years, I still hadn't read it all the way through; maybe I'd better. "Kip's getting carried away. And you, my dear . . . you're going to Mrs. Trask's, too, so you need to come straight home after school so you can get ready."

"I want to study. Can't I stay here in my room? You know I won't bother you guys—I'm not interested." She mopped up the last of her egg with the toast and zipped up her new parka.

Would it be dangerous to let her stay here? She wasn't going to burst into the middle of the séance and demand to be part of the action. In fact, if I knew Miranda, she'd hide out in her room all evening without so much as a squeak. But what if something went wrong? With a nagging feeling, I shook my head.

"I trust you, but after what happened with Kip the other night, I don't want to take a chance. You're going to have to bite the bullet this time." I picked up the phone receiver and dialed Ida Trask. Her schedule was free for the evening, and I made arrangements for the kids to spend the night at her house.

Miranda grabbed her books. "I'm going to be late. Look at it snow."

I pushed back the lace curtains and peered out the window that overlooked our front walk. The snow was piling up faster than my neighbor across the street could shovel it. He was wrapped in a big overcoat, fighting a losing battle with his shovel, but I knew that he wouldn't stop. Horvald Ledbetter was one of the few truly compulsive people we knew. Once, Miranda caught a glimpse of him weeding his petunias at two in the morning. She was about to come in from her stargazing when he tiptoed out of his house in a bathrobe, armed with flashlight, trowel, and cultivator. She slipped in through her window so quietly that he never noticed her up on the roof. She watched him work under the stars until she grew weary and fell into bed.

"Nasty. Okay, I'm ready to head down to the shop. I'll drop you off. Grab my purse and keys while I make sure the stove's turned off." A little O/C, I always checked and double-checked the burners to make sure they were cool whenever we left the house.

I managed to drop Randa off at school and still make it downtown by nine o'clock. Usually we didn't open until eleven, but with the holiday rush, I took advantage of every merchant hour I could. The door was locked. Cinnamon was late. Great, the holiday rush and she probably had car trouble again.

I quickly flipped the sign to "We're Open" and put water on to heat for tea. The sisters Farrah Warnoff and Sheila Smythe rushed in, breathless and covered with snow. Both had placed special orders, both of which had arrived yesterday right before I closed up. Farrah had begged me to find a Spode cream and sugar set, while Sheila wanted a Dresden figurine. The Dresden had taken some hunting, but I managed to fill both requests at a reasonable price. The pieces had arrived intact. I wrapped up their purchases and bustled them out the door.

I quickly whipped the shop in order for customers. First things first. I poured the steaming water into the thermoses. Besides the usual Earl Grey, we would have apple cinnamon and orange pekoe. As I arranged a large platter of gingerbread and molasses cookies, chalking "Spice Is Nice" on the menuboard, Cinnamon came rushing through the door, three shoppers on her heels. Any more thoughts about murders and ghosts would have to wait until the shop closed. Taking a deep breath, I dove into my day.

Nine

✢

MIRANDA WAS SCARFING down a bowl of pudding when I got home from work. Her book stood propped open against the center pillar candle on the table. I quietly walked up behind her, removed the book, and marked the place before I closed it. "Talk to your mother, child."

"Aw, Mom! I was in the middle of a chapter." She rolled her eyes.

"Yep. But we have more exciting things to discuss."

"Like what?" She wrinkled her nose. "How many china patterns you can guess with your eyes closed?"

"Smart-ass." I grinned and slid into the chair opposite her. "We're going out this weekend and buying a Christmas tree."

She perked up. "Really? Did we keep the ornaments when we moved?"

I frowned, mentally sorting through the boxes in the hall closet. "I'm not sure, but I'll buy a few more just in case. The garland is probably shot, and all the lights were tangled together last I looked . . . oh, hell, let's get rid of everything except the special ones and buy all new stuff."

Miranda did a happy dance in her chair. "Kip will be

glad to hear that. He was awfully sad last Christmas . . . and the one before. Umm, Mom, will Daddy be sending us gifts this year, or are we going to get money from him again?"

I thought about the note I'd received the other day. She didn't need to know that Roy's gift "checks" were coming from me instead of from her father. The kids would see right through me if I bought the gifts and labeled them from him; they always picked up on that little trick. So I got them gift certificates to their favorite stores and said they were from Roy, hoping it would ease the pain of being ignored. "I think your dad is pretty busy lately. But I know he'll send you something."

She thought about it for a moment and in her mouse voice asked, "Does Dad ever really think about us?"

I dreaded that question, and it came up every few months. How could I answer when I didn't know, myself? How could I possibly craft an answer that wouldn't hurt? Miranda was vulnerable. Roy had been the world to her until he so abruptly trashed our family. "Randa, hon . . . your daddy went through some changes. He still loves you, even if he doesn't show it. Someday he might be more involved in your life, but we can't make it happen simply because we want it to."

She rubbed her head, and when she looked at me, the loss in her eyes made my stomach ache. "Why did Daddy have to bring her into our house? Why did he do that to her in *my* bed? He knew I was coming home early from school!"

I rubbed my neck. The familiar twinge of a tension headache loomed at the base of my skull. "I don't know. I don't know what he was thinking. He didn't mean to hurt you; he was trying to hurt me." Nursing a wanton desire to beat him senseless, I again tried to neutralize the damage, but the truth was that Roy had traumatized Randa to the point of nightmares. If there was a hell, he'd burn like a torch. He'd burn as brightly as Randa's little wicker bed had when I chopped it up with an ax and set it on fire in the front yard, along with Roy's entire wardrobe, including his Armani suits.

She finished her pudding and pushed the bowl away. "It wasn't your fault."

I filled the sink with soapy water. The breakfast dishes were crusted over—we hadn't had time to rinse them. Sometimes I enjoyed doing the dishes by hand instead of stacking them in the dishwasher. The bubbles lathered gently against my skin, giving me time to think. I began to scrub the scrambled eggs off the frying pan.

Miranda grabbed the dishtowel and dried as I washed. We worked in silence until she put the last plate in the cupboard. "So you like this Andrew guy?"

I thought about it for a moment, wanting to give her an honest answer rather than some glib comeback. After a moment, I dried my hands and untied my apron. "Yes, I do, but I'm going to take it slowly. What do you think of him?"

She hung the dishtowel over the bar on the oven and grabbed a handful of cookies out of the strawberry cookie jug. Scooping up her books, she headed out of the room, stopping for a moment by the door. "He's okay, I guess."

As she disappeared up the back stairs to get her stuff, Kip called from the front door. His backpack in the one hand, Game Boy in the other, a sullen pout clouded his face. "I want to help. Why can't we stay home? It's not fair."

"Listen, kiddo." I knelt down so we were face-to-face. "You're already in enough trouble, so no more complaining. First: you've got to earn my trust back before I'll let you help me out again with magic. Second: I don't trust the spirit that's following Susan. It possessed you once already, Kipling. I won't put you or your sister in danger."

Kip shuffled, scuffing his shoe on the floor. "I guess I messed things up, huh?"

I pulled him to me and gave him a quick hug. "I know how much you love all of this. It's exciting. But when you get enthusiastic, you don't listen. You rush off half-cocked and someday you're going to get hurt or hurt somebody else. Remember when you decided to build a volcano for science class and Miranda tried to help you with the recipe for the lava? You ignored her and turned the kitchen into a disaster area." The hardened combination of baking soda and mud had taken me days to clean up.

He plopped himself on the bench against the foyer wall and played with one of the philodendron's leaves. "Sly and I were supposed to camp out in the living room tonight and watch *A Christmas Carol*. His mom was going to make cocoa and popcorn balls."

I ruffled his hair. "And now you're going to miss it because you're grounded. Kip, when you do something wrong, you have to accept responsibility for your actions. You don't live in a vacuum—what you do affects other people. You and Miranda can watch the movie at Mrs. Trask's, and I'll bet she'll make hot cocoa if you ask."

"It's not the same."

"No, it's not. But everything will be okay. Next week, we'll watch *A Christmas Story* here together, like we always do." *A Christmas Story* was a family favorite; we watched it every year. I lifted his chin and gave him a soft smile. "We'll go out this weekend and get a Christmas tree and decorate the mantel and light a fire and roast marshmallows."

A ray of delight broke through his gloom, and he threw his arms around me. "Yay! I was wondering if we were ever gonna have fun again."

I gently disengaged him and knelt down by his side. "I'm sorry. I haven't been a very good mom for a while. Things have changed, though. I promise."

He sniffled a little, then gave me a peck on the cheek. "It's okay. Randa and I aren't good at helping out, either."

Miranda came galloping down the stairs with a book bag that was almost as big as she was. She motioned to Kip. "Come on, slowpoke, let's get moving." She gave me a quick hug, and they headed out the door. Ida lived just a few houses away; I didn't need to drive them over there.

Kip waved. "See you tomorrow, Mom. Will you tell us what happens?"

I agreed. "It's a deal. Remember, unless there's an emergency, both of you stay right with Mrs. Trask. No going over to Sly's or to the library or anywhere else. Have a good night and I'll see you after school tomorrow." As they shut the door, I leaned against the window, watching them trudge through the swirling snow. The world was so big. I hoped I was preparing them for it.

I HAD AN hour before Harl and Andrew were due. I jumped in the shower for a long rinse. I had finished dressing in a caftan of flowing black linen with silver threads running through the weave when the doorbell rang. I gave my hair a last brush-through and answered the door. They had come together. Andrew carried a box of chocolates and a bouquet of flowers. Harlow shoved a bottle of sparkling cider into my hands.

"I didn't know what sort of hostess gifts were appropriate for a séance," Andrew said as he helped Harl with her coat and boots. I carried the cider and candy into the living room and found a vase for the flowers. Roses, winter-white as the snow drifts outside the window. I pressed my nose into them and inhaled deeply—they had a clear scent, light and fragile. It had been a long time since a man had given me roses.

We moved the coffee table out of the way and set up a small wooden card table. I arranged a pad of paper and a pen in case Susan decided she wanted to dictate another note. Andrew suggested that we also set up a tape recorder in case somebody commandeered one of us for use as a mouthpiece. I agreed, though with a little luck and Nanna's charm, *that* wouldn't be happening again.

Andrew and Harlow joined in, first with mirth, then with a growing sense of sobriety as they realized we were actually going through with this. I set out glasses of water in case we got thirsty; it wasn't a good idea to interrupt the flow of a séance in order to run into the kitchen for a drink. After dimming the lights, I unplugged the phone so we wouldn't be interrupted.

"Should we use a Ouija board?" Andrew held our chairs for us as we sat down.

I nixed the idea. "I won't allow one in the house. They

attract wandering spirits, and you never know who you're going to dial up on the great cosmic chat line." They laughed. Good. It was important to break the tension. This was a first for both of them, so I had to keep control of the situation without making them nervous. "Okay, a lot of things might happen; the hardest part is when you hope for contact and nobody shows up. Spirits are notorious for not showing when called, but I have a hunch that Susan is hanging around. I can feel her energy."

"If she does show up, what will you ask?" Harlow jumped up and took the gum out of her mouth. She dropped it in the wastebasket and returned to the table.

I held out a list of questions I'd written up earlier, when I had a free moment at the shop. "If there's one thing I've found, it's that you must be prepared. When the supernatural hits your doorstep, it's way too easy to forget what you wanted to ask." I lit the candle in the center of the table, and we joined hands. Nanna had taught me this, too, but she seldom performed the invocation of spirits except on All Souls' Night, when we paid our respects to our dead relatives. "I'm going to invoke her like Nanna taught me, except I'll be using English. God knows, if I tried to conjure up somebody in German, I'd probably end up with Genghis Khan or Attila the Hun and we'd be in deep shit."

One breath. Two breaths. Lower into trance. The familiar feel of the energy swept around me and I let it engulf me, draw me under. I could feel Harlow's nervous anticipation crackle through her fingers into mine, and Andrew was emanating a light that I hadn't noticed before. He seemed to step in, to buoy me up with his support. He probably didn't even know what he was doing. I rode on his energy for a moment and decided it was stable enough to rely on, though if Susan appeared, who knew whether he could keep his focus? People folded over the simplest things.

When I felt ready, I took another breath and spoke in a loud, clear voice, forcing my intent into my words. *"I invoke and implore you, spirit of the night, Susan Mitch-*

ell, appear at this table and grace us with your presence. Give us a sign that you hear us."

I waited. Nothing. Not a peep. I could feel Andrew and Harl tense, and I knew from experience that they were holding their breath. I led them in taking another slow, deep breath and repeated my request. I was almost ready to cash it in for the evening when the candle flame wavered and flared high into the air. A rush of icy wind raced through the room, dropping the temperature where we sat by a good twenty degrees.

Harlow squealed. "Oh, my God, she's here!"

The table began to clatter against the floor, and it took all that I had to grab hold of their hands and not let go. My first thought was earthquake, but the hairs rose along the back of my neck, and I knew that Harlow was right. Susan was here. I caught my breath, waiting. Sure enough, she wasn't done yet. The dimmer on the light switch began to spin, first flooding the room with light and then plunging it into candlelight. Roller-coaster time—my stomach began to flip-flop and, as I gulped air to calm the stirring nausea, it dawned on me that the séance was actually working.

Cool! Nanna's teachings had held up over the years. I hadn't led a séance since I was a teenager, and then had called in some musty old spirit whose only request was that we leave him alone. Then, as the table continued to quiver and shake, I began to think that maybe this wasn't such a bright idea after all. Harlow and Andrew both looked a little green, and I knew that I was going to have to take charge. If anything too disturbing happened, they'd drop me like a hot potato and I'd go splat—no friends, no help.

"Susan, is it you? Are you here? If so, show yourself." We'd come this far, there was no going back. A cold chill hovered over the table, and my breath filtered out from between my teeth like mist caught in a frozen tableau. The temperature had dropped again. It had to be close to thirty degrees inside the living room. The windows were beginning to ice over.

A bud vase went spinning off the shelf over the computer and crashed against the opposite wall, missing the window by a fraction of an inch. Shards of the delicate glass showered down on the carpet.

"What's happening?" Harlow was starting to panic, and Andrew was a close second behind her. "Emerald, do something!"

"Stop this *now!*" My voice echoed through the whirl of energy, and there was an immediate hush as the lights stopped flickering and the table came to rest.

One beat, two beats . . . a swirl of vapor formed near the archway that led into the dining room, and out of the vapor we could see the ghost of Susan Mitchell materializing. Andrew gasped, just enough so I knew he recognized her. Harlow faltered and dropped my hand, pushing her chair back.

There is a peculiar quality to the dead when they appear in spirit form—a translucent, not-quite-human-anymore feel. Susan had faded since I had last seen her; now she was more vaporous than material. She turned her gaze to me, and I hesitated a moment, sensing less of the pleading victim I'd first met, and more of some subterranean creature who lives in shadows and haunts old houses with memories long gone by.

"Why is she looking at us like that?" Harlow scrambled out of her chair and was now pressed against a wall.

"She's starting to lose what's left of her humanity. Spirits grow farther away from the mortal realm the longer they've been dead, and it gets harder for them to take physical form for very long. But I wouldn't expect her to be moving away this fast. I wonder what's been happening to her over there." Privately, I thought that Mr. Big & Ugly was responsible. I had the feeling he was feeding on her energy. Or maybe she was going through some sort of internal war—wanting to move on but unable to let go because of her unfinished business. I cleared my throat. Susan stayed where she was, not moving, lightly hovering above the floor. Andrew took a tentative step forward, and I motioned for him to stay where he was.

"Susan, we want to help you. We need more information and were hoping you could point us in the right direction." She slowly inclined her head. I relaxed a little. She could still understand me, which meant she wasn't totally trapped between the worlds. "Do you need a pen? Can you still write like you did the other night when you first came to me?"

One beat. Two beats . . . and the vaporous form moved forward toward the table, where the pen and paper were waiting. As we watched, the pen rose to hover above the surface while Susan stared at it intently.

I glanced at the list of questions. "We need to get in touch with Diana, your daughter. Where is she?"

The pen hesitated for a moment, twitching, then scrawled something on the page, and the paper flew off the table and feathered its way to the floor. I didn't feel like getting close enough to retrieve it while the ghost was still standing there, so I thanked her and tried to figure out how to phrase the next question. The last thing I needed was an angry spirit railing at me.

"Susan, Walter has an alibi—" I had barely begun to speak when a roar came pouring through the room. Susan reared back, eyes blazing with a brilliant blue fire, and the pen went flying behind the sofa. A dark cloud began to take shape behind Susan and she turned to me, mouthing something I couldn't hear. The fire in her eyes had turned to fear and she tipped her head back, shrieking in her silent world as she vanished through the ceiling. The cloud raced after her.

"What the hell is going on?" I watched both Susan and the cloud disappear through the ceiling. As we sat there, staring at one another, hesitating, a thin cry pealed through the house from the second story.

What? Was that Susan? A second shriek, razor-sharp, echoed through the room, and I knocked over my chair in my rush to the stairs. "Miranda!" It couldn't be—she was over at Ida's, but I knew my daughter's voice, and that had been her screaming. Andrew was fast on my heels, Harlow behind him. As we pounded up the stairs, yet a third scream sliced into my heart.

Ten

✦

"RANDA! MIRANDA!" IF ripping out my lungs could make me run faster, I would have willingly done so. As it was, I shredded them, screaming as I took the stairs two at a time. Andrew and Harlow were right behind me.

The railing shook as I propelled myself up to the second story. I slammed open the door. Randa's CD player was sitting in the middle of the floor, next to an open book. I didn't see it in time to slow down and my foot got caught in the coiled cord, sending me sprawling. A shower of sparks crackled through the air as the plug tore itself out of the wall. The soft movements of Bach skipped and fell silent. I pushed myself to my hands and knees. Andrew crowded into the room behind me, with Harlow dogging his heels. They grabbed me by the arms and yanked me to my feet.

"Where is she?" I had to find Randa. I didn't see her anywhere in the room. Her daybed was mussed, but the covers hadn't been turned down. The computer was on. An old toy chest stood open in the corner with one of her childhood dolls sitting next to it, but Miranda was nowhere in sight. I started to panic, blood pounding in my head. Then I saw the window. It was open, curtains waving in the icy breeze. I shot toward it, but Andrew beat me to it.

"Holy hell!" He scrambled over the sill. "She's out here." He held her in his arms, my Miranda. She was unconscious, her hair limply trailing in the snow. "She was lying near the edge of the railing."

Harlow and I lifted her through, and he climbed back in and shut the window behind him. We got her into bed. She was ice-cold, but she was breathing. She twitched, moaning.

"Is she okay? What is she doing here? She was supposed to be over at Ida's." I knelt by her side, brushing the hair away from her face. Snowflakes still clung to her eyelashes but had started to melt, and now they shimmered like tiny diamonds. I gently lifted her wrist and felt for her pulse. There it was, too fast but strong. She coughed, as if she were starting to come around, but only turned her head to the side.

"Randa? Randa! Wake up!" I shook her by the shoulders. "Get me another blanket. She's freezing." Harlow retrieved a bedspread off of the brass quilt stand that had belonged to Nanna, and we spread the bedspread over my daughter.

Andrew raised Miranda's head to slip in an extra pillow as Harlow scrunched in behind me on the bed, her right foot balancing on the floor, her other knee tucked against my left side. She began to rub my shoulders. I could feel knots of tension ripple under her fingers. Using her thumbs, she dug into a pressure point on the muscles near my collarbone.

"Jeez, that hurts!" I would pay dearly for the fall and the stress, but right now all that mattered was Randa. "Harl, there's a bottle in the medicine cabinet that says "Lung Ease" on it. Could you get that for me?"

"Whatever you need, babe." She patted my shoulder and popped a quick kiss on my head. "I'm going to call James to tell him I'll be late." She took off out of the room again.

As she clattered down the stairs, I looked up at Andrew. "Those spirits came right through Randa's floor." I felt her forehead. Her skin was so cold, and she looked so vulnerable. "What the hell is she doing home?"

He examined the window again. "Want to make a bet she ran for the only way out she could when they appeared? She probably fainted from fright. Can ghosts really hurt people, I mean . . . physically?"

"Some ghosts." I shrugged. "Not Susan—I don't think Susan would hurt anybody, but Mr. Big & Ugly is mean. Not only does he have a nasty temper, but he's also powerful. He got through my warding when Nanna's charm should have kept him out. Andrew, will you get the paper that Susan wrote on? We don't want to lose it."

We were facing a can of worms, all right, and, as Murray had predicted, there was no going back. I thought about her reading. I'd done everything right and still, fate had intervened and put my child at risk. I racked my brain for the rest of what Murray had warned me about. Andrew leaned over the banister and called downstairs to Harlow, asking her to grab the note Susan had written. I made room for him on the little daybed. Miranda didn't fill but half of it. The distant ring of the phone startled me, but then it cut short, and I assumed Harlow had answered.

Andrew whispered, "Everything will be okay" and slipped an arm around my shoulders. I rested my hand on Randa's chest, feeling her breathe, reassuring myself that she was alive.

Harlow jogged into the room and handed me the bottle of Lung Ease. "Ida called. She just went in to check on Randa, to ask if she wanted a snack, and found out she was gone. Apparently Randa snuck out without anybody knowing. I told Ida that she was here so she wouldn't worry."

Randa and I were going to have a serious talk once everything had settled down. "Andrew, could you please stand over there?" She might just be thirteen, but I respected my daughter's privacy. I took the bottle and pulled the cork. The lotion flowed onto my hand, wafting up a cloud of eucalyptus and camphor as I rubbed it onto Randa's chest. I made a bottle every year for colds and coughs, and it worked better than any remedy I could buy on the shelves.

"Will she be okay? Should we call a doctor?" Harlow took the bottle and sniffed it, then winced. "Jeez, that's strong stuff."

"It works." I closed my eyes and tuned in to Randa's energy. There, a bright spot surrounded by a lot of fog. But that central core was burning bright. I touched her with my own energy, blew a mind kiss to her, and gently withdrew. She would be okay ... my baby was safe. I began to relax. "Randa should be waking up soon." Even as I spoke, she began to stir. She shook her head and opened her eyes. I helped her sit up as she started to cough.

"What happened?" Her voice was thin and scratchy.

"That's what I want to know. What are you doing up here? I told you to stay with Mrs. Trask unless it was an emergency, and what happens? I find you here, out on the roof, unconscious. Miranda, answer me: Why did you sneak around like this?"

She squinted, blinking to brush away the light. "I forgot my book and came home to get it. I knew you'd be mad since you told us to stay at Ida's for the night, and since you were in the shower, I thought I could sneak in and out without you knowing. Then, when I got up here, I figured that I had time to print out my history report that's due tomorrow. I'm really sorry, Mom."

I tried to remain calm. "You disobeyed me and you snuck out on Ida. She was frantic when she found out you were gone. You knew what we were doing tonight! You know that we have a dangerous ghost. You could have been seriously hurt."

"I said I was sorry! Jeez, what happened to me? I ache all over." She struggled to stand up, but I pushed her back down on the bed.

"Stay where you are. I told you, we found you out on the roof, unconscious. How did you get there? What happened?" Feeling on the verge of losing control, I struggled to breathe deeply to keep my temper reined in. A layer below the anger, I could feel anxiety churning away. Did the ghosts come through her room? She didn't seem to remember them, if they did.

Miranda quit trying to force her way out of bed and fell back against the pillows. After a moment she sniffed, wiping her nose with a tissue from the box on the nightstand. "I don't know. I don't remember what happened. By the time I got everything I needed and was ready to go back to Mrs. Trask's, I could hear all of you downstairs. I didn't want you to find out I was here, so I decided to stay in my room until after you finished. I was reading. That's all."

I glanced at Harlow and Andrew. Great. Just great, how wonderful. The evening had gone so far astray from our plan that I began to wonder if we weren't jinxed. Harlow motioned me over to the desk. I asked Andrew to sit by Randa and joined Harlow, who was dangling a piece of paper in her fingers.

"Susan gave us an answer," she said.

I took the page. In answer to my question about Susan's daughter, the spirit had scribbled, "Ask Karri B . . ." The rest trailed off into an unintelligible scrawl.

"Karri B . . . well, that gives us something to go on." I handed it to Harlow. "Who on earth is Karri?"

Harlow took the paper back and tucked it in her pocket. "I was thinking about that. It must be Karri Banks—the librarian. She was probably one of the closest friends Susan had, if you can use the word 'close.' Karri and I meet once a month to discuss the literacy campaign; now and then she's mentioned Susan to me."

"Find out anything you can, babe." Miranda coughed and I joined her again, adjusting her covers and tucking them in. Her cheeks were a bit rosier, the color was starting to come back into her face now that she was warming up. She would be fine. "Harl, could you call Ida back and tell her that Randa will be staying at home the rest of the night? She's number three on speed dial. Tell her that Randa's come down with a little cold?"

Harlow nodded and took off down the stairs. There was no sense in taking Randa back into the cold just to go to Ida's. I didn't want to tell her yet that I thought that Mr.

B & U might be responsible for what had happened. And the truth was, I couldn't be sure. Nobody had been upstairs except Miranda herself; there was no way of being certain about what happened. In my heart, though, I knew this was the work of the spirits.

Randa sniffled. "I'm sorry to be so much trouble." I relented then, unwilling to put her through any more stress than she already had experienced. I gave her a long hug and kiss, then asked Andrew to step outside. When he left the room, I helped her into her pajamas and brushed her hair like I used to when she was a little girl.

"We have to talk about the fact that you disobeyed me, but we can do that tomorrow. For now, I want you to get back in bed." I held up the covers for her, and she crept into the brass daybed we had bought when we first moved to Chiqetaw.

"Stay here?" She reached out for me, as if she were afraid I was going to leave. I took her hand and gave it a squeeze.

"I'll be right out in the hall, saying good night to Andrew. I'll sleep in your room tonight, sweetie. Meanwhile, you close your eyes and rest."

Andrew was waiting for me. "Is she okay?"

"Yeah, I think she'll be fine. She doesn't seem any worse for the wear, but I'd sure like to know what the hell happened up here. Okay, well, that about caps it for the night. I'm sleeping in her room. Where's Harlow?"

He pointed to the stairs. "Downstairs. You know, until tonight, I would never have believed such things possible. You've opened up a scary new world for me, one I don't know if I'm ready to face. One that exists outside the pages of a book." He reached out to stroke my face with a gentle hand.

I kissed his fingers as they ran over my lips. "You don't have to come back if you don't want to. I know this must be terrifying. I deal with things like this enough to be used to it, yet these forces still scare even me. Some of us have no choice but to cope with being able to see and feel these other worlds, regardless of whether we enjoy it."

He reached down and planted a kiss on my forehead. "I'll stay as long as you need me to tonight. What I'm trying to say is that when I thought of ghosts before, I thought of Casper and Beetlejuice, but not anymore. Now I have more respect. A lot more. For both the spirits and for someone who can handle them like you do."

I looked at him silently. There wasn't much to say. He didn't smile, just stared back solemnly. When had life gotten so complicated? I swallowed a throatful of tears. "What am I going to do? Ghosts are threatening my family. But as angry as I am, I can't help but feel sorry for Susan. Something's wrong—she wouldn't show up like this if there wasn't unfinished business."

Harlow reappeared, and when she did, she was carrying a tray containing a teapot, two cups, and a plate of vanilla wafers. "I thought you and Miranda could use something to eat."

"You're such a sweetheart." I held the door open for her. She carefully maneuvered the tray onto the worktable that Randa had convinced me to get for her instead of a vanity. I poured a cup of what turned out to be chamomile and took it over to my daughter. Randa pushed herself up in bed and sleepily accepted the tea and cookies. I rejoined Andrew and Harlow near the door, where we spoke in low tones so Randa couldn't overhear us.

"Okay. Harlow, why don't you talk to Karri, see if she can shed any light on what's going on." I turned to Andrew. "Meanwhile, I need to talk to Walter. I don't know what good it will do, but I can read most people; maybe I can tell if he's hiding something. However, I need to be physically near him to do so."

He nodded. "I might be able to help. My writing group has been talking about putting together a small affair for those of us who loved Susan. If I host it, I can make it a public event. Walter can't avoid coming to something like that—it wouldn't look good if he snubbed us, especially not to her devoted readers."

"We could use that excuse to contact Diana, too. We could invite her up to her mother's memorial," Harl interjected.

"Good idea." I squeezed both their hands. "This week is insane. I promised to buy a tree and ornaments, and the shop's annual sale starts tomorrow at noon." We were offering a 25 percent discount on all tea-related items . . . teapots, teas, and teacups. I was also holding a drawing for a free teapot. Great promotion, and it brought people into the shop. Even though the teapot wasn't "fine china," it had a pretty sunflower pattern, and a lot of people had entered the contest.

"I wish Nanna could help me. I need her advice." Nanna had been one of the few I could turn to during a crisis. "Since that isn't an option, I think I'll call Murray again, ask if she'll come over and get a feel for the situation. She's a damn good psychic as well as a fine cop."

"Cop? Are you talking about Anna Murray?" Andrew sounded surprised. "I met her when she questioned everyone in our writers group after Susan died." Andrew inched toward the door. Fatigue clouded his eyes. Harlow looked just as wiped.

"Both of you go home. Harl, call me tomorrow if you find out anything. I'll either be here or at the shop, depending on how Randa feels. And guys, thanks for being here tonight."

Andrew pressed his lips together. "Em, I won't run again. Not because of ghosts or spooks or anything else like that. Would you like me to stay over tonight? I can sleep on the sofa downstairs."

"Let me know how Randa is tomorrow, babe." Harlow gave me a quick kiss and took off down the stairs as we followed her out into the hallway.

"Thanks for the offer, Andrew, but it's not a good idea. I have to take things slow. Do you understand? I come with a lot of baggage. Two kids, a nasty ex . . . a ghost who has revenge on the mind." At the last, I couldn't help but laugh. "That sounds absurd, doesn't it?"

Andrew snorted. "At least you don't look like Dan Akroyd!"

"Hey, we may still end up turning into Ghostbusters." My giggles subsided, and I yawned. Every muscle in my body hurt. It even hurt to think.

He edged toward the stairs. "I suppose I should get on home."

"Go, sleep, rest. We'll be okay." I blew him a kiss, and he reached out and let his fingers linger against my cheek. "Lock the door behind you?"

"Will do, ma'am." With a salute, he handed me the cordless phone that Harlow had left on the upper hall table. "Get some sleep. I'll call you tomorrow." Before I realized what he was doing, he leaned over and caught me in a lingering, thigh-melting kiss and slipped downstairs. The sound of their voices echoed, and the front door shut with a loud click.

I took the cup from Randa, and she burrowed under the covers and promptly fell asleep. After making sure she was tucked in, I crept over to the rocking chair that sat in the corner of the room and pulled an afghan over me as I leaned back and rested my feet on the footstool. The chair had been Nanna's. When she died, she willed it to Miranda. Randa loved it, curling up on it with books and boxes of cookies and glasses of milk. As I drank my own tea, resting my head against the wooden frame, I understood why she spent so much time in her room. It was quiet and calm here. Somehow my daughter had managed to create a little haven of peace for herself.

I focused on Nanna's energy, her winks and the quarters hidden in her pockets and tiny dolls she sewed from bits of rags. "Nanna? Nanna—if you can hear me, please watch over us as I sleep. Please watch over my little girl and make sure that nothing hurts her. And please, let Kipling be safe."

The prayer was halfhearted. I really didn't expect an answer, but the curtains fluttered even though there were no drafts and I felt a firm, guiding hand on my shoulder. Miranda stirred again, and a smile broke out on her face as she slept. I squinted, peeking through half-closed lashes, and saw a golden outline standing near the bed. Nanna. Nanna had come in response to my plea. Content that we would be safe the rest of the night, I closed my eyes and fell asleep, drifting into a deep and dreamless slumber.

Eleven

❖

I WOKE BEFORE dawn. My night in the rocker had left me no worse for wear—I was used to it, though when I stretched and yawned, I could feel a sharp twinge in my side from sitting too long. As I rubbed the sleep out of my eyes, I remembered—Nanna had been there, watching over us. No wonder the room had been so comfortable. I had slept so deeply that I couldn't even recall one speck of a dream.

Randa was resting peacefully.

A peek out the window showed that the ever-present clouds had decided to take the day off. A glimmer of light promised a clear morning, although at these temperatures, clear weather meant cold weather. We'd be turning the furnace up another notch before dinner tonight. The dawn was settling in—vague streaks of pale yellow infused the horizon with the illusion of warmth. The combination of the ever-growing snowdrifts against the robin's egg blue sky seemed both beautiful and surreal.

Ice layered thick on the outside of Miranda's window, but the inner sill was warm to my touch. I stood for another minute, watching the world wake before I padded back over to her bed and knelt by her side. Her breathing was shallow, and she was close to waking. I shook her gently by the shoulder and she dragged herself into a sitting position and looked around. Her mouth puckered with the beginnings of a frown.

"What happened? What time is it?" She squinted at the alarm clock. "Seven-thirty?"

"Do you remember much of last night, honey?"

She scratched her head, frowning. "Not much. I came back for a book and . . . I guess I got sick?"

I didn't want to scare her, especially since I wasn't even sure myself what had happened. She'd be terrified if I told her about the ghosts. I felt her forehead. Her skin was slightly warmer than it should be, but I didn't see any other signs that she was the worse for wear. "I think you were, sweetie. We found you on the roof in the snow. You fainted. Probably overexhaustion—all the studying tired you out."

She rubbed her eyes and quietly laid back against her pillow. "I guess I am feeling a little strange. I was out on the roof last night?"

"Yeah, that's where we found you. Remember, Andrew and Harlow were here?" She nodded. "Okay, well, I'm keeping you home today. We'll drop by the doctor's office later on. Would you like to lie on the sofa and watch some TV while I make breakfast?" Cinnamon would have to handle the shop for the day. She was a good clerk; she would call me if there was a problem.

"You're staying home?" Miranda allowed me to help her up and into her bathrobe. "You never stay home."

"I do when you go fainting on the roof during the middle of the night." I grabbed her Nanna quilt as we headed toward the hall. Miranda stopped long enough to retrieve Mr. Sanders from her keepsake trunk. She hadn't hauled out that old bear in quite a while. She must be feeling a bit shaky. In the living room, I tucked her in on the sofa and turned on the television. Miranda didn't usually like kids' shows, but she did love Bugs Bunny. I found a Looney Tunes special on the Cartoon Network and left her laughing at the antics of Elmer Fudd.

It worried me that she didn't protest when I told her I

was keeping her home. Randa never cut class, she was a homework machine, and the few times she got sick I practically had to tie her down in bed to make sure she wouldn't sneak off to school. Her easy capitulation was out of character.

As I filled the kettle for tea, I remembered the raffle at the shop today. Damn! I couldn't afford to miss that. My customers expected me there. I glanced at the clock. Almost eight. The drawing was set for one this afternoon. Maybe I could drop Randa off at Mrs. Trask's after the doctor's office and pick her up on my way home after the drawing. I'd better call Ida to see if she was going to be home.

While the water was heating, I grabbed my Day-Timer and scribbled down the phone calls I needed to make. Ida, and Cinnamon . . . the doctor to schedule an appointment . . . also, I wanted to ring Murray to see if she would come over. While I was thinking about it, when I called Mrs. Trask, I'd better speak to Kip, see how he was doing.

I chose a bright blue teapot for the morning and tied together four bags of Moroccan Mint, looping the strings around the handle to keep them from settling on the bottom. Moroccan Mint was my favorite—it was good for almost anything that ailed you. On top of everything else, a quick survey of the refrigerator convinced me I needed to go grocery shopping. We were out of eggs and bread. I didn't want to feed Miranda cold cereal, so I dug out the oatmeal and started boiling water. I found a package of sausages and tossed them in the frying pan, then set up the tea tray I always used when the kids were sick. On Mother's Day they covered it with a doily and served me breakfast in bed.

When everything was ready, I carried the tray in and set it on the coffee table next to the sofa. Miranda scooted up, and I propped a pillow behind her back. "Ready?"

"I'm cold. I have a headache, and my back aches." She wrapped her bathrobe around her and tied the sash tighter.

"Wait a minute before you put anything in your mouth." I hunted in the downstairs bathroom where I kept most of the medications, fishing through the drawer until

I found the thermometer. A quick tuck under Randa's tongue, and sixty seconds later I was staring into her hundred-degree face. "You have a little fever. Eat your breakfast, and I'll call the doctor."

As she sprinkled brown sugar on her oatmeal, I retreated to the kitchen and dialed Dr. Adams's office. He wasn't in yet, but his nurse scheduled Randa for a ten-o'clock appointment. I thanked her and called Mrs. Trask.

Ida Trask was not a woman whom one blithely called by her first name, at least not to her face. She had been married once. Her husband had been drafted into the Korean War. A chopper pilot for a medical unit, he crashed during a rescue mission after saving sixteen people from a wrecked cargo truck they had been riding in. His chopper went down when he made one last run to make sure everybody was out.

After his death Ida left her young son with her mother and enrolled in Western Washington University. Two years later she returned to Chiqetaw to raise her son, and she raised half of the town along with him. Feared and revered, Ida Trask had become an institution in this burg. After retirement, she took care of children from her home. I felt safer leaving the kids with her than with anybody else.

I told her that Randa had gotten sick last night after she'd dashed home for a book and asked if I could drop her off after the doctor's appointment. Ida still sounded miffed over Randa's little escape, but she accommodated us. I would tuck in a little extra when I picked Randa up; there was no way I could afford to lose her as a baby-sitter.

Kip came on the line and prattled on about their evening. Mrs. Trask had managed to wean him out of his bad mood, and they'd had a good time; they played two games of Life and watched a movie and ate thick deli-sliced roast beef sandwiches for supper. Relieved, I told him I'd see him after school and hung up.

Randa had finished her oatmeal, but she left the sausages. "I'm kind of queasy. Can I have more tea?" Both of my children had learned the art of tea drinking at an early age, though I only allowed Earl Grey on special occasions; otherwise they got caffeine-free herbal teas like Wild Berry Zinger or Lemon Spice. I gathered up her dishes.

I poured her another cup and carried it back into the living room. Daffy Duck was trying to outfox Bugs and, as usual, was losing. Satisfied that Miranda had everything she needed, I returned to the kitchen and put in a call to Cinnamon.

"I'm going to be late coming in and early leaving. Miranda is sick, and I really want to be home with her today. Can you open up the shop?"

I could hear her cover the receiver in order to yawn. "Sure, I can handle it. Take care of her and I'll see you when I see you. Will we still hold the drawing at one?"

"Yeah, I'll be there by noon unless something goes wrong. Go ahead and drop by the bakery to pick up the box of sugar cookies I ordered. There's a big box of chocolates and a bag of candy canes in the storeroom. Arrange them on the clear crystal platter. The cookies can go on the cake-plate tower—use the holiday plates I bought for it. They're in the NFS cabinet. Make up a trio of mint teas—wintergreen, spearmint, and peppermint flavors. Mark the board Yuletide Joy. That should do nicely."

The NFS china hutch had been Cinnamon's idea. We kept shop pieces in there—plates for setting out pastries, teacups we served the customers' tea in, special trays and items I loved and wasn't sure whether I wanted to sell. Clearly labeled "Not for Sale," the hutch served as eye candy for the customers.

The sound of scribbling told me she was jotting down my instructions. Good. Cinnamon was a bright girl, but I was glad she wasn't relying on her memory. It wasn't that I didn't trust her, but sometimes smart people don't always have it together in other areas. Her memory was on the blink as often as her find-a-good-man meter.

The kettle whistled and I filled the teapot a second time, this time with a chamomile-and-lavender tea. I carried it out to where Miranda could serve herself. "Drink this and rest a little if you can. We've still got a couple of hours before your appointment, and I think the extra sleep would do you good." She was already yawning; the tea would put her out gently but firmly. She nodded, eyes heavy. I returned to the kitchen, where she couldn't hear me.

Even when she worked swing shift, Murray was one of those up-with-the-sun people which, in western Washington, doesn't say much most of the year. But overcast weather or not, she was usually awake and in full gear by first light. I punched in her number and waited. On the fourth ring, she answered. I told her what happened and begged her to come over to do what she could to help me sort out this mess.

"Damn, I wish I could get away, but sugar, I don't have a spare minute, not until the weekend. White Deer is coming to visit today, and I've got a stack of paperwork to finish at work that's so high I can't see over it, as well as my regular beat. Can you last until Sunday, when I'm taking a few days off?"

"Yeah, I guess so. Thanks anyway, hon." Disappointed, I dropped the receiver back onto the phone base. Waiting until the weekend wasn't my idea of comfort, but there was nothing I could do. Murray was always busy; it was a wonder the woman hadn't put herself in the hospital with a stroke. We'd have to manage on our own until then.

I decided to take a shower. When I peeked in on Randa she was asleep, with the quilt tucked up under her chin. As quietly as I could, I edged the remote out of her hand and turned off Daffy Duck. I placed it on the table in easy reach in case she woke up while I was upstairs.

The sting of the water felt good on my back. I was playing with my health, losing too much sleep. Sore from the fall last night, it was obvious the tension was starting to get to me. Add to that the hectic schedule at the store and I knew that my body would make me pay, sooner or later. I scrubbed my skin with the loofah, hoping the bracing scents of ginger and pineapple would wake me up, but all they did was make me smell like a Hawaiian fruit basket.

I leaned out of the shower and reached for the towel, then realized that I'd forgotten to grab one. The steam coiled thickly around my arm, and a rash of goose bumps puckered up along my skin. As I fumbled, trying to get my bearings, another hand about the same size as my own but cold—icy cold—covered my fingers. What the hell? Someone was in the bathroom with me!

I jerked back, slipped, and landed in the tub on my tailbone. Another inch and I could have split open my skull, but luck held. Shaken but not seriously hurt, I scrambled to my knees and cautiously stood. I needed my clothes. Naked equaled vulnerable equaled danger. Even a scrap of a washcloth would give me some protection.

There were no sounds beyond the shower curtain. Maybe I was being paranoid? Maybe all the stress had brought this on?

Nope, not a chance. As I calmed myself so I could focus, I knew someone was in the room with me. Susan? Mr. Big & Ugly? Given a choice, I'd opt for Susan any day, but I wasn't going to bet my life that it was her. What next? I covered my breasts, tucking my arms tightly around me, and waited, listening. At first the only thing I could hear was my own breathing, but a faint squeaking noise, like fingers on a wet window, echoed through the mist-shrouded room. I had to get out of here, had to go check on Randa . . .

Randa! Randa was alone downstairs. As I yanked open the shower curtain, the vinyl liner ripped under my frenzy. I stumbled out of the tub, waving away the mist until I could see the door, but when I reached to open it, my hand slipped on the handle. The ceramic knob began to turn against my grip, rattling as it did so.

"Oh, hell! Leave me alone!" The power behind the force on the doorknob was tremendous, and I knew it couldn't be Susan. My hand slipped off the knob, and I fumbled to regain my grip. Low mutterings began to re-verberate around me—I thought I could hear a woman calling for help and the deep laughter of a man, low and menacing. Shit—they were both here. I couldn't catch the words, but from the tone of his voice, his intentions were clear, and it sounded like he was terrorizing Susan.

I had to get out of here. I grabbed the nearest piece of cloth I could find—a hand towel—and used it to get a better grip. As I threw myself against the door, bracing so I could leverage the knob with more force, a high, thin shriek echoed, and deep laughter pounded in my ears. The energy blocking the door swept away and I yanked it open and raced into the hallway.

As I thudded down the stairs I wanted nothing more than to scream, to wake Randa and get her out of the house, but I didn't want to scare her. I barreled into the living room, trailing a mist of water behind me. Just as I saw that Randa seemed safely asleep, a brief wave of laughter echoed behind me and strong hands pushed against my back, sending me flying across the room to land on the floor near the sofa. My shin slid along the edge of the coffee table, hard, scraping a long gash into the leg, and my knee managed to smash right against the corner. A gut-wrenching wave of pain sent me face down to the floor, where I stayed.

Startled, Randa woke and sprang into a sitting position, staring at me with that cool, unwavering gaze that made her such a formidable foe on her school's debating team. "Uh . . . are you okay, Mom?"

I lay plastered against the carpet, butt in the air. After a moment, I managed to catch my breath and pushed myself up. My breasts were covered with tiny flecks of dirt. The thought that maybe I should vacuum more often ran through my head before I could clear my mind.

Miranda crawled out from under the covers, dragging her quilt over to cover me. She knelt beside me. "Mommy, you're bleeding—should I call 911?" A look of concern spread across her face.

I didn't want to scare her, didn't want to tell her that a ghost had knocked me senseless, but it was either that or let her think I was going nuts. I shook my head and pushed myself into a sitting position, wincing as I tried to straighten my leg. "No . . . no . . . just bumped my knee. The cut stings, but it's superficial. I think I'll be okay. How about you? Are you okay?"

She gave me one of her you-really-are-out-of-it looks. "I was resting, like you told me to. What's going on?"

I used the coffee table for leverage and forced myself to stand up. The room wobbled a bit but settled down as I limped over to sit on the sofa, wrapping the quilt around me. My knee protested the moment I put weight on it and was turning a serious shade of blue. The scrape down my shin was bleeding. Lovely. With my luck, I'd probably dislocated something.

"Uh . . . the ghost—the nasty one who followed Susan's spirit—was in the bathroom with me. I was scared that you'd get hurt, so I came running down to check on you. I guess I don't make such a great athlete, huh?"

She raised one eyebrow in her best Mr. Spock imitation, and a smile spread across her face. Here I was hurt, and my daughter was actually laughing at me. "Mom, I could have told you that years ago." Then she seemed to comprehend what I'd said, and her smile faded. She nervously twisted the blanket in her hand. "Is it still up there? Is the ghost here now?" She stared at me, begging for me to answer her next question with a *yes, I can*. "Mom, you can stop the ghosts from doing what they want, can't you?"

I pressed the back of my hand against her forehead. Her fever was about the same. I didn't want to think about what she'd say if she knew I thought that the spirit might be responsible for her illness. "I don't know, honey. I'm trying. Okay, back under the covers while I go clean up." I gently tucked the quilt back over her. "Do me a favor, Ran. Don't go to sleep, okay? Wait till I come back down before you nod off?"

"I don't think I could go to sleep even if I wanted to." She scrunched into the corner of the sofa and hugged Mr. Sanders to her chest.

I limped over to the stairs. It never occurred to me before what a wonderful invention the railing was, but I was grateful for it now. By the time I hauled myself to the top, I began to think I had seriously wrecked something.

I cautiously pushed the bathroom door open. The mist

was gone, vanished into whatever ozone hole mist disappears into. "Anybody here?" I kept my voice low so Miranda wouldn't hear me. As I turned the corner to face the mirror, I saw my image—studded with carpet dirt and little bruises. Across the face of the mirror, across my reflection, someone had written in the steam. The steam was gone, but the words were still readable.

A delicate hand had written, "Help me!"

This was too much. Not only did I have a frantic ghost on my hands, but also Mr. Big & Ugly had taken it upon himself to terrorize everyone in sight—Susan, me, my family, and my friends. Enough. He was playing hardball, and he was going to find out just who he was playing it with. That is, if I could figure out how to beat him at his own game.

Twelve

❖

WITH A BACKWARD glance at the house, which now loomed ominous and brooding, we headed out to the doctor's office. Miranda was fine, he said, she had a little cold and needed to rest. I, on the other hand, wasn't in great shape. My sprawl had left me with a severe bruise on my knee and rug-burn abrasions from my breasts to my shins, as well as the cut on my leg. I wasn't going to be running any marathons for a week or two.

I pulled up in front of Ida's house and turned to Randa. "I'm sorry I have to go in to the shop. I forgot all about the drawing."

She patted my arm. "It's okay, you've had a rough morning." She gave me a sneaky grin. "Besides, Mrs. Trask makes the best oatmeal chocolate chip cookies I've ever tasted."

I kissed her head and made sure she got inside okay, then headed for the shop. Frieda Halston won the raffle, and almost knocked over a display of teacups and saucers. Quick reflexes on Cinnamon's part saved the day, but I was in no mood to stick around after we managed to get Frieda and her new teapot out the door.

Before I left the shop I bit the bullet and made arrangements for Lana, one of Cinnamon's friends, to come in on Thursday and Friday. It wasn't the ideal solution—I really should be working during the Christmas push—but there was no way I could handle the holiday rush at the store and evict my ghostly visitors at the same time. After finalizing that Lana would help during the rush hours on both days, I put in another call to Murray. As I tapped my fingers on the countertop, waiting for her to answer, I could feel a tension headache working its way into my neck. Ibuprofen, I'd give anything for a couple of ibuprofen. When she came on the line I spilled out the morning's events.

Before I could ask for help, she offered to take Kip and Randa for a few days. "My schedule is nuts, but with my aunt here, she can help watch out for them. They like White Deer, so there shouldn't be any problem."

I breathed a sigh of relief. Knowing they were safely out of the way would allow me to focus all my attention on exorcising Mr. B & U. With both Murray and White Deer keeping track of them, I'd feel a lot better.

I was still searching for a bottle of Advil when Harl called. She had managed to dig up some info from Karri Banks. I grabbed a pen, ready to jot down what she found out. "What did she say?"

Harl snapped her gum. "Karri and Susan went to school together. They were in the same class. Karri was hesitant at first, but since Susan's dead, she agreed to talk to me."

"Good going." Once again I marveled at Harlow's ability to worm her way into any social gathering and walk away with a pocketful of news.

"I asked her if Diana had been notified of Susan's death. She said she wasn't sure, so I fished around. Turns out there are some interesting skeletons in Susan's closet, and nobody knows whom they belong to. It seems that Susan ran off when she was seventeen. She was crazy over some guy but wouldn't tell anybody who he was. Nobody heard a word out of her for a couple of years and then suddenly she shows up again—very pregnant."

"I take it with Diana?"

"Yeah," Harl said. "And within a few weeks Susan married Walter."

I thought for a moment. "Then is Diana even his daughter?"

"Rumor has that up for debate, but he *is* on the birth certificate. Bernard, Walter's stepfather, gave his seal of approval to the marriage—baby and all—but Walt's mother was heartsick. Karri said Eunice wouldn't even go to the wedding."

"Weird. So they have the baby and—"

"From the beginning, the marriage seemed a little rocky. At one point Susan told Karri that she'd made a terrible mistake but that she couldn't talk about it. By the time Diana was six, Walt and Susan sent her to boarding school. Over the years, they shunted her from one school to another. I guess she only came home for Christmas and Thanksgiving. When Diana turned eighteen, apparently she told her parents to go to hell and took off on her own."

"Any chance Karri has Diana's address?" I crossed my fingers.

Harl snickered. "O mighty leader, ask and receive. Actually, Karri said she tucked it away somewhere, that Susan gave it to her at one point in case anything should happen. Apparently she didn't trust Walter to bother getting in touch with Diana."

"Weird way to treat your own kid." I could never treat my children like that.

"Yeah, I know. Anyway, Karri's going to look for the address and let me know when she finds it."

I asked Harlow to call Andrew and fill him in. I would tell her about this morning's little debacle later on. Luck held, leading me to a bottle of pain relievers in the back room, and I popped a couple before heading out to pick up Randa. We swung by Kip's school and nabbed him before he got on the bus. He noticed the brilliant colors purpling my knee. I told him I'd tripped and hurt myself, and left it at that. Randa remained helpfully silent, appeased by the promise that as soon as they came home, we'd go pick up a Christmas tree—a big blue spruce.

The kids seemed excited over the prospect of a few days at Murray's. Randa gave me a knowing look, but Kip was preoccupied making sure he had his Game Boy and cartridges. As they packed everything they'd need for the next few days, they chattered away about how good it would be to see Sid and Nancy again. Kip wanted to get a snake but both Randa and I nixed the idea.

"A snake would try to eat the cats," Randa said. She gave Samantha a last tummy rub and begged me to watch over the furbles. I crossed my heart and promised to keep both Mama and babies in cat bliss while they were gone.

Murray's shift started in an hour, but she was prepared to take time off if White Deer didn't arrive before she left. I felt bad about interrupting her work, but she told me that she had plenty of leave time accumulated and she would call in with a "sour stomach."

"They need me, but they can wait a couple of hours if they have to. White Deer is on her way; she's past Bellingham according to her last cell call and should be here within half an hour." We tucked the kids into her guest room and left them watching some sort of holiday special on the television in there. Murray fixed herself a sandwich and some espresso. "Do you want a shot?"

"Nah. It's too late, and I've had too little sleep. One drop of caffeine and I'll be a basket case tomorrow morning. Tea would be nice, though."

She fixed me a cup of Wild Berry Zinger and added honey and lemon. "I told my aunt enough so that she knows the general situation." She settled into the overstuffed chair she kept in place of a table in the breakfast nook. I curled up in the matching recliner opposite her. "White Deer won't pry unless you offer her information, and even then, she's sticky-handed about giving out advice. So, what are you going to do?"

"I haven't the faintest idea." Things were so up in the air that I wasn't sure what was going to happen. I just hoped none of us would be standing directly beneath when Mr. B & U came in for a landing. "Meet Walter? See if we can contact Diana? Exorcise a demon? I guess most of all, try to make sense of this whole mess."

Murray absently stirred her coffee. "So Susan piggy-backed in an astral nasty. You have to be careful with spirits, Em. My people know a lot about them—we take them seriously. More seriously than most of you psychics do."

Astral nasty. I shuddered. Nasty was *the* word, all right. Etheric stowaways were like parasites, feeding off of energy. "I thought I could deal with them, Nanna taught me how, but I'm in over my head on this one. And I'm still not sure what to make of Susan. I think she might be hiding something; she took a lot of baggage with her when she died."

"Walter didn't kill her, Em. He has an airtight alibi. I checked over it again, and there's no way he could have been in that house."

"Does that mean that he couldn't have had anything to do with it? There might be somebody else involved, or maybe he masterminded the whole thing. Anyway, Susan gave us the right lead to get information about Diana. Do you happen to have her address? Are you guys supposed to notify her that Susan's dead?" And, I thought, how much would Murray tell me before warning me to back off?

She laughed. "Still digging? I don't think anybody from the department has been in touch with the girl. Since this was an accident, it's not our policy to notify family members unless there's nobody else to do it. Walter's her father; it's his responsibility to inform her. I didn't even know about Diana—Walter sure didn't mention her when we talked to him. Most of us in the department are transplants, you know—none of us lived here back when Susan was young."

I took a quick sip of the tea. "We can go see her without the cops getting mad at us, right?"

"Of course you can visit Diana. There's nothing illegal about it—just don't tell her you think Walter killed her mother. That could get you into trouble if he wanted to push the issue. So the family is estranged to the point of where he didn't even mention having a daughter? It may seem abnormal to us, but people with as much money and power as Walter and Susan usually play by their own rules. Just remember, Susan's death was an accident . . . or suicide. Her spirit's either confused or trying to play tricks on you."

It was clear that as far as Murray and the Chiqetaw police were concerned, the case was closed. Evidence cleared Walter, his alibi held, and I knew Murray well enough to know that she would get cranky if I hounded her on the subject. I pushed the cup away and reached down for my purse.

"You heading out?"

"Yeah, I should. I ache all over. When Mr. B & U slammed me against the floor this morning, it really jarred me up. I've hired somebody to help Cinnamon out at the shop the next couple of days, so that's taken care of, but there's a lot to do, and I'm not sure where to begin. Gotta buy Christmas presents tomorrow, for one thing. Andrew and Harl are due over tomorrow evening, so I'll probably go shopping in the morning. That is, if the damned ghosts decide to leave me alone tonight."

"Sleep here. You're welcome to stay over along with the kids. Why put yourself in danger?" She reached forward and put her hand on my arm.

I choked up, welcoming the comfort of her generosity. The offer was tempting. I swallowed one last mouthful of tea. "Thank you, babe. I wish I could, but if I stayed here I'd be admitting defeat. Also, Samantha and her kittens are alone in the house. I have to watch over the fuzzies as well as my own chicks, you know? Okay, I'm ready to shove off. Tell White Deer thank you for me."

I popped in to give Randa and Kip good-bye kisses. After giving me a hug that I never wanted to end, Murray escorted me to the door.

"Take care of my babies—they are the most precious gifts in the world I have."

"You think I don't know that?" She looked at me as if I were crazy. "Get moving, drive safely, and call me when you get home. I want to make sure you get there."

* * *

I GAVE HARLOW and Andrew quick calls and we all touched base and made sure we were on the same wavelength. We agreed to meet the next day—Wednesday—during the afternoon. Andrew wanted to come right over when he heard what had happened and I was tempted, but I also knew that I needed a good night's sleep. I wouldn't be able to close my eyes if he stayed with me. His presence had far too strong an effect on my underutilized libido. I promised to call if anything happened and made up the sofa bed after hanging up. I wanted a fast retreat out the door if Mr. B & U decided to pay me another visit.

The whispers started the minute I turned out the lights. They went on all night, echoing through the house. I curled into a little ball on the sofa; the cats snuggled uneasily around my feet. My slumber came in fits as I tossed and turned, skirting the edge of consciousness. Once I woke up and thought I saw a bright light go skittering across the ceiling, but then as I shook my head and rubbed my eyes, it disappeared and I wasn't sure if it had been the remnant of a nightmare or if it had been real. With a shiver, I turned to press against the back of the sofa, and pulled the covers over my head. By morning I had managed to eke out enough sleep to leave me groggy but functional.

Unwilling to step into my shower so soon after yesterday's fiasco, I used the downstairs bathroom, but I still had to go upstairs to get dressed. I hesitated a moment before opening the door to my room. Everything felt out of place, though nothing had been touched, and I had the eerie feeling of being watched the entire time I got dressed. I hurried as fast as I could and decided to eat breakfast out.

After a quick stop at Starbucks for my special—a triple grandé iced mocha, organic milk, no whip—I gave the kids a call to say hello. They were fine, they missed me and I missed them, but they sounded like they were having fun.

I hit the only mall in town, elbowing my way through the crowds at the local Target and Bon Marché like Moses parting the Red Sea. I had promised the kids Christmas this year, and damn it, we were going to have one. Shopping for them was easy—sweaters and an astronomy program that Randa wanted, a high-powered telescope to blow the dinky one she had out of the water. Kip would be happy with video games and a selection of Transformer and Harry Potter action figures.

I loaded up the cart with decorations and ornaments, too. I decided to settle any potential arguments over ornament color by using gold and silver balls. Crimson bows, multicolored twinkle lights, and brilliant ropes of gold and silver bead garlands completed what we would need for the tree. Along the way to the cash register, I picked up stockings—one for each child and cat. By the time I reached the cashier, I sighed and handed over my card. Resigned to being in debt forever, I watched her swipe it through.

BY THE TIME I got home, Harlow and Andrew were waiting on the front step. They huddled together like conspirators planning a Third World coup. I dragged them into the kitchen and they scribbled notes about my watery encounter with the spirit as I phoned in an order for pizza. Cooking was out for the night; I wasn't wasting time or energy on it.

"Ha!" Harlow laughed and pushed a length of golden crimped hair out of the way. "We should call you 'Showers with Spirits.' "

"Funny, lady, funny. Go answer the door; here's a twenty. Tip the delivery boy." Pizzarama was running a special that included two three-topping pizzas and a two-liter bottle of soda for a flat fifteen dollars. Andrew divided the slices with a knife while I handed out paper plates. Once we were settled, Harl picked at her dinner as usual, while I dove into a thick wedge. I was hungry and didn't care who knew it, though I felt conspicuous next to Harl's eat-like-a-bird approach.

She pulled out her Day-Timer and opened it to a page of notes jotted down in brilliant red ink. "Karri called me about an hour before I came over. She finally found a phone number that Susan gave her." She held out a thin slip of paper.

"Diana's?" I held the paper up to the light.

"Not quite. It belongs to the girl's landlord. I called and said that I was Diana's cousin and I wanted to surprise her by coming to visit but didn't have the exact address, only this number. The landlady is chatty, let me tell you that. I have the feeling that if Diana finds out *how* chatty, she's gonna find a new place to live right away. Within the course of our ten-minute conversation, I managed to find out that Diana's a rather unstable young woman who has a job in a bookstore, or owns a bookstore or something like that. She doesn't have any close friends, and her landlady thinks she's been drinking too much as of late."

"So what do we do? Go up to her door and knock?" Now that we had her address, I was starting to get cold feet. "What on earth do we say? 'Did your father tell you that your mother's dead? Oh, and by the way, your mom's haunting us until we help her out'?"

Harlow gently patted her lips with her napkin. I marveled that her lipstick stayed put with only a faint trace of a Cupid's bow showing on the linen. "I think we can come up with something more diplomatic than that if we put our heads together."

I waited for a moment, testing to see whether any brilliant deductions would surface, but the only thing that came out of my pause was a delicate burp. I blushed. "I talked to Murray. She said Walter never mentioned Diana when the cops talked to him about Susan's death. I bet he hasn't told her about her mother."

"I know." Harl grinned at me. "We'll simply tell her that we were her mother's friends, that we're paying our respects and are sorry about what happened. Karri told me that in the past few months, Susan mentioned that she and Diana were trying to rebuild their relationship."

That was an interesting tidbit. "One way or another, we'll find out if Walter contacted Diana when we talk to her. Why don't we invite her to the memorial for Susan?

You can bet Walter won't, if they're at odds as much as Karri says they are. Speaking of which"—I turned to Andrew—"how are plans for the service going?"

"Got it all set up. I've notified the paper about the event, so he can't back out. Prepare for a deluge—people loved Susan, and the affair is going to be swamped. But we can watch him in action then."

"Murray's convinced he's innocent." I made a decision. "Harlow, how about we just get this over with? Let's drive down to Seattle and visit Diana tomorrow." I wasn't looking forward to being the bearer of bad news, but our options were limited. I dreaded thinking about what would happen if we got there and the girl hadn't heard of her mother's death. How were we going to tell her?

Harlow's eyes were bright, and I noticed that her pupils were a little dilated. "Are you feeling okay?" I asked.

"Hmm? Oh, yes. I didn't sleep very good last night."

Andrew filled us in on the memorial party. He had persuaded the writers group to host it so soon by offering to coordinate everything himself. After a short speech on what Susan had meant to her fans, apparently every eye in the room had been watering, and he had his go-ahead. I wondered how much he was spending out of his own pocket for this but wasn't sure how to ask without seeming nosy or, worse, patronizing. I had no idea whether Andrew made a good living from his work. His car was nice but not fancy, his clothing well kept but not the latest fashion. He said he wasn't as well known as Susan, and I assumed that meant he didn't sell as many books as she did.

"So, we're set. Tomorrow we visit Diana and on Saturday we see what we can find out from Walt."

"Okay. I'll be here at eight-thirty sharp tomorrow. Be ready to go." Harl pushed back from the table and picked up her dish, depositing it into the sink.

"Sounds good."

Andrew caught me near the refrigerator. "Can I stay for a while?" His whisper told me that he wanted to be alone.

Together. Just the two of us. My mind weighed the

question, but my heart answered. "Sure," I whispered back. Was I falling for him? Or was I just infatuated? I pushed aside the question, it didn't matter; all I knew was that I wanted him to stay.

Harlow left, giving us both a tentative hug. Something was out of sorts with her, but she didn't seem in the mood to talk. We would catch up on our way to Seattle.

Andrew sat on the sofa and cautiously pulled me onto his lap, taking care not to bump my knee. "No protests." His arms found their way around my waist and I relaxed, leaning against his shoulder. "Let's not talk about Susan or ghosts or danger. I want to kiss you. I want to nibble on your ears. I'm telling you this in case you want me to leave, because once I get started, I'm not going to want to stop. Tell me how far I can take you, Emerald. If I can take you at all."

He traced a line from my breasts, where the top buttons on my shirt were open, along my neck, gently grazing the skin. I shuddered. It had been so long since a man had touched me, had made me tingle and zing along every nerve in my body. His hand slid into the depths of my hair and he turned my head so I was facing directly into his eyes. "I don't know where this is going and I can't give you an answer. But I want you more than I've wanted any woman in a long, long time."

I bent my head, taking his lower lip between my teeth and sucking gently. Black eyes flashing, he let out a quiet groan. I wrapped my arms around him as he lifted me higher onto my lap. He buried his face in my breasts and I pulled him to me, my breath coming in gasps as he slid one hand up my shirt and fingered my nipples through the silk of my bra. Delicious and dizzying—no one had touched me this way in so long. I tugged at my blouse buttons as he reached around to unhook me.

"Ripe," he murmured. "So round and heavy." He cupped them, squeezing gently, as if he were testing peaches; then with a firm grip, as if he owned them and me along with them. As he sucked greedily, I shifted to allow him access and he flipped me over, looming above me and I lay flat, pressed against the sofa, with his tongue flickering against my nipples as his fingers slid under my skirt to make the ache between my legs grow. I fought for control, fought to retain some sense of self, but his energy threatened to embrace me, to overwhelm me.

"No—no—not yet!" A shiver of despair echoed up my spine.

Andrew stopped where he was, staring at me through those dark and brilliant eyes, hair falling out of his po-nytail to trail down against my skin. His lips were set, not in a smile, but in a firm line, and when he looked at me I felt that he was searching for a path into my soul.

"I can't make love to you tonight. Andrew, I have to take it slow. I want you, but I can't get lost in you yet." I held my breath, praying that he would understand, wouldn't go charging off in a huff.

He took my chin in his hand, gave me a single nod, and kissed me sweetly on the lips before pulling away. "We'll take it slow."

I slipped on my shirt and pulled the ends together, tying them under my breasts. "I'm sorry, I didn't mean to go so far—but your arms feel so good."

That made him laugh, a smile breaking through his severity. "That's a compliment I don't hear often enough." He brought his fingers to his nose. "I can smell you on my fingertips. It makes me hungry."

I shivered, once again feeling as if I were with a wolf that was prowling the night. Not a player—no, a wolf in the northern mountains tracking the scent of his mate who was unaware she was being followed. I realized how little I knew about him. He was still a mystery.

"Emerald, tell me something: Are you afraid of me? Or are you playing it safe?"

I thought for a moment. He did frighten me a little, though I didn't know why. I hadn't seen this side of him before, strong, demanding, and yet—and yet, he had stopped when I asked, and he was still sitting here, not rushing away with his ego crushed. "I'm playing it safe. I need to. For the kids. For myself."

With a nod, he stood and pushed back the strands of hair that had come loose. His ears were burning red. He was as pent up as I was. "Do you want me to sleep on the sofa? After yesterday morning—"

"The spirits weren't quiet last night, but they left me alone. I slept down here with the phone right next to my head, and I plan to again tonight. If they come back, I'll be out the door and into my car before they can lay a hand on me. Everything should be fine."

He acquiesced. "Be careful. I want you whole, intact, in my bed. Actually, I want you whole and intact no matter what." He picked up his notebook. "Get some sleep, Em. Tomorrow is a big day. You and Harl want to be fresh for your drive." We shared a lingering kiss at the door. He patted my ass. "You're gorgeous, you know that? Lock the door after me."

After he left, I stretched out on the sofa, replaying the scene over and over in my mind. Only in my fantasy, we didn't stop.

Thirteen
❖

ONCE AGAIN, THE whisperings started shortly after I went to bed. Samantha complained, setting up a steady series of yowls and growls until I turned on the lights. The mutterings died down, as did her discomfort, and we all dozed off until shortly before dawn, when a loud shriek startled me out of my slumber. I shot up, blinking as the light hit my eyes. The sound hadn't actually been audible so much as kinetic, reverberating through my body.

Susan hovered in the archway, clutching her head as tears poured down her cheeks. I pushed my way out from under the covers and looked for Mr. B & U, but he seemed to be contenting himself elsewhere for the moment. She shot me a despairing glance, lips twisted, and wept silently in her world of vapor and mist. Then, with another look at me, her gaze so obviously a plea for help, she vanished slowly as a ray of morning light broke through the window.

Shaken, I forced myself to get dressed and to grab a quick breakfast. I didn't like the idea of leaving the cats alone in the house, so I put in a quick call to Andrew. I woke him up, but after he'd cleared his thoughts, he was gracious enough to accept Samantha and her babies into his home. Harlow and I would drop them off before we hit the freeway. I managed to corral the calico and her kittens—Nebula, Noël, and Nigel—into their carrier, and gathered together their litter box, a bag of clumping litter, their food dishes, and a couple of cans of food. By the time Harlow pulled up, all we had to do was drop the whole kit 'n' caboodle off at Andrew's.

WE TOOK HARLOW'S car. Relieved that, for once, I wasn't the one driving down I-5, maneuvering through the nasty gridlock that built up miles before we reached the Seattle area, I took the time to relax. Colliding images from the night before vied for space in my thoughts . . . Andrew and his embrace, my own sexual tension, the terrified appearance of Susan Mitchell this morning. I felt trapped in a kaleidoscope that was spinning out of control.

Harlow wove in and out of traffic. She was skilled in the art of opportunistic driving and we made progress, slipping into openings I didn't think possible to navigate.

"This is one thing I don't miss about living in the city," I said, breaking the silence. "Planning ahead, leaving two hours early when traffic is bad."

Harlow nodded, ducking into the HOV lane as she sped up. After a while I noticed that she was being unusually quiet. I had the feeling that whatever had been wrong the night before was still bothering her. I broached the subject. She shook her head. "I don't know if I can talk about it."

"C'mon, Harl, you know you can tell me." I knew that she wasn't good at handling high stress, that it could cause a relapse into behaviors best left in her adolescence.

After a few minutes she took a huge breath and let it out in a shuddering sob. "I'm pregnant. I've been suspicious for a few weeks, but yesterday I went to the doctor and he confirmed it."

"Pregnant!" I jumped as far as the seat belt would let me and would have hugged her if we hadn't been barreling down the freeway at seventy-five miles an hour. "Oh, Harl! Why are you upset?"

She squinted through tear-clouded eyes. "I'm so scared. I haven't even told James yet—I'm terrified about what he'll say, what will happen."

We swerved to miss some joker who had decided that a slow crawl would do in the express lane, and I pointed ahead to a sign advertising a rest stop. "Pull in there. I'll take over the driving." She did as I instructed. When we were parked in the wooded rest area, she unfastened her seat belt and leaned forward, head on the steering wheel.

I patted her back and brushed her hair off her forehead. "Shush . . . quiet, babe. Everything will be fine. Everything will be okay." She hiccuped twice and stopped crying as I handed her a tissue. She blew her nose and looked at me, bleak and frightened. And I knew why she was afraid. "You're worried about the anorexia, aren't you?"

She bobbed her head. When she spoke, her voice was full of phlegm. "I don't know if I've conquered it, or if it's still out there, waiting for a trigger. But that's not the only problem. Goddamn it, Em, I was hooked on coke for years. Is that going to affect the baby? I've already had two abortions. . . ."

"When?" I hadn't heard about those.

"When I was modeling. Sex was everywhere and so was cocaine. Heroin, crack, you name it, I could score it. Sex and blow went hand in hand—they were great separate, but man, put them together and *wham, bam, thank you, ma'am* meant a fine ol' time. A couple of times I was so out of it that I didn't use any birth control. The pill made me gain weight, so I didn't take it." She hung her head. "It's all a nightmare. I don't know if I can be a good mother. Lola sure didn't set a good example for me." With a grimace, she wiped her nose and brushed her hair back from her face.

"Do you want to be a mother? Do you want a baby?" Strange, but I realized Harlow had never, in all the time we had known each other, mentioned wanting children.

She shrugged. "Part of me does. Part of me is afraid to think about it."

"How do you think James will feel?" I'd never seen her so low and thought, *this is what I used to be like*—depressed, terrified to move, terrified to do anything because everything seemed wrong.

She coughed, and a bubble of spit appeared on her lip. I handed her another tissue. "Oh, James will be thrilled. If he knows I'm pregnant, there is no way on this Earth that I will be able to convince him I shouldn't have the baby. I'm stuck, Em . . . either I get an abortion and never mention it to him, or I tell James and have the baby because I refuse to lose him. I love him too much."

There wasn't much I could say. I wasn't about to tell her what to do—that was a recipe for disaster—but I did decide to give her something to think about. "Did it ever occur to you that you have good friends who will help you through this? That James will be here to support you? Harl, you aren't eighteen anymore. You are so much stronger than you give yourself credit for."

"Really?" She looked at me with that schoolgirl wonder that spoke volumes about her self-esteem. Or lack of it.

"Really, truly, and honest, too." I slid out of my seat and motioned for her to change places with me. I slid up into the driver's seat of her gargantuan Suburban and buckled in. "Let's go see Diana. If you want to talk more about this, I'm here to listen. If you want to let it be, that's fine, too. Whatever you need, Harl. Whatever you need."

I shifted the car into gear and pulled back out on the freeway. The traffic had thinned somewhat; rush hour was almost over for the morning. We would hit Seattle in another twenty minutes. "Where are those directions?" I asked and Harlow busied herself by digging out the map. She sniffed a couple more times, but the haunted look that had been dogging her all morning had eased up, and I thought that she would manage to get through this. I would do my part to make it as easy for her as I could.

*   *   *

A STEADY RAIN was falling by the time we exited off the freeway and zigzagged our way to the U-district. Ah, rain. Rain in the springtime. Rain in the autumn. Rain in the winter. The only time it didn't rain in Seattle was during the month of August, and even then we kept an umbrella nearby.

No matter how hard I tried to get away from this city, I always ended up coming back for one thing or another. I wished that one of those reasons would be Roy's desire to see his children, but he hadn't asked for visitation rights in months, and the kids were slowly but surely beginning to see his true colors. As much as I hated the man, I wanted Kip and Miranda to think their father loved them.

Harlow guided me through the labyrinth of one-way streets until we found ourselves parked in front of an old brick apartment building. Five stories high, the brick was cracked in several places, and the paint on the window trim was worn and weathered. Two large juniper bushes shrouded the front entrance, and I made an educated guess that we wouldn't be finding an elevator inside. Harl started to pull out a cigarette but stopped as I shook my head.

"Don't do it, not until you make up your mind about the baby."

She growled something under her breath but shoved the cig back in the pack and jammed it into her purse. We made our way up the walk. "What floor does she live on, again?" I prayed Harl wouldn't say "five" . . . or even "four." Come to think of it, "two" wouldn't be that great, and "three," even worse. The bruise on my knee was hurting, and I didn't look forward to climbing a bunch of stairs.

The gods of bliss were with me.

"The first—115." Harlow stuffed the paper into her pocket and opened the door. I limped into the dimly lit hallway and blinked. We stopped for a moment to allow our eyes to adjust, then trekked down the narrow hallway. No sounds filtered into the hall; the rooms must be fairly well insulated or else nobody was home during the day.

110, 112 . . . 115. As I approached the apartment I noticed that the door was slightly ajar. Maybe Diana had stepped out to the laundry room or the incinerator, but it still seemed strange for someone in Seattle to leave her door unlocked. I looked back at Harl, uncertain whether to knock. I rapped lightly on the molding of the door-frame.

No answer. I knocked again.

Still no answer.

"What do you think? Should we wait, or leave a note?" I fished in my purse for a notebook and pen.

"I don't know. I wouldn't think that she'd go far and leave her door open."

It seemed odd to me, too. Something felt off—wrong. *Take a deep breath. Count to five. Knock one more time.* Still no answer. A wave of tension played up my spine, and I noticed that the hairs on my arms were standing up. Diana hadn't stepped out—I knew it as sure as I knew that the other side of the door led to a place I didn't want to go. Using the corner of my jacket, I gently pushed the door open.

"What are you doing?" Harlow hissed from behind me, but I waved for her to be quiet. The door creaked on its hinges, then gave way and opened another few inches—enough so I could peek around the corner.

I stuck my head in, as quietly as I could, and looked around. The room was furnished with antiques. A claw-foot sofa; dark, heavy end tables; art nouveau Tiffany lamps. For all I knew, they were real. I noticed the art decorating the walls: poster-size reproductions of Susan Mitchell's book covers. Maybe Diana had forgiven her mother after all. I was about to turn around and leave when a bright red object poking out from behind the sofa caught my eye. At first, in the dim light, it was difficult to make out what it was. In a brilliant flash, with startling clarity, I realized that I was staring at a foot covered by a red stocking.

"Oh, my God!" I limped forward. There might be somebody still hiding in the apartment, but I didn't have time to think about that.

Harlow pressed behind me. "What's wrong?"

I stopped by the edge of the sofa and motioned for her to back away. "Don't touch anything. Don't even sit down." Like a storm waiting to break, nausea welled in my stomach, and I swallowed the rising bile as I took in the scene.

Sprawled on the floor like one of those victims on *Justice Files* or *America's Most Wanted* lay the body of a woman surrounded by a pool of drying blood. The resemblance to Susan was uncanny, and I knew that I was standing over Diana's corpse. She lay on her back, and the look on her face was one of terrible surprise. The carpet around her was slick, saturated with blood from what looked like a single, deadly stab wound penetrating her heart. She had been dead several hours, from what I could guess.

I took a deep breath and let it out slowly as I slipped into "action mode" and everything became distanced, surreal. I turned back to Harlow. "Out in the hall. Get out your cell phone and call 911. Ask them to send the paramedics and the police." Even though I knew it was hopeless, I gingerly leaned down and felt for a pulse. Her skin was cold marble. "Diana's been stabbed. She's dead."

Fourteen

❖

NORMALLY I WOULD have expected her to freak out upon finding a dead body, but Harlow remained surprisingly calm. She tucked the hem of her coat around her hand and nudged the door open a little farther. Good, she was being careful. I heard her murmur into her cell phone before she stuck her head back through the door. "The cops will be here in a few minutes. I'm going to try to find the owner of this joint."

As I took another look around, it occurred to me that perhaps the murderer was still hiding in the apartment. I peeked in the kitchenette and the closet-size bath. Nope. The studio was clear. The rolltop desk sat open, drawers toppled every which way, empty except for a scattering of calligraphy pens and pencils and splattered ink. With a queasy feeling, I noticed that the closest wall had been dotted with tiny drops of red—blood. Diana's blood.

As I traced my steps back toward the door, a glint by one of the end tables caught my eye. I bent over to look. The shimmer was a silver cufflink in the shape of a crown. I longed to pick it up, check it for engravings, but the cops would have my head if I did.

Harlow hissed at me. "Someone's coming. Get your

butt out here!" Apparently she hadn't found the landlady yet.

I hurried out to join her. Two uniformed men were striding down the hall.

"Over here, officers. We're the ones who called you." Harl's voice was steadier than I trusted my own to be.

The cops gave us a long once-over, then turned their attention to the apartment. "Where's the body?" The older cop had a knowing, tired look in his eyes, and I had the feeling he'd seen too many bodies lately.

I pointed. "The door was open when we got here. I went in, hoping to find Diana at home but instead I found her on the floor. I'm pretty sure she's dead. There's no pulse. We called the paramedics just in case, though. They haven't gotten here yet."

He and his partner took opposite sides of the door and motioned us away. I knew there was no one inside but didn't want to admit that I'd rifled through the apartment, so we retreated far enough to be out of range. The older man pushed the door fully open and they went into what I had taken to calling their "search and secure" mode when I watched the police programs on the Discovery Channel.

After a few moments, the younger man—Officer Nelson—returned to the hall. He pulled out a notebook. We would have to go down to the station and give statements. The front door to the brownstone burst open, and the paramedics raced down the hall. It was too late, I thought. Diana wouldn't be needing their services today.

We could hear them working on her as Nelson began to question us. After looking at our identification and noting our names and driver's license numbers on his pad, he asked, "How do you know the deceased?"

"We don't."

He looked confused.

"We knew her mother, Susan Mitchell. Susan died last Thursday, and we weren't sure if Diana had been notified. We wanted to make certain that the girl knew about her mother's death."

"Her mother died last week? What was the cause of death?"

I thought for a moment before I opened my mouth. Here was a chance to plant a seed, but I'd have to be careful. "Apparently she died of an overdose of insulin. The police are *calling* it an accident."

"Her mother lived in Chiqetaw?" I nodded. Nelson scribbled this information down. "When you got here, did you touch anything?"

I squinted. "I don't think so, but we can't be totally sure—I did push the door open so I could go in. I also felt Diana's wrist to see if she had a pulse."

"We'll need to get your fingerprints to eliminate them from any we find at the scene. What about people? Did you see anyone entering or leaving the apartment or the building?"

Both Harlow and I shook our heads. "Nobody."

The officer paused as the other policeman emerged from the apartment.

The older man, whose nametag above his badge read "Leary," flipped his notepad shut and tucked it into his pocket. "Coroner is on his way. There was nothing they could do. She never had a chance."

Nelson handed Leary his notes. "Ladies, I'm sorry to detain you, but we need you to come down to the station and give your statements."

I looked at Harl. We really didn't have a choice. "We'll do whatever we can. What's the address? We can drive there." They put in a call to the station. Within moments another prowl car had shown up to escort us to the precinct.

On the drive downtown, Harlow and I got our stories straight. We didn't have anything to hide, but I didn't want the subject of Susan's spirit to come up. We would stick with the fact that we wanted to make certain Diana had been informed of her mother's death, that Susan had given Harlow the phone number for the apartment building.

The station was crowded, but so were most big-city precincts. We gave our names to the officer on duty and were led into a back hall, where they led me into one room while Harlow was taken to another. The woman taking my statement dutifully recorded everything I told her.

"Your relationship to the deceased?"

"She's the daughter of a friend who died last week."

She jotted that down and said, "Do you know if she has a husband or fiancé or children we should notify?"

"I don't know." I shook my head. "We came down to make sure she knew her mother had died. I've never met the woman before."

"I see. Can you recall anything that might be useful? A vehicle, a person outside the building?"

I answered as carefully as possible, sticking to what we had seen, which was nothing. After fifteen minutes, the interview was over and both Harlow and I emerged from our prospective rooms. The police thanked us and said they'd be in touch.

Harlow grabbed me by the elbow and we headed out of the precinct.

My stomach rumbled. "As Miranda would say, 'that was fun . . . NOT.' I suppose we should eat. That good with you?"

She was a little too pale for my comfort. "I think I could manage a salad. It's hours past lunchtime, and I thought we'd be on our way back by this time."

We stopped at the Keg. There wasn't one in Seattle proper, so we braved rush-hour traffic and crossed the 520 floating bridge over to Bellevue, where we could find a franchise of the steakhouse. I shook my head as the line of cars grew longer and longer. "God, I'm so glad I don't live here anymore. I think when we reach the restaurant, I'll give Murray a call. See how the kids are."

The hostess led Harl to a booth while I put through the call. I didn't want the kids to know I was in Seattle or what had happened. Murray said they were fine, having a great time. They were both home from school and Miranda was studying while Kip was helping Murray finish the birdhouse for her mother. As I sketched out the details of the afternoon, I could hear the wheels turning in her head.

"Well, someone got to her before you did. The questions are: Who? and Why?"

"I'm thinking that Susan knew Diana was murdered—hence her drastic appearance in my living room this morning. That would put Diana's death at about 5:00 A.M. How's White Deer holding up with the kids?"

"Fine. She's going to teach them how to weave a potholder. Miranda even put down her book when White Deer was talking about life on the reservation."

"Who says miracles can't happen? Okay, I'll give you a call tomorrow. Kiss them for me, would you?" I made my way back through the crowded restaurant.

Harlow was munching on breadsticks, looking slightly green around the edges. "I'm queasy—I guess I waited too long to eat. Well, what do we do next?"

We put in our orders for chowder and salad. After the waitress left, I sipped the raspberry lemonade I'd ordered and thought about her question. "I suppose we might be able to get her neighbors to talk to us. If we do, are the police going to be upset?"

"Did you want to stay down here for the night?"

The waitress brought our bowls of steaming soup. My stomach growled. "Nah. I'm going to take a stab at exorcising Mr. B & U tomorrow. Maybe you can call her landlady? Find out a little more?" I buttered a roll, surprised at my appetite, but as the image of Diana's corpse flashed through my mind and I pushed it away, I realized that coping with this was going to be harder than I thought.

Harl unfurled her napkin and laid it across her lap. "Let's finish dinner and head home. This situation is getting more and more convoluted."

AS SOON AS I arrived home, I called Andrew and asked him to come over. Harlow didn't hang around; she was too tired and preoccupied with when and how to spring the news that she was pregnant to James.

By the time Andrew opened the door, I flew into his arms. "Diana's dead."

"What?"

"Somebody stabbed her . . . we found the body. It was awful, Andrew."

"What? Are you okay? Is Harlow okay?" He braced my shoulders. "Emerald, this is getting too dangerous. You need to back off—I don't want to see you hurt. Do a banishing or exorcism or whatever you need to chase the ghosts out of the house and let it drop. I don't want to see anybody get hurt." His fretting was both comforting and irritating.

"Andrew, stop." Didn't he realize that I wanted to back off, more than I would ever admit to anyone? I was in over my head, and the waters were rapidly becoming a whirlpool of confusion and danger, but there was no way I could untangle myself, not after everything that had happened. "If I could only wave a wand and say, 'Poof, go away' and make everything that had happened with Susan vanish in a puff of smoke, I would. But life doesn't work like that." I took his hand. "Spirits don't work on a time-table or with laboratory precision. I made a promise to myself that I'd help her. I'm not giving up. And now . . . with Diana . . ."

I stopped, bringing my hand to my lips. In all the confusion, I had managed to push away the brutal image of her murder, of her petite frame sprawled on the floor, but the memory crashed into my mind, trampling my thoughts. I had seen plenty of TV shows and movies, but nothing could have ever prepared me for the real thing.

"I can't forget the way she looked. The way the blood smelled." I leaned against Andrew's shoulder. "She was so young, she couldn't be much more than twenty years old. I keep thinking how the cops wrote off Susan's death as an accident. What if they're wrong? What if the same person who killed Diana, killed her? Shouldn't we do everything we can to make sure the murderer is brought to justice?"

He sighed. "When you put it like that, it's hard to debate you, but I don't want to see you get hurt, or Harlow, either. And *I* don't look forward to any scuffles."

"Don't worry. We won't do anything stupid." I paced the length of the room.

"What is it?" Andrew asked.

"Do you think Walter might have something to do with Diana's death? They didn't get along. Susan was in the process of patching up the mother-daughter relationship. I don't know."

"You didn't see anyone there, did you? Don't be too quick to jump to conclusions. Coincidences *do* happen."

Grumbling, I retreated to the kitchen and spread several slices of French bread with butter and Parmesan and popped it in the toaster oven. While I was waiting, I turned on the kettle and fixed a pot of Winterberry tea. Yes, coincidences did happen, but so did murder conspiracies. Bad guys were real, not pencil-drawn villains in a comic strip. I set everything on a tray for easy carrying and returned to the living room. "Take my mind off of the murder—tell me about your party."

Andrew brushed my hair back. He poured our tea while I curled up in the rocking chair. "I didn't mean that you should forget what happened, Em. I'm not heartless. Anyway, the memorial will be at 8:00 P.M. on Saturday, in the high school cafeteria. They agreed to let us use it when I explained that it was a benefit for the memory of Susan Mitchell. She had a lot of teen fans—mostly girls. So it's going to be a snarl of people. I ordered a couple of sheet cakes, gallons of punch, and several party trays of olives and cheese and crackers . . . the usual fare."

"I guess Diana won't be coming." The thought that the young woman wouldn't be there to attend her mother's funeral memorial made me incredibly sad. "We don't even know if she ever knew her mother was dead."

Andrew sobered. "I guess we won't ever get to know."

With a deep breath, I shook off the mood as much as I could. "Didn't the preparations set you back a bit? Those trays and cakes aren't cheap." I still wasn't sure what Andrew's financial situation was like but didn't want to ask outright.

"The Chiqetaw Players offered to foot the bill for the

food. Sort of their way of saying good-bye to her. The writing group chipped in, and we're funding the center-pieces and the flowers. I'm supposed to make a speech about Susan, that I haven't worked on at all. I'll go over to the school Saturday afternoon and supervise the ar-rangement of the tables." Andrew put his arm around my shoulder, pulling me close.

"When I think that you might have come in on that murder if you'd been a little bit earlier . . . my dear Ms. O'Brien . . . I do not want to lose you now that I've found you. You're crazy as a loon, a contradiction in today's world, and the sexiest woman I've met in years. I'm not going to take a chance on losing you before I truly get to know you." He covered my lips with his own, and I shifted in his arms. "Emerald," he whispered, his lips on my hair. "Emerald, is Harlow coming over tonight?"

My breath caught in my throat and I sounded throaty, sexy, so unlike my usual self. "No, she wanted to go to bed early."

His hands slid up under my shirt. "May I? I'll stop whenever you want."

A knot formed in my stomach, and all the tension from the past few days screamed to be released. "All I could think after you left last night was how much I wanted you in my bed." Two years without sex was two years too long. I tried to think of the kids, tried to think of respon-sibilities, but when he rubbed a light finger over my nipple and gently bit my lower lip, the battle was over. I capit-ulated, the willing prisoner. "Oh, God, don't stop."

Andrew made it easy. He held his fingers to his lips. "Ssshh . . . let me undress you? Please?" I wondered what he would think of my body. He lowered me onto the sofa and slowly undid the buttons on my blouse, then gently slipped it off my shoulders. I shivered as he hovered over me, taking me in, gazing at me with those dark pools of light before he unhooked my bra and folded it on top of my shirt. His lips took over for his fingers and he began to kiss me from the hollow of my throat, delicate kisses tracing a line down to circle each nipple. I moaned, feel-ing the fire build.

I started to pull down my skirt, but he grabbed my wrists and raised them above my head, pinning me with one hand. "Let me." With his free hand, he unzipped the waistband and I lifted up enough so he could slide the skirt over my hips. Ever so slowly, he worked my panties down and dropped them on top of the pile.

It was all I could do to keep from crying out with hunger and fear as he let go of me and pulled off his sweater and jeans. His chest was matted with dark, curly hair, and his muscles rippled under a sleek layer of skin. I wanted to taste every inch of him.

Suddenly I was in a hurry—hungry for touch, hungry for contact. It had been so long since I had last been touched by a man's hand. I pulled him down on top of me and he maneuvered his head down between my legs, nosing gently, his tongue flickering with butterfly kisses. As I began to soar, he crept up, looming over me, and I pulled him to my breast. He drove deep, and for the first time in years, I remembered what it was like to be a wanted woman. I pushed out the image of Diana, of Susan's spirit, of everything except this man who wanted so much to make love to me.

We fell asleep on the sofa, curled in each other's arms, untouched by the whisperings of the spirits that I could feel lingering, just beyond earshot.

A FLURRY OF wind raged against the window outside, waking me up. I glanced at the clock. Six o'clock . . . we had slept all night. I slipped out from beneath the afghan that I'd pulled over us during the night and shivered my way into the downstairs shower.

As I was lathering up, I heard a knock. A rising swell of panic rose up, but Andrew laughed as he opened the door. He was naked, and climbed into the stall with me, lathering me all over with bubbles and scrubbing my backside until I grabbed the loofah away from him.

"Twit!" I towel-dried and ran upstairs. He joined me in my bedroom while I hunted for something to wear. The room felt odd, and I was struck with a longing to spend the day there, to make my presence known. I almost felt as if I had stumbled into some strange woman's boudoir where I had no right to be.

I selected a jersey knit dress and slid it over my head. Andrew zipped me up. He sprawled on the bed, winking at me. "Hey, lady, how about a hug?" As I leaned down, he pulled me on top of him and grinned. "On second thought, what about an early-morning snack?"

"What about it?" I slipped out of his arms and searched my jewelry box for my emerald studs.

"I'd like my breakfast in bed. C'mon, give me breakfast, woman. . . ." He patted the quilt beside him, flashing me an ungodly leer.

"You're sneering."

"No, I'm leering. Big difference."

"You need a refresher course." I sniffed and turned back to the mirror, but I could see his reflection. He knew I was watching him, and so he began to make suggestive gestures. I started to laugh. "You're crazy, you know that?"

"Oh, yeah, *un lobo loco. Deseo tu cuerpo.*" The next thing I knew, he was naked and standing by my side. He unzipped me and trailed kisses down my back. "I'm hungry, and I feast on only the finest. Come give me what I want."

I slipped out of the dress. "Be careful what you ask for," I whispered as he led me to the bed. "You might be surprised by what you get in return."

Fifteen

❖

AS SOON AS Andrew left, I pulled out Nanna's trunk and hauled it into the kitchen. While the water was heating for a pot of tea, I carefully emptied the contents of the trunk onto the table, lifting out Nanna's journal, piles of charms and incense, and other paraphernalia. Once it was empty, I felt around the edges of the black velvet lining. The smell of old wood, polished with scented oils, made me shiver. Here, in my hands, was living history and tradition, but not one that most people would ever read. This was what lineage was all about.

After hunting for a few minutes, I found the hidden trigger. The velvet-lined bottom gave a little *pop* and came loose. I lifted out the cushioned insert and set it aside. Nanna had taught me about the false-bottom trick before she died; I was the only one who knew about it, besides the carver of the trunk, who was long dead.

Hidden inside, within the folds of a thick satin wrap, rested a scabbard, worked of leather blackened with age. Every month, under the light of the new moon long after the kids were asleep, I oiled this scabbard, rubbing the amber-scented unguent into the leather. Now I unwound the peace binding that held the blade firmly within the sheath. As the leather thong dropped away, I withdrew a gleaming blade. It, too, received a thorough cleaning each month. I would take a soft cloth and polish the dagger, as Nanna had taught me, as her teacher had taught her.

More than five hundred years old, the dagger was known as a seax. Single-edged, the blade stretched out a good twelve inches from the hilt, which was carved of antler, and the patterned welding had left a brilliant weave of darkened knotwork along the steel. Whether the sheath was the original remained a mystery. I didn't know and neither had Nanna, but the dagger was old, and she had given it to me on her deathbed.

I grasped the hilt. It felt heavy, slightly awkward in my hand. I seldom used it except when things felt out of control, and then the heft of the blade, the feel of tradition, passed through the steel to calm and give me a boost of courage. Magical blades sliced through energy; they also amplified and directed it. Attuned to their owners through years of use, they were sacred objects of tradition, treated with respect and care.

I set the dagger on the counter and stopped what I was doing long enough to pour the water over the tea bags. While the tea steeped, I replaced the false bottom and shifted everything back into the trunk again. The dagger might help me evict Mr. B & U. Then again, it might not, but either way, it wouldn't hinder my workings.

After I poured myself a cup of tea, I began a list of everything I could remember about exorcising harmful spirits. There wasn't much—Nanna had done such a good job of keeping them out in the first place that she hadn't had much call to evict them. Most of what I knew came from recent texts on the subject.

Unlike the Catholic exorcisms, folk magic tended to use a variety of herbs and charms to evict the unwanted visitors. I jotted down some of the more common elements used in clearing space: sage, cedar, sweetgrass, rosemary, rue, heather, lavender. Most I had on hand, but since I wasn't clear on what had drawn Mr. B & U to our home in the first place, kicking him out was going to be

more complicated than lighting a stick of incense and
showing him the door.

I was leafing through Nanna's journal when it occurred
to me that since the astral entity had shown up along with
Susan's spirit, perhaps he was related to her. Maybe he
was some nasty relative waiting on the other side for her?
No, a little voice nagged. If this was true, then he would
be focused on her, not on my family, I thought, doodling
circles on the paper. Why should he care about us if he
was really after her? No, Susan had nothing to do with
Mr. B & U except that they were both haunting my house
at the same time. Susan could stay, but whatever the
source of *his* power, it was time to take care of it. I wanted
the kids home. I wanted the cats home.

I finished my tea and dug around in the box until I
found what I was looking for—an old Egyptian ankh that
Nanna used to wear underneath her apron. I slipped the
symbol of eternal life over my head and poked around in
the pantry drawer for a new white taper candle, then took
it and the dagger and a stick of frankincense upstairs. It
was time to sort out what I was dealing with.

Since Mr. B & U had first appeared in Kipling's room,
that should probably be my base of operations. I wandered
into his bedroom. A miracle—it was still clean. Though
he had cleaned it only a few days ago, I expected it to be
a mess again.

As I lit the stick of incense and set it in an empty quart
jar that I assumed Kip used for catching various bugs, the
smoldering tip released a whiff of fragrant scent, rich and
as ancient as the hills. Frankincense, used in rituals since
the time of the pharaohs. Nanna had used it to purify and
cleanse space. As the smoke began to fill the room, I lit
the candle. After taking my seat on the end of Kip's bed,
I held the dagger in my left hand, took a deep breath, and
lowered myself into a trance. Without the kids here to
worry about, it would be easier to do what was necessary.

Down, once again, lower and lower until I felt myself
drifting, felt my mind floating. I hovered gently on the
edge of consciousness, losing the veneer of panic and fear
that had built up over the past few days. I took another

deep breath and slowly exhaled, listening as the air whistled through my teeth, taking the last remnants of worry with it. Everything felt calm—I had reached a level of stillness that always awed me, always reminded me that the world was so much bigger than we could see with our eyes.

I reached out, searching for something to tell me I was on the right track, that Mr. B & U had made this room his home base, but nothing seemed out of place. Had I made a mistake? But then, faintly—on the very fringe of earshot—I could hear some sort of drumming, a steady pounding. At first I thought it might be my heartbeat, but when I checked, I realized my pulse was tripping along faster than the drumbeat. No, this was the cadence of some other entity.

And then I saw it. A brief glimpse, a quick glance. Dark and shadowy, something that was hiding under the bed, unable or unwilling to come out. Startled, I pulled away and with a jolt shot out of my trance. I blew out the candle, snuffed the incense, and leaned down, shaking as I moved Kip's quilt. There, just out of reach, rested some sort of bottle filled with dirt, and I could feel a glimmer of energy from it. So, Kip had been playing at magic again without my permission. I would whip his butt for this.

With a glance toward the door to make sure there wasn't anything coming through, I reached under the bed with the dagger, using it to maneuver the bottle out to where I could get ahold of it.

It was a witch's bottle, all right, but not a thread bottle. Thread bottles were filled with snips and clips of leftover thread from sewing. I'd taught Kip how to make one, how to charm the threads within so they captured and confused negative spirits within the chaos of tangled pieces. But this bottle was one I'd never seen before, packed with dirt, and a few pieces of garlic and other herbs. So Kip had been in my stash, had he? As I moved the jar, I thought I saw something else inside—one of Nanna's charms!

"Oh, you are in for it now." I grabbed the bottle and

stomped into my room, where I cleared off the top of my desk. Nanna's silver ouroboros, a snake with its tail in its mouth, was clearly visible, stuck in the dirt to one side. The top was sealed with melted wax and I hesitated, not willing to break the seal just yet. If there was something attached to the charm, it might be freed to cause more damage if the jar was opened and the spell broken.

"Damn it!" I had told him time and again to leave the trunk alone unless I was there to supervise, and what did he do? Steal Nanna's talismans and proceed to disobey every rule I had set for him. That was it—Kip would be leaving the magic to me until *I decided* he had bailed himself out of this mess. As I turned the bottle over and over in my hands, a shiver raced through my arm. I heard a faint laughter, and something inside told me that whatever this was for, creating it had been a horrible mistake. How, I didn't know, but I was all too sure that we would find out.

When I called Murray to tell her what I'd found, she suggested we have a little talk with Kipling. The exorcism was on hold until I knew what I was dealing with. "I'll be over in a few minutes." I packed up the bottle, Nanna's journal and trunk and anything else I thought we might need and headed over to Murray's. My hands were shaking as I grasped the steering wheel, and I knew that we were in more danger than I had believed possible.

MURRAY SCRUNCHED HER forehead as she eyed the bottle. The kids didn't know I was there yet, and I didn't want them to until we had a chance to talk. "You know, I've been thinking. Ghosts don't invade a witch's house in such a thorough and frightening way without help," she said. "Have you been doing any sort of magic lately, other than the warding and general cleansing?"

I thought back over the past month and shook my head. "Nope . . . nothing. Earlier this autumn I made a wishing-bone charm for a prosperous Christmas season at the shop, but that's it. I should have been able to feel the wards ripping if something tore through my protection."

"Then maybe this is the key." She called Kip and Randa into the room. After a round of tight hugs, I motioned for the kids to sit down and, once they were comfortable, held up the bottle. "Recognize this?" I asked Kip.

He paled, pulling back so fast that he almost knocked his chair over. I set the bottle down in front of him and he pressed his lips together and hung his head. I could hear him breathing, too quick and too loud. My son was terribly afraid of something.

"Kip," Murray said, giving him a contemplative look, "your mom and I were talking about the ghosts. We were thinking that maybe somebody tried to do some sort of spell and it backfired. I wonder if that might have happened?" She flashed me a warning smile to keep quiet and let her talk. "Do you think you can help us? Do you think somebody might have tried to cast a spell that backfired? Maybe it was somebody who realizes now that he made a mistake? What do you think?"

His bottom lip began to quiver. "Maybe . . . maybe I know somebody like that." Eyes tearing up, he bit his lip.

Murray tipped his chin up so he was looking into her eyes. "Kipling, this is serious—we aren't dealing with very nice entities here, and there are dangers that you can't take care of on your own. Did you try to open some sort of gateway?"

He attempted to speak, but his teeth were chattering so hard we could barely understand him. "I—I'm sorry. I didn't mean to! Honest, I didn't mean to hurt anybody." He broke into loud tears. I'd never seen him so upset before—even when his father left, he managed to retain some sense of composure, but now he was falling apart. I started to reach out but stopped when Murray shook her head at me.

After a moment, she lightly touched him on the arm; her fingers barely brushed his sleeve. He began to quiet down. She handed him a paper napkin and he coughed into it, then blew his nose loudly. It was obvious that he was afraid to tell me what happened. How bad could it be? I wondered. Then I stopped myself: Mr. B & U was bad news, big bad news.

"Kip, you have to tell us exactly what you did. Don't leave anything out. We might get mad, but we still love you. Your mother loves you and you know I adore you, even when you make mistakes."

I reached out and took his hand, clutching the still-so-small fingers inside my own. He was trembling, but I could feel him start to calm down. "Honey, she's right. Whatever you did, we'll deal with it, but you have to tell us. We can't do anything if we don't know what we're facing."

Kip took a deep breath. "Well, a couple of weeks ago, when Sly stayed overnight . . . remember?"

I remembered, all right. Sly had wolfed down two huge servings of stew and bread, and I wondered what they were feeding the scrawny runt at home.

"I was telling Sly about Nanna. He said that spells have to be like on the movies—like that old show *Bewitched,* and like *Charmed.* We got in an argument and I told him I'd show him real magic. So . . . so . . . I got out Nanna's book and a charm and we cast a spell after you went to sleep." He ventured a look up at me.

I sat very still, remembering his admission that he'd been in the trunk. If I'd only insisted on him telling me the whole story that day, we might have saved a lot of time and worry. Torn between wanting to kill him and wanting to snatch him up and protect him, I could only wonder what the hell we were going to do now.

"What did you do?" Murray sounded like she'd swallowed a frog.

Kip frowned. His lip was so chapped that it was going to be a mess in a few days when the skin started peeling. "I-I-I tried to call Nanna in to visit."

"Nanna!" I shot up like a bolt. "You tried to summon a spirit? You know better than that!"

Murray sighed. She knew, as did I, that invoking entities was work best left to advanced practitioners, never beginners. I thought I'd taught Kip this lesson, but obviously my influence wasn't as strong as Sly's. "What spell did you use? Do you remember what you said?" If Kip had said something in such a way that it could be misunderstood, or twisted by some force stronger than he was, then all hell could break loose, and obviously it had.

Kip stuttered a little while I sent Miranda off to carry in Nanna's trunk from the car. He watched as I flipped through the pages of her journal, then jumped when I came to a page with a long incantation written on it, in a mixture of English and German. The spell was titled "Summoning Spirits."

As I scanned through the words, a lump began to form in my stomach. "This is a charm for summoning the ghost of a person who has been murdered, and it calls on the astral forces for vengeance!" I set the book down, unable to continue. "Why on earth did you use this for summoning Nanna? She wasn't murdered, she died of a heart attack."

"I didn't know. The title says it's for summoning spirits. I didn't know it meant ones who'd been killed!"

He was right. The parts in German gave the specifics but Kip didn't know German. He wouldn't have known that the spell wasn't a general summoning charm, and if he mangled a couple of the German phrases he would have been calling for the astral forces to *attack* our home rather than avenge the murder. I finished reading the pages and then closed the book. "That explains a lot. What talisman did you use? It says to use the Celtic cross encircled by an ouroboros, but that's inside this bottle, and I don't see any mention of making a witch's bottle in the instructions."

His cheeks reddened. "The next night I got scared and made the bottle. I put the charm in there, hoping to tangle up anything that showed up. Since I didn't have time to save thread pieces, I used some dirt, thinking that maybe it would bury the spirit again. I guess it didn't work."

"Damn! Damn it, damn, damn, damn." Whatever he'd done, we were seeing the ripple effect as the spell backfired all over the place. "You screwed up, big time. We're in trouble here. I hope you realize how much havoc you've managed to cause."

He hung his head, weeping silently. I had tried to drum into his head the same cautions Nanna had taught me.

Obviously it hadn't worked. He was either too young or too reckless to handle the energy.

Kip slowly met my gaze. "I'm sorry. I'm so sorry."

Murray was reading the invocation. "This is a nightmare. You used this to invite your Nanna?" He nodded. "Em, I don't speak German and obviously Kip doesn't either. Tell us what the words mean—and Kip, you better listen so you can learn what you conjured up."

I took the book and struggled to translate. "Let's see. . . . here it says . . . *the gateway is open, enter you unsanctified and wandering spirit, avenge our household.* If you read it wrong, you probably asked it to *exact revenge on our household.* Essentially, Kip, you managed to extend an open invitation to any nasty spirits who might have heard you."

Miranda freaked. She turned to him, shrieking. "You did it! You're the reason that ghost came, and you're the reason why we aren't safe anymore!" Before I could stop her, she jumped up from her chair and landed on Kip, knocking him onto the floor. Startled by the sudden squall, it took me a moment to realize that my sweet, brilliant Miranda was actually straddling her brother, slapping him soundly on the face and chest while she screamed at the top of her lungs.

Murray was quicker than I was. She leaped in and grabbed Randa by the shoulders, dragging her off even as Randa continued to scream. "You're an idiot! You're an idiot, and if the ghosts kill us, it's *all your fault!*" The last was uttered in a shout filled with spit. She sprayed him square on the face, and I didn't know who to feel sorrier for—my terrified daughter or my son who was reeling under the impact of the attack.

"To your corners!" I shouted as Murray tightened her hold on Randa until she lost her fight-or-flight stance. Meanwhile, I trundled Kip back into his chair and handed him a tissue. I took a deep breath. "Okay, listen to me— both of you. I'm in no mood for this. Murray and I will try to figure out how to undo the damage you've caused, Kipling. Meanwhile, if you two get into another fight I'll have you grounded in your rooms until next Thanksgiving. Understand?"

They both stared at me, Kip in tears and Miranda fuming. I gave them my look that basically threatened to feed them to the sharks if they so much as said one more word. Kip was the first to test the waters. "Randa? Randa? I didn't mean to do this. I'm sorry. I didn't mean to do anything that would hurt you."

She brushed him off like she would a cobweb. "If you're so sorry, how come you did it in the first place? Why didn't you listen to Mom? Do you think you know more than she does? You think she's stupid?"

I raised my hand. "Enough. Kip, I know you're sorry, and I know you didn't mean any harm. But you screwed up and now somebody else has to try to clean up your mess. You've put all of us in danger, you know?"

He hung his head. "I know. What are you going to do?"

"About the ghosts? Try to get rid of them. Meanwhile, you thought being grounded for getting into Nanna's charm box was bad—well, buster, guess what? Bad just got worse. You're grounded for three months, and you're working at the shop every Saturday until that time is over. No after-school sports, no hanging out with Sly—in fact, that friendship is over except when you're on school grounds. And—no more magic for at least six months. Now get your butt in the other room and get busy on the homework. Those grades better go up since you won't be spending time goofing off."

He nodded, speechless, and trudged off to the living room. As I watched him go, I almost felt sorry for him. My temper was running full tilt, but I still couldn't help it—he had wanted to prove himself an adult, and the backlash had been far worse than he ever expected. Still, when I thought of the situation we were in because of his stupidity, I wanted to beat his butt raw. I took a deep breath and held it in for a moment, then let it whistle slowly through my teeth.

Miranda's turn. "Randa, answer me this: How many times have I told both you and Kip that I won't tolerate

violence from either one of you, whether it be to a
stranger or to someone you know?" Self-defense was one
thing; outright aggression wasn't going to wash.

She started to protest, but I shot her a look that put a
stop to any outburst. "A lot of times." Her voice was
petulant, but I could tell she knew she was in trouble.

"You know that I refuse to tolerate thugs in my house."
A hard-and-fast rule since they were babies, this was one
area where Roy had agreed with me.

"Yeah, yeah . . . so what's my punishment?" She stared
out of the window, sullen. I could tell she knew she'd
been fingered.

I reached out and grabbed her chin, turning her head
back to face me. "Don't you look away when I'm speaking. I'm your mother and you *will* show me respect.
You're spending three months of Saturdays with Kip,
down at the shop. Both you and your brother will behave
decorously and be very helpful to each other, to Cinnamon, and to me. If I catch you fighting about this again,
whether with words or with fists, I'll pack you up and
send you off to go stay with your father. He won't put up
with any crap, not now that he and his new wife are so
happily married."

She knew I meant business. No copping attitudes while
living under my roof. She swallowed. "I'm sorry."

"Don't tell me—tell Kip. You owe him the apology.
I'm your mother, I set the punishments around here. It's
not your place to decide what to do to him when he makes
a mistake, and that's exactly what you were doing." I
knew I was being a real hard-ass, but she had to learn
that she didn't set the rules. She fled into the other room,
and all we heard were the scribbling of pencils and the
turning of pages as she dove into her homework.

I leaned my elbows on the table and rested my head
on them. "Oh, Murray, I think I just lost it. What are we
going to do? Mr. B & U pretty much has a license to kill,
and he seems bent on using it."

Murray let out a shuddering sigh. She glanced at the
clock—almost time for her to go on shift. "I don't know,
Em, but I wouldn't break this bottle right now if I were

you. Who knows what might happen if you try to undo Kip's spell that way?"

I nodded. The holiday season had suddenly become a nightmare, and I wanted only to wake up from it to find everybody safe again.

Sixteen

❖

I WAS SO ready to go to work the next morning, if only to get away from thinking about the ghosts for a while. While I knew a little more about what we were dealing with, knowing about them and finding a way to get rid of them were two different things. I wasn't sure just how much I trusted my abilities.

Cinnamon and I were swamped, but my mind kept wandering back to Susan and Diana. Who could have wanted them both dead? And why? And what had Kip managed to unleash on us all? Had his spell attracted Susan as well as inviting Mr. B & U in for a rampage?

I mulled over the string of events, still shaken and a little off kilter. It was hard to even take pleasure in the new shipment of cut crystal stemware that I always ordered this time of year. I held one of the delicate glasses up to the light, watching as rainbows skittered across the finely polished surface. The stem on the goblet was so fragile that if I held it the wrong way, it would snap. *Snap* . . . I flashed back to Diana, lying dead in a pool of blood.

With a shiver, I pulled myself out of my thoughts and finished the display just in time to take a call from Kip. He sounded subdued, but told me that they were helping

Murray finish her Christmas gifts; then Miranda came on the line and bubbled over about how White Deer was teaching her some of the native legends of the stars.

Murray had some news of her own for me. "I did some digging, Em, since you're so sure Walter was behind Susan's death."

"And? Don't leave me in suspense."

She hedged a moment and then said, "This will be public knowledge soon enough; it won't be long before it gets around the grapevine." After another pause, she dove in. "Susan cut Walter out of the will a couple months before she died, and he knew about it. He gets squat."

"Then who inherits?" I was confused. There went Walter's one motive for murder down the drain.

"Diana. She left most of her money to her daughter."

"I suppose that makes sense. What happens to the money now that she's dead, too?"

Murray's voice was strained. "I don't know, but it won't go to him. That was one of the stipulations—the money will never touch Walter's hands."

This put a whole new spin on things, and I wasn't sure what I thought. I glanced at the clock. Four-thirty. "I've got to get ready for tonight. Are you going to be there?"

"Nah, I didn't know her very well, and anyway, I'm on duty tonight. A couple of the guys from the force will be there, though. Their wives were in Susan's theater group."

I thanked her and hung up. The store was actually quiet for a change. "Cinnamon, I'm leaving early. Close up at six, please."

She was counting cookies, wrapping them in tiny cellophane packages for our customers; just a little "thank you" for their patronage. "Sure thing. Mom's taking the kids to a movie so it doesn't matter if I'm a little late."

I gave her a big smile. "Thank you for helping me so much this season. I hope you know how much I appreciate it."

She slid the basket of cookie packages under the counter. "I know. I'll take all the hours you can give me. I like this job, and the extra money sure makes it easier."

"I understand. I've been there, Cinnamon, I know what it's like. Okay, I'm out of here." I headed out into the flakes that were starting to fall. Wouldn't it ever stop snowing this year?

I APPROACHED THE house cautiously. The night before had been relatively quiet, but I didn't trust the silence. The peace could shatter at any moment. I hurried upstairs, and after a whirlwind shakedown of my closet, decided on a floor-length hunter green velvet dress that I had tucked away. I'd worn it often when Roy and I went from one corporate shindig to another. After the divorce, I stuck it in a garment bag and hung it in the back of my closet. Now I'd be wearing it with Andrew.

I held the dress up to the light, eyeing it critically. Hmm, not bad. I could probably still get into it, even though I had gained fifteen pounds since we moved here. I hunted around for a pair of shoes that would work and finally decided on a pair of black ankle boots. I dropped the gown and boots onto my bed and crawled in the shower, leaving the curtain and door open. I'd clean up the puddles later. Still leery of the bathroom, I wasn't anxious to participate in a repeat performance with the bad boy of the astral realm.

As I lathered my arms and back, I thought about the upcoming party. What would Walter be like? My intuition was honed with years of practice, but there was a lot riding on this meeting, especially with what Murray had spilled this afternoon.

After I dressed, I started to sit down at my vanity to make sure that my eyeliner was on straight and that my lipstick wasn't bleeding. Whoa—the woman staring back in the mirror couldn't be me. If she was, then I washed up pretty damn good. My hair cascaded down my back in a nimbus of curls, the faint hints of silver giving me just a touch of refinement. The dress set off my eyes, which were as green as my name. Irish. I inherited my father's looks but my mother's tongue. I patted my belly. Some folks might think that I could stand to lose a few pounds, but I liked my curves. Apparently Andrew did, too, and tonight I could finally see why he found me attractive.

I opened Nanna's trunk and pulled out a small wooden box. In the box, wrapped in a piece of silk, rested a brilliant palm-sized spike of amethyst crystal. I gently shook away the material and, settling myself on the bed, clenched my fist around the hard, cool gem. I closed my eyes, letting my thoughts drift randomly until the energy around me felt quiet and calm. After a moment of silence I reached inward, searching for answers. What should I do? Had I bitten off more than I could chew when I decided to help Susan?

My thoughts fluttered lightly around me. *Patience,* Nanna seemed to whisper. *Have patience. Give it time. Wait. Listen. Don't rush the spirits.*

A buzz began to hum at the edge of my perception, like static along a phone line. A voice, feminine and shimmering, otherworldly and ethereal, sparkled out from the crystal. "You must see this through. Unwrap the layers one at a time. You cannot expect to find your way through the mists until you discover the right path."

The voice was gone. *You must see this through. . . .* So I couldn't get out of the mess with a simple exorcism. *Unwrap the layers. . . .*

Was I looking in the wrong place, for the wrong reason? Murray's news had blown my theory that Walter had been after Susan's money. At a loss, I brought the amethyst to my lips and kissed it gently. Nanna gave it to me on my twelfth birthday and told me that if I ever lost it or gave it away she'd redden my backside no matter how old I was. I later found out that on her own twelfth birthday, a Gypsy from a nearby village gave the crystal to Nanna and told her to use it and pass it on when she felt it was time.

Six o'clock. Half an hour left before I had to leave. I hunted through my closet and pulled out a mandarin jacket embossed with a golden dragon pattern. A quick traipse through my jewelry box and I fastened a diamond solitaire pendant around my neck. Roy had given it to me for our third anniversary. I seldom wore any gifts he had bought for me, but tonight I wanted to look beautiful.

I thought of Andrew and blushed. I didn't want to fall in love; love was messy, love could hurt. And yet, I couldn't help my feelings. So far he was everything I had fantasized about. Promptly at six-fifteen I stepped outside.

I stopped and stared up at the expanding panorama above me. Sweeping across the heavens like the train of a velvet cloak studded with diamonds, the night sky wavered as chill and unyielding as the ice and snow that covered the sidewalk. A faint glimmer of lights flickered from the north . . . a rare vision of the aurora borealis. The northern lights danced across the horizon in a shimmer of green and white, waves radiating like pale ghosts riding the winds.

With a shiver of anticipation—a prescience, perhaps—I cautiously made my way to the car. My boots were slick on the ice, and I made a note to call the Schroeder boy from down the block and pay him to shovel out our walkway. I clutched the tall juniper branches next to the house for support, and their scent mingled with the chill. The smell of Christmas and northern lands and reindeer.

The parking lot was already partly full by the time I eased into a spot near the entrance. I swept through the doors, blinking under the glaring fluorescent lights as I was transported back to my own high school years. Rows of lockers reminded me of the contraband I had stored in my own, praying that no one would search it—nothing too serious when I looked back, a little pot, a switchblade that I didn't even know how to open but carried so I'd look cool and make bad-boy Jimmy Salver want to date me. At the time, it had all seemed so daring and dangerous.

Would Miranda do the same? Or would her locker be full of technical journals and notebooks? Instead of pictures of her favorite music groups, I had no doubt that she would plaster up photos of comets and astronauts on the inside of her locker door. Kip . . . Kip was an enigma. I had no idea how he would turn out.

The party in the cafeteria was in full swing, the tables

boasting delicate arrangements of hors d'oeuvres and centerpieces of white lilies surrounded by yellow tea roses. A large easel on one of the tables held a publicity poster of Susan, and people had bordered it with flowers and sprigs of holly. Faint music caught my ear—I thought I recognized *Swan Lake* but wasn't sure. People milled from group to group, teenagers staying pretty much with their own crowd, the adults congregating near a makeshift bar, where a waiter served wine and soda.

Andrew stood in a corner, talking to two men and a couple of women who I assumed were either part of his writing group or theatrical colleagues. They were dressed in dark suits—the women, too. I changed my mind. Writers wouldn't be dressed so formally; they had to be doctors or lawyers. Harlow and James waved me over. Her eyes were unnaturally bright; she looked like she'd been crying. James looked worried. I wondered if she'd told him she was pregnant.

She kissed me, and James caught me in his arms for a quick hug. "I hear you've captured my buddy's heart. Don't you go breaking it. He's a good person!"

I blushed and Harlow laughed. "James, you're embarrassing her!"

"No, I'm not." James winked at me. "She looks delighted and delightful. Emerald, I've never seen you looking quite so lovely as tonight."

I grinned at them. "Must be the romance. So, how goes the work, James?"

"Wonderful! I just wish I could get my wife to cheer up and share my good mood, though I guess it might not be appropriate at a wake, you think?" He didn't sound wonderful.

I wanted to ask what was wrong, but Harlow slipped her arm through mine. "Come on, let's go to the powder room and make ourselves even more glamorous than we are." She strolled me across the room and out the door. I leaned on her arm a little; my knee was hurting, and the high-heeled boots only exacerbated the pain. Why had I given into vanity?

We found the rest room; it was empty.

Harlow sighed and looked around. "You'd think they'd put a divan or something in here. All ladies' rooms should have them." She dropped onto the hard little bench against the wall, and I gratefully joined her.

"What's wrong? Something seems up." I could sense it . . . she was just a big old ball of despair and worry and tension.

"Oh, Em, everything's a mess. James has been offered a six-month assignment in Africa. He's been trying for this job for months and I'd made plans to go with him should he get it. Eco-safari . . . environmental films, stuff like that. What can I do? If I keep this baby, there's no way I can go jolting around the savanna for six months in a bumpy Jeep. If I tell him, he probably won't go, and this is the chance of a lifetime. It could send his career soaring!" She buried her head in her hands.

"Mess" was the word for it. I raised her chin so she was looking directly into my eyes. "Listen to me. If you have an abortion and James finds out later, it will end your marriage. I guarantee it. He loves you, he worships the ground you walk on, and if you do something like this, he will never trust you again. Are you willing to destroy your marriage because of your fear? You have to talk things out and he has to have a say in the matter."

She nodded, sniffling. "I'm so confused."

"Think straight, woman. You know James loves you. You love James. Whether or not you choose to have this baby, the two of you must make a united decision. He's the father, and he's your adoring husband." I dropped my hand and she searched my face, hungry and afraid. "Tell him tonight. Don't wait any longer."

"I guess I should. But what if he wants it? What if I get fat? What if I develop anorexia again and hurt my baby? I couldn't live with that."

"Maybe you will have the baby. If so, then yeah—you'll get fat while you're pregnant, so don't even bother worrying about it—it won't be forever. Look at Jane Seymour; she not only has her twins, she still has her gorgeous hair and figure. You love working out so much that I doubt if you'll have any problems at all." I didn't tell her that I still carried around my pregnancy fat. I had been too thin due to Roy's urging, and I decided after I had the kids that I wasn't going to let him push me around. Just another of our many conflicts. "As far as the anorexia, well, you have James and Andrew and me to lean on. We'll help you make it through the rough days so that your baby can be as healthy as possible."

She splashed some cold water on her cheeks and dabbed at her eyes, careful not to smear her mascara. "I don't know what I'd do without you, Em. I really don't."

"Everything will be okay." Even as I said it, I could see Harlow standing there, with a blond-haired chubby little girl beside her. They were laughing as a butterfly settled on the girl's nose. The vision disappeared as quickly as it came. "Come on, let's get back in there before they think something's happened to us." I squeezed her hand, and we headed back to the cafeteria.

As we reentered the room, I caught sight of Walter Mitchell. He was easy to recognize, standing with the little group that had congregated around Andrew. Something about Walter's demeanor—as if he owned the room—made me give him the once-over. So that was what Susan had seen in him. Though not a handsome man by traditional terms, he emanated power, and power was an aphrodisiac.

I kept hold of Harlow's arm as we sauntered over to meet and greet. I knew she didn't feel like coping with Walter tonight. He glanced at us as we approached, and a flicker raced across his face bordering somewhere between a rattler coiling to strike and a stalking lion. I immediately thrust myself forward and held out my hand.

"Mr. Mitchell, may I extend my regrets? Susan will be deeply missed."

He accepted my hand with a firm but reserved shake. "Thank you. I'm sorry. Have we met?"

"Oh, yes, at some party last year." I was surprised by how easy the lie came to my tongue. "I can't remember which affair it was offhand, but I do remember you." I let go of his hand and turned to Andrew. "I told you I'd be here by six-thirty."

I gave him a grin and waited for his cue. Some men were skittish about displaying affection in public, but he leaned down and planted a firm kiss on my cheek, avoiding my lipstick as he pulled me to his side. Walter stepped a little closer, crowding us while at the same time jostling Harlow out of the circle. A predator. He was a predator. I knew it as certain as I knew that Andrew was a protector. Walter leaned toward me. Bells rang—*warning signals.* I stood my ground, but took a step closer toward Andrew.

"Tell me, what is it you do?" Walter's tone was too friendly, his eyes too cold.

"I own a shop." I decided to divert his energy, throw him off guard if I could. "We're also terribly sorry about your daughter. Coming on top of her mother's death, it must be a great shock. I hope that Harlow and I were helpful to the police and that they catch the maniac who killed her."

If I hadn't been able to feel his energy shift, I wouldn't have known that my words had any impact at all. Harlow managed to keep herself still, but she stared at me like I'd lost my mind. Andrew gave me a tight squeeze that left me breathless.

Walter straightened his tie. "Thank you. I'm only glad that Susan didn't have to hear the news. How is it that you and Mrs. Rainmark knew the girl?"

The girl? He referred to his daughter as *the girl?* Definitely a cold man. "Susan mentioned her. We wanted to give our condolences to Diana about her mother's death and ended up walking in on the murder scene." He was watching me too closely.

"Diana chose to keep her life separate from ours," he finally said. "Only recently did she reenter Susan's life, and I suspect it was for selfish reasons. You have to understand, Diana was emotionally unstable. She had the bad habit of picking the wrong friends. My guess is that this time, she chose someone dangerous as well as unsavory."

Harlow cleared her throat. "Seattle seems like a dangerous city. I'd never move back to a big city. Would you, Emerald?"

"No, no. I wouldn't." Uncomfortable with the awkward pause punctuating our conversation, I asked, "When is Diana's funeral going to be held?"

Walter pointed to a younger man across the room. "My assistant is taking care of that matter. I believe it's being held next Tuesday. If you're interested in attending, I suggest you call my office and ask for Toby Gilmore. He can give you the information. And now, if you will excuse me, I have other guests to talk to."

After Walter was out of earshot, both Harl and Andrew pounced.

"What on earth . . . ?" Harlow leaned close so James wouldn't hear.

Andrew took hold of my elbow, jostling me. "That man is dangerous! He may not seem like it now, but I guarantee you, don't mess with him. I don't want you hurt."

I cautioned them to lower their voices. "I wanted to see how he would react."

"And at what conclusion have you arrived?" Andrew folded his arms. He wasn't smiling anymore, and I had the feeling that I was two seconds away from a lecture.

"We can't talk about this here. How long is this party supposed to last?"

"Until nine. Since I organized it, several of the group's other members volunteered to clean so we can be out of here by nine-fifteen." He sighed. Loudly.

I slid my arm around Harlow's shoulders. "I got some information for both of you about Walter and about why Mr. B & U showed up in the first place. I'll fill Andrew in tonight and tell you tomorrow."

She shrugged. "I could come over tonight—"

"Don't you have something to tell James?" I said pointedly.

She frowned. "I guess. I don't know if I'm brave enough, but I'm going to have to sooner or later."

I patted her arm. "Go on, go talk to him. If he flips, call me."

She swallowed, close to tears. "I'll talk to you later. Night, Andy." With a quick peck on our cheeks, she whisked herself off to where James was talking with a few of the theater people. She whispered into his ear, and a few moments later they were bundled up and bustling out of the door.

Andrew frowned. "What was that all about?"

I shook my head. Harl was one of my best friends and deserved my loyalty. "I can't say anything right now. I promised."

"You sure?" I nodded. Andrew kissed me on the forehead and pointed to a group of people standing near Susan's picture. "I'd better get ready to give the speech."

I waved him off. I needed to think, anyway. I'd been worrying about Harlow ever since finding Diana's body. Since she was pregnant, I shouldn't let her help me out. Bad enough with Mr. B & U on the loose, but Walter was a whole 'nother category of dangerous. What kind of friend would I be if I let her get hurt? Let her take a chance that might put her at risk?

Andrew was preparing for his speech when a strange man entered the auditorium. He caught my attention from all the way across the room; his energy was disturbing—chaotic, like a whirl of clouds and mist. His hair shimmered like white gold, and he wore a suede jacket, jeans, and a pair of motorcycle boots. He silently pushed his way through the mingling guests to where Walter stood. At his approach, Walter reared back, clenching his fists. I maneuvered close enough to hear what they were saying.

"What the hell are you doing here? I told you never to come back to Chiqetaw."

The stranger eyed him, guarded and aloof. "Thought you could get away with it, did you? Thought you could kill your daughter and nobody would be the wiser?"

"What?" Walter backed up, but a crowd had gathered, keeping them both from moving too far. "What the hell are you up to, Joshua?"

"You killed her because she was going to tell the police you molested her when she was a teenager." Walter let his fist fly and, with a triumphant grin, the man danced out of range, managing to evade the blow. Someone shouted for help, and I could see Andrew motioning to Gary, one of the cops Murray had mentioned was going to be at the service. They headed our way.

The stranger continued. "Didn't count on me, did you? She told me all about it, Walt, all about how you used to sneak in her room at night and make free with the fingers. She was going to write a letter to the pig boys in blue. By the way, do you still beat your wife?" Walter blanched. "Oh, so sorry—my mistake. Now that she's dead, you don't have to." Walter lunged again, but the man had already backed away, heading for the door. Andrew and Gary caught up to him and escorted him out of the room.

Walter tried to shove through the throng. "Get out of my way. It's time to put an end to this—"

Another man, obviously a friend of Walter's, stepped forward to calm him down. "Calm down, Walt. Come on, the guy must be out of his mind."

Eyes blazing, Walter pushed him away. "Keep out of this; it's my fight. If he wants to rumble, then bring it on—there won't be enough left to mop up the floor when I'm done with him." He looked around at the crowd gawking at him. "What do you all think you're looking at? Don't you have lives of your own?" He stomped out of the room. Nobody made a move to stop him.

The whispering started almost immediately. I slipped to the side of the room, unnoticed by the milling guests. What the hell had just happened? Who was that man? Joshua . . . the name sounded familiar, but I couldn't place it. Whoever he was, he'd made some pretty ugly accusations against Walter. Great, I just thought Walter killed Susan. Now another specter had risen its head.

Andrew entered the room again and launched into damage control. There wasn't much he could say. "Thank you for attending. Due to . . . uh . . . unforeseen circumstances, we'll have a moment of silence for Susan and then fold up the reception early."

Thank heaven we didn't have to be on cleanup duty, too. While I waited for him to find his notes and jacket,

I mulled over everything that had happened. One thing I knew for sure: Walter had dark secrets locked behind those steel-shot eyes, and I wasn't sure just how many of them I wanted to know.

Seventeen

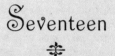

BY THE TIME Andrew and I made it through the front door, I was so sore and tired that I didn't even bother to go upstairs; I just grabbed a spare robe that I kept hanging in the guest bedroom and disappeared into the bathroom. I belted the terrycloth robe around my waist.

As I scrubbed off my makeup and brushed out my hair, I fingered the gray strands that were firmly entrenched amid the darker brunette. Thirty-six and already turning silver. Should I break down and dye my hair? Maybe Andrew would like it? With a quick laugh, I decided that if he wanted me to, he could pay for it to be professionally done. He hadn't complained about my looks yet.

He had taken off his shoes and tie and was sprawled on my sofa. I grinned. "Nice to see you so comfy." And it was ... nice to see a man on my sofa. I wasn't sure how we'd handle this when the kids came back, but for tonight I was going to enjoy myself. He patted the sofa, and I dropped into the seat next to him. He reached down and gently lifted my feet, rubbing my aching toes with the gentlest of fingers. "Mmm ..." I leaned back against the arm of the sofa and closed my eyes, enjoying the pampering. "Now, talk. Who was that man? Why was he accusing Walter of killing Diana?"

Andrew snorted. "That was quite a scene, wasn't it? That man happens to be Joshua Addison, Walter's stepbrother. As to where his accusations came from, I have no idea. Gary took him down to the station before I got a chance to talk to him."

"So, we're not the only ones who suspect Walt of foul play. I have to say, though," I said, remembering Joshua's ice-filled eyes, "there's something a little out of whack with Joshua. I don't know what it is, but he's kind of scary."

"I think they're both warped. I'd like to forget that this whole night ever happened, everything got so out of control. Next time you try to talk me into anything like that again, remind me to hit the streets before I let you convince me to play along." He tickled my arch, and I playfully kicked at him. "Can you imagine the rumors circulating through the phone lines right about now?"

I couldn't help it, I had to laugh. "Oh, God, too bad Harl wasn't there. She would have given anything to see that little scene. Walt hit on her sometime back, you know—tried to spread rumors about her when she refused him."

"That sounds about right." Andrew stroked my leg. "On another subject, I'd like to ask you a question, and I hope I'm not being forward. If I am, just tell me to shut up."

"I always reserve the right not to answer." I yawned. "But please, don't stop with the foot rub. That feels so good."

He laughed and began to knead the pads behind my toes. Ooo . . . I opened one eye and gave him an appreciative wink. "This is as good as sex. At least right at this moment it is."

"We'll see about that later." His grin was devilish and, not for the first time, those wolflike eyes captivated me. "Okay, now for the question. Please don't take this the wrong way. I just want to understand you better."

"Ask away."

"Why don't you keep any alcohol in the house?"

How to answer? I didn't have anything against drinking, but sometimes I was afraid of how easy it was to down a glass of wine whenever there was a problem. "My taste for booze started to grow right after the divorce; I got scared, so I quit keeping it around except for special occasions. I'll have a glass of wine when I go out to dinner, but that's about it. And . . . Roy drank a lot; he was a jerk when he was drunk."

Andrew leaned over and kissed my cheek. "I understand. Okay, I was just curious."

The doorbell rang. I glanced at the clock. "Who could that be? It's ten o'clock." Andrew answered the door and came back, trailing a bemused Harlow. She glanced at his loose tie and at my bare legs.

"Did I interrupt?" Her eyes darted from Andrew to me and back again.

What was she doing here? She was supposed to be home with James, celebrating the baby. "I didn't expect to see you tonight. Did you tell him yet?"

She curled up in the overstuffed chair and stabbed a finger at Andrew. "I suppose *he* knows?" She glared at me.

"Nope, didn't say a word."

She looked surprised but grateful. "Truth is, I chickened out."

Andrew gave her an inquisitive look. She sighed. "Andy, I need you to keep quiet about this. I appreciate that Em didn't tell you, but it's going to come out sooner or later. I'm pregnant. I'm just waiting for the right moment to tell James."

"Wow!" Andrew gave her the thumbs-up sign. "Jamesy will be proud as peaches! You guys will make fantastic parents."

"I hope so," she said, shrugging. "Anyway, I promise, Em—I'll tell him tomorrow. I just—too much emotion tonight, with Susan's memorial and all."

I let a short burst of air whistle through my teeth. "Okay, but it better be tomorrow. You're going to start showing soon, and you have to tell him something."

She gave me a brittle smile. "No problem. How did
the rest of the service go?"

We filled her in, and halfway through, her jaw had
dropped lower than my boobs. "So ... you know a lot
about the goings-on. What do you know about Walter and
Joshua's relationship?

She nodded, still gape-mouthed. "Trust me, that's a
real case of bad blood. Walter inherited Joshua's share of
the estate from Josh's father. That had to hurt. Joshua left
town during high school, he was a real troublemaker, and
one day he just took off. He didn't come back for years,
I understand, and then he only stayed for a little while
and was gone again. I have no idea what he was doing
or where he went. I don't know if anybody does, except
maybe Walter himself. But if he's back in town, he's
probably here to stir up trouble. The two hate each other."

"Do you think Walter would molest his own daughter?"

"Even though he's a sleaze, I don't think he'd resort
to that. But what if she was going to tell the police that
he did? What if he found out? Would he kill her?" Harl
leaned back in the rocking chair. "True or not, an accusation of child abuse would destroy his reputation."

Andrew leaned forward. "Walt hit Susan, or so she
said. Joshua seemed to know about that."

"That's still rumor—nobody ever saw the bruises. I
believe Walt hit her," I said slowly, realizing that I firmly
believed Walter capable of violence. "*You* heard him
screaming at her like she was dirt. And tonight he threatened Joshua. But molesting a child's far worse than hitting
an adult. Harl's right. Joshua could destroy Walt's life just
by making an accusation."

"So," Harl said, "what's next on the list of things to
do?"

I licked my lips. This was going to be harder than I
thought; I didn't want to tell Harlow she couldn't play.
Part of my reluctance stemmed from the desire to keep
her help, but I couldn't let her put herself in danger. "Harl,
I've been thinking about this all evening. I don't want to
throw a damper on you, but since you're pregnant, maybe

you shouldn't be involved. I don't want you getting hurt. The ghosts have proved dangerous. Walter already caused trouble for you in the past. Now look at the charges against him—he might be involved in two murders."

Harlow regarded me solemnly. "Walter is dangerous," she said. "He did his best to destroy my reputation. Everybody knew his rumors were lies, but they were willing to accept them until they figured out that I have more money stashed away than he does and I'm more willing to contribute to community causes. But I still can help."

I was torn. I wanted her input; she was a ticket into parts of society that I couldn't enter without a guest pass. "I don't know—"

"Hold it," Andrew interrupted, stopping me before I crumbled. "Em's right—there's no way we can let you endanger yourself. However, you *can* help by feeding us information you might know. Other than that, I think you should steer clear of this whole situation."

"Aren't you the take-charge man. I guess I have to start thinking about somebody besides myself now, huh?" She sniffed. "I hate being left out of things, and you really do need my help. But I'll back off." She patted her stomach. "Hard to believe that there's somebody growing inside, huh? Kind of freaky. Speaking of Walter, did you see that near stumble when you mentioned Diana?"

"I noticed that, all right. There's more. Murray told me that Walter isn't going to inherit a single cent from Susan. She cut him out of her will before she filed for divorce. What it boils down to, folks, is that since Walter knew about both the divorce and the change in her will, two of his main motives are gone. He wouldn't inherit if Susan died, and since she was leaving, he had no reason to get rid of her."

Harlow let out a low whistle. "If he had no motive and his alibi holds, then are we barking up the wrong tree? Why would Susan lie?"

"I don't know. Revenge maybe, for having affairs on the side or for beating her up? Revenge for him abusing Diana, if he did?"

Harlow mulled over the situation. "He's not a stupid

man. He wouldn't just go down to Seattle and kill Diana and hope nobody made the connection."

"No, not unless he thought that he got to her before she contacted the police. If he didn't know she was in contact with his stepbrother, then maybe he thought nobody would make the connection. Just a random coincidence—mother and daughter dying close together, but in two unrelated circumstances?"

Andrew joined in. "Want to make a bet he's got an alibi for the time of her death, just like he has one for the time of Susan's death? But the pieces have to fit together somehow. And we know one thing for certain: Somebody murdered Diana, and whoever did it probably won't hesitate to kill again."

I thought about it for a moment. There were so many questions, so many loose ends. But when I closed my eyes, I couldn't shake the brittle stare that Walter had given me, nor the feeling that he knew more than he let on. Murray had said to watch out for deception and subterfuge. The obvious answer was that Walter was the source of all of this, but then . . . was he? And would we recognize the deceit when we found it?

Andrew leaned back, his arms behind his head. "How about some tea? You've got me hooked on the damn stuff."

I gave him a grateful smile and we adjourned to the kitchen, where I put the kettle on to heat. Andrew leaned on the counter and picked up the witch's bottle I had found under Kip's bed. "What's this?"

I took the bottle out of his hands and put it back on the counter. "Leave that alone. Trust me, you don't want to mess with it." I supposed this was as good a time as any. I told them about my aborted exorcism attempt and what had followed—finding the witch's bottle, and Kip's confession. "Susan may have been drawn by the spell, too—she says she was murdered, and the spell is intended to summon a murdered spirit and to use the astral forces to bring vengeance for that death. Unfortunately, the astral force in question—Mr. B & U, that is—is bent on tar-

geting our household because Kip messed up the word-
ing."

They both stared at me for a long minute, then Andrew
muttered something under his breath. I didn't ask what he
had said. I didn't want to know. I went on making the tea
and getting out the cups.

Harlow was the next to break the silence. "So I get to
play spy?"

Andrew and I looked at each other, and then he gave
me a little nod. I shrugged. "Consider yourself our internal
operative." I rifled through the junk drawer until I found
a notepad and pen. "We need to make a list of our priorities. The kids are due back tomorrow night, and I still
haven't got a clue how to handle Mr. B & U, especially
now that I know why and how he showed up here."

Harlow grabbed the side of the table, and her face took
on a peculiar shade of green. "Hold on—I'm gonna
puke."

She made a mad dash toward the sink. As she rushed
by Andrew, she bumped into the counter. The witch's
bottle had been sitting near the edge; it wobbled once and,
before I could catch it, tipped and fell to the floor, shat-
tering. Dirt and herbs spilled every which way, and the
ouroboros skidded across the tile, coming to rest directly
at Harlow's feet.

I stared at the shards of glass. This was *so* not a good
thing. Murray had cautioned against breaking the bottle,
and I seconded her concern.

Harlow urped but there wasn't much in her stomach to
cough up. She rinsed out both the sink and her mouth as
I leaned over the pile of dirt, wondering what to do next.
Before I could stop her, she reached down and picked up
the charm.

"Here you go." She held out the ouroboros.

"Drop it! Don't touch that." I scrambled to her side
and grabbed the silver pendant out of her hands. "Harl,
you shouldn't have done that."

"What? What did I do?" She looked alarmed. Andrew
stood beside us, uncertain.

I fingered the charm—the energy was thick around it,

oozing like old honey, and I didn't like the feel of it. "Let me clean up this mess—don't either of you touch any part of the dirt, herbs, or glass. Andrew, please get me the dustpan and whisk from the pantry. Harlow, I want you to find a box of salt in the cupboard, and wash your hands with salt water. Just do as I say." Maybe we could negate any possible ill effects.

After sweeping up the dirt, I asked Andrew to open the door for me. I took the dustpan outside and scattered the contents in the lot next door that was filled with snow-covered brambles, then covered the whole mess with salt and an entire package of sage. I went back inside and scrubbed the floor with Florida water, then carefully put the ouroboros in a saucer and set it aside. By the time we gathered around the table again, everyone's nerves were shot.

I washed my hands and dug through the cupboards for a box of saltines. "Here," I said, handing a packet of them to Harlow. "Eat a few of these. Then go home and go to bed. You need all the sleep you can get. Trust me, later on you'll be grateful for whatever sleep you've managed to snag. You're lucky, you know—most of your pregnancy will be spent in the cooler months. Thank timing for that."

"I'm sorry about the bottle, Em. I hope I didn't cause any trouble." Harlow looked despondent. "What about our list of priorities?"

"We can deal with that later," I said. The bottle was history; there was nothing I could say about it that wouldn't frighten her. I had my suspicions but could only hope that I was wrong, and chances were, nothing would happen.

She sighed. "You know, a lot of people have a lot of grudges against Walter, including me. We just never get to have our say because he buys the players in the town off with his donations and public image. I hate to say it, but you know, the idea that Susan's attempting to frame him might not be as far-fetched as it sounds . . . revenge from beyond the grave?"

At that, we called it a night. Andrew walked her to her

car, and she drove off into the icy night. The weather was still clear; at least she wouldn't have to contend with snow on the winding drive through the gorge to her home.

I washed out the mugs and cleaned up the counter while Andrew made sure the doors were all locked. He pressed against my back, curling his arms around my waist. "Is it all right if I stay here tonight? I'd really like to be with you again."

"I think I'd like that."

He nuzzled my ear. "So what do we do when the kids come home?"

"Honestly? I don't know." I leaned against the counter. "They like you and I'm not ashamed to have you here, but I have to know where we're going before the kids get used to you staying overnight. I don't want them getting attached and then have you disappear out of their lives. They already suffer from enough abandonment issues with their father."

"Fair enough. Then I suppose I'll just enjoy tonight for what it is—a rare gift. Once Kip and Miranda come home tomorrow I'll go back to trying to earn your trust. Especially since I've had a taste of what life with you is like."

We finished cleaning the kitchen, then curled up on the sofa. At a quarter of midnight, the phone jangled. I immediately thought of the kids. Please don't let it be Murray with bad news! I snatched the receiver. Something was wrong; I could feel it.

James was on the other end, and he sounded frantic. "Is Harlow still at your place?"

"No, she left forty-five minutes ago. She was headed home." I covered the mouthpiece and glanced over at Andrew. "Did Harl say anything about stopping anywhere on her way home?"

He shook his head. "She just said she was tired and couldn't wait to get to bed. She's not there yet?"

I took a deep breath and spoke into the receiver. "She was headed straight home, James. It's cold tonight, icy. You might want to call the cops to see if she broke down by the side of the road or something."

"She has a cell phone; she would have called me.

Something's wrong, Emerald." His voice was shaking in earnest now.

"Hold on, hold on—we don't know that for sure. Call the police, give them her license number, and ask if there have been any reports of accidents tonight involving her car. Meanwhile, Andrew and I will come over. Call us right back if the cops know anything."

While Andrew waited by the phone, I quickly got dressed. By the time I got back to the living room, Andrew had just finished talking to James again. "No reports of any accidents. They're going to keep an eye out for her. Let's go. Do you know what route she normally takes?"

"Yeah, she has one shortcut in particular she uses—up old Route 93. I'm worried. Harlow's never irresponsible like this. She would have called James if something was wrong. If she *could* call, that is." I pulled on a pair of low-heeled boots and buttoned up my parka. "We'll take the Cherokee. Your car, as nice as it is, doesn't have enough get up and go."

The temperature had been dropping steadily. With clear skies, it was going to be a frozen wonderland. I estimated we were already in the low twenties and still plummeting. We buckled up and I pulled out on the road, cautiously gauging how bad the buildup of ice was. The pavement glittered: rhinestones instead of cobblestones. I inched along the route that I knew Harlow always took. One place in particular had me worried.

Along the dark drive to her house, which sat a little out of town on ten acres, ran a gorge. A ravine really, dark and very steep, that led down to Alder Creek. During the summer it was prime blackberry territory, but this time of year, the creek was frozen solid. During spring the runoff from the snow turned it into a raging river *en miniature,* and several kids had almost drowned there. The road that wound by the ravine was narrow, without any real shoulders. With few lights out this way, if a driver made one wrong move, he—or she—could easily slip over the edge. The town council had been after the county for years, begging them to put in a series of guardrails, but the county always found one excuse or another for ignoring the requests.

As we neared the ravine, I slowed down, keeping my brights on so we could hunt for any suspicious clues. "Do you really think she had an accident?" Andrew was peering out of the window, trying to see something in the darkened night.

"I don't know, but if she did, this is probably where it happened. Use the cell phone—call James and see if she's shown up yet." As we crept along at all of twenty miles an hour, he put through the call. Harlow wasn't home, and James sounded on the verge of hysteria. My hands began to shake. This wasn't supposed to happen. Harl was going to have a baby. She wasn't supposed to just disappear like this.

Andrew shouted. "A light—I think I see a light down there!"

I pulled off to the side of the road as much as I could and flipped on my hazard blinkers. We got out of the car and cautiously approached the edge of the road. Sure enough, there were headlights coming from down there— faint, but they were reflecting up at us. "Hello! Is anybody down there?"

First there was an awful silence, then a faint noise, a call that seemed to come from miles away. Hard to make out—but then we both heard what sounded like a woman's voice. "Harlow! It's got to be her!" I started toward the edge of the ravine, but Andrew stopped me.

"You're not going anywhere. You call 911. I'll see what I can do about going down the gorge, but you stay up here. I don't want both of you down there needing help. That ravine is slick and dangerous."

I grabbed the cell phone and punched in 911. Andrew found a mile marker a few yards up the road and I gave them instructions, warning them that we were on the side of the road but that there really wasn't a shoulder so please would they not ram into my car. They assured me help was on the way.

Andrew was rooting around in the back. He popped back out with a long coil of clothesline. "This is the closest thing to rope that I could find. Do you have a flash-light?" He found my box of flares, and while I grabbed the flashlight from the glove compartment, he set up the warning lights on the road to direct the emergency vehicles.

I could only watch as he secured the clothesline to a tree that was near the edge of the ravine. He wouldn't let me get any closer. He tied the line around his waist and, the flashlight in one hand, clothesline in the other, began to lower himself down the steep embankment. As the darkness enveloped him, I rubbed my gloved hands together, cold in spite of the layers of clothing I had on. "Hurry, hurry, hurry . . ." I muttered under my breath, using the words like a mantra in hopes of speeding the rescue units along.

As carefully as I could, I crept to the edge of the ravine and peeked over. I could see the pale glow flicker in and out as Andrew descended into the darkness. The head-lights from the car below were fading, and I guessed that the battery was either damaged or losing its charge. I couldn't hear anyone calling up the hill now, and I prayed that whoever it was who had tumbled over the cliff was simply too tired to answer. But what if it was her? What if Harlow was down there in a pool of blood? Or gaso-line? What if she lost the baby? What if she lost her life?

Before Andrew could reach the bottom, I heard the wailing of sirens, and a paramedics unit, a police car, and a fire truck pulled up behind my car. I directed them to the edge and told them Andrew was already on his way down. The paramedics and firemen sprang into action, pay-ing out rope from one of the trucks. Two of the men, guided by a set of bright lights attached to their headgear, imme-diately set out over the edge, following roughly the same path Andrew had taken.

Just then we heard a yell. Andrew had reached the bottom. "It's her! It's her car! I don't see her—she still must be inside."

Harlow. Harlow was at the bottom of the ravine, freez-ing and hurt. She had to be hurt; otherwise she'd be out of the car, trying to get up the hillside. Harlow was an athletic woman; if she *could* get free, she would have by now. As the truth began to impact, a wave of nausea swept through me. Stomach roiling, I leaned over, struggling to keep my balance as everything I ate that afternoon came up in a huge gush of bile onto the side of the road.

Oh, God, oh, God, Harlow was down in the ravine, and it was all my fault. "N-n-no. . . ." I stuttered, trying to make my way to the edge.

One of the paramedics rushed up beside me. "I'm Captain Files. You know who is down there?"

"Y-y-yes, she's my b-b-best friend." I was shaking now, my lips frozen from both the icy chill and a growing terror. "She didn't make it home and her husband called and we came out looking for her and saw the lights from the ravine below and now she might be down there dying—"

He put his hand on my shoulder to steady me. "Take it easy, ma'am." He handed me a handkerchief from his own pocket and I blubbered into it, blowing my nose. "Can you tell me her name?"

"Harlow . . . Harlow Rainmark." I managed to choke out James's number and the fact that Harl was pregnant. The squad leader's radio crackled and he held it up, looking at me before he pressed one of the buttons on it. As we listened, I held my breath. Was she okay? Was she dead?

"We have reached the victim, over."

"Copy, 120. Be aware that the victim is pregnant. What is her condition?"

"Victim is unconscious, breathing labored with normal pulse. BP is 145 over 99. She's trapped in her car but Lopez and I should be able to get her out. Possible broken leg, possible concussion. We'll need a stretcher. We're sending Mr. Martinez up the line so wait until he gets there before you send anybody down."

"Copy, 120." He turned to his crew. "Get a stretcher ready to go down the line. Whitman, head down to make sure that guy Martinez gets his ass up here without breaking something, too." One of the men began belaying down the rope, his headlamp shining into the dark maw of the

ravine. Files looked me over. "You don't look too good."
I was struggling to keep my emotions under control. "Are
you all right?"

I stopped, leaning against the car. "I'm just so scared.
What if she dies?"

He opened the door to my car. "You should sit down
for a moment." I dug through the front seat to find my
water bottle, then rinsed my mouth and spit onto the
ground, clearing out the taste of the vomit.

I begged him for news. "How is she? Do you know
how she is?"

He shrugged. "No, but my men will get her up here in
one piece. Her vitals don't sound too bad at this point."

"The baby?"

Once again, he shrugged. "That I can't tell you,
ma'am. We won't know the full extent of her injuries until
we get her to the hospital. By the way, what's your name?
You do have one, don't you?"

He leaned closer, giving me a big-brother smile. I sniffled, grateful for the support. "Emerald. Emerald O'Brien."

"O'Brien . . . oh! You own the china shop, right?"

I nodded. "Yeah, I do. What's going on? Why aren't
they headed down to her?"

"They need to make sure Mr. Martinez gets back up
first—there he is. Take it easy; your friend Harlow is in
good hands with our men."

A fireman guided Andrew as he crawled back over the
edge. Then the crew members who had been standing by
with a stretcher disappeared, on their way to rescue Harlow. I hurried over to Andrew, aching with every fiber of
both body and heart.

"How's Harlow? You saw her? Are you okay? Did you
hurt yourself on the way down?" Worries crowded in,
shoving aside everything else.

He pushed himself to his feet and brushed himself off.
"I'm fine. Yes, I saw Harlow, and I don't know how she's
doing. They said she's unconscious, she probably has at
least one broken leg. I think she'll survive."

"The baby?"

He shook his head. "I don't know, Em. . . . I just don't know."

I jammed my hands in my pockets. If only she'd stayed at home and talked to James like she was supposed to, but no, she had to get cold feet and come over so late. I shook off that thought. It wasn't her fault—it was mine. If only I'd put that goddamn bottle away like I should have, she wouldn't be in this predicament now. She wouldn't be hurt. I shook my head and looked up at Andrew. "Harlow's hurt. How soon before Miranda or Kip take it on the chin because of me? Every person I love has been put into danger because of this mess. I've got to get rid of this ghost." The wind sprang up, and a jet of cold air nearly froze my ass off. I pulled my coat tighter.

"Emerald, listen to me. Harlow didn't just accidentally slide off the cliff."

"You mean somebody broadsided her?"

"No. I mean she was startled into driving off that cliff. Somebody wanted her dead."

"Someone deliberately ran her off the road?" I stared at him in horror.

He glanced around to make sure no one was eavesdropping. "Harlow was awake when I got down there. She passed out a minute later, but I got a chance to talk to her. She told me that she saw a woman standing on the road, the woman raised her hands and then something dark, I don't know what, leaped in front of Harlow's car and when she swerved to miss it, the car wheels wouldn't hold on the ice and she went tumbling into the ravine."

My jaw dropped and I started to speak, but the excited clatter of voices stopped me. They were bringing Harl over the edge now. I rushed over to check on her. She was bruised, and her lip was cut. They had splinted her right leg and her left wrist.

One of the paramedics told us that she'd been drifting in and out of consciousness the past few minutes. Now she opened her eyes and they widened when she saw me hovering over her. "Em . . . Em . . . James? The baby? Is my baby okay?"

"James is on his way to the hospital. You just hush,

be quiet and rest. You need to rest." I took her other hand in mine and held it as they carried her over to the ambulance unit.

She tugged me to come closer. I leaned down before they slid her into the back and put my ear near her lips. She whispered, throaty and hoarse. "Susan. Susan was on the road. She tried to warn me but then something appeared. Something huge and dark and I was so scared. I tried to swerve, tried to get away. I couldn't stop the car . . . Susan . . ." Her eyes fluttered, and she drifted back into unconsciousness.

As they loaded her into the rescue unit, they told us where to meet them at the hospital. I could barely hear what they were saying. Numb beyond the point of exhaustion, I was sick with the realization that if anything happened to Harlow or the baby, it would be my fault. I had no reserves left and had to ask Andrew for help in getting back in the Cherokee. He drove.

We were halfway back to town when I remembered. Harlow had grabbed the charm—the one from the witch's bottle. Could that have been the catalyst for the attack on her? One thing I was sure of: "We've got a rogue spirit on our hands. Next time, somebody could die." I thought of Miranda, out on the roof, and of Harlow and how she would have died if we hadn't found her. I had been so casual, so sure we could handle this without any trouble. I had forgotten Nanna's strictest rule: *Never underestimate the powers you work with, and never underestimate the powers you encounter.* I had no choice. It was time for war, and I was on the front lines, leading the troops.

Eighteen

✤

WE ARRIVED AT the hospital shortly before the medics. I called James while en route and told him that Harlow was alive and going to be okay. By the time Andrew and I got there, he was waiting by the emergency room entrance, his face a mask of ashen gray. I thought that he could probably use a wheelchair and some oxygen himself. The minute he saw us, he raced over, begging for information.

"All they could tell me is that they're bringing her in and that she seems to be in stable condition." His gaze darted from Andrew to me, then back to Andrew. "Is she okay? What's going on?" Andrew put his arm around James's shoulders and led him into the waiting room, where we could see the moment they brought Harlow in for treatment.

I took a deep breath, wanting to prepare him. There was no easy way to do this. "James, they think she's got a broken leg and maybe a broken wrist. She's pretty bruised up. There's something else."

He looked at me, worry filling his eyes. "What?"

"Harl is pregnant, and we don't know how the baby is

doing. She was going to tell you tonight but was too afraid—"

"Pregnant? I'm going to be a father?" A look of wonder lit up his face.

"Yeah, she'll tell you all about it when she can. But James, we don't know how the accident affected the baby. We'll have to wait and see what the doctor says." It occurred to me that I hadn't even had a chance to congratulate him on becoming a father, and here we were, waiting to see if it was going to happen at all now. Damn it.

Andrew held up his wallet. "Going to get us all some coffee and something to eat." He disappeared out the door after giving James a quick pat on the back. I sat next to James, holding onto his hand.

"Why didn't she tell me?" He sounded so confused that I wanted to take him in my arms and rock him like a child. "I don't understand. I love her so much and I don't think I could stand it if something happened to her. She has no idea just how much I need her. She's so caught up in worrying that she won't be good enough, and all along, I'm the one who hasn't been good enough for her."

I wondered what it would be like to have someone love me the way James loved Harlow. Even in the beginning, Roy hadn't felt that way about me. I pressed a tissue into James's hand and leaned back. "Listen to me, babe. She needs you as much as you need her, and she adores you. That's why she was so afraid to tell you about the baby. All sorts of issues have come up—fear about her anorexia, about what will happen while she's pregnant, about how she's afraid you'll miss out on the trip to Africa since she's pregnant. But she'll get through this, and everything will be fine. Accidents happen and people recover." I wasn't about to tell him what caused the wreck. Let him think it was just bad timing, bad luck, for now.

He wiped his eyes. "Thanks. You're a good friend. No wonder Harl thinks the world of you."

I shivered. How would he feel when he found out what really happened? I saw the flash of metal as the doors burst open. "Here she is—come on, but don't get in their way."

James jumped up. The medics did their best to keep him out of the way without making him feel useless. He pelted them with questions, and they patiently answered as best as they could. Harlow was still drifting in and out of consciousness. A couple of doctors and nurses whisked her off into an ER. James was turned away at the door, and the nurse brought him back to the waiting room. He sat down, looking confused but a little less panicked.

"They won't let me go back with her."

"That's so you won't get in their way while they're working. They need the room to fix her up, hon. Just be patient. They'll let you know what's going on as soon as they find out." I wished that I felt as calm as I sounded. For James's sake, I couldn't break down like I wanted to. He needed the strength of friends right now and, though I might have let Harl down, I sure as hell wasn't going to do the same to him. I let out a shaky breath as Andrew returned with a tray of coffee and doughnuts. The coffee smelled good, and the sugar would help keep us going. When the doctor finally came out to talk to us, James leaped up. Andrew and I followed.

"How is she?" James leaned close, fear and hope waging war in his eyes.

The doctor consulted his chart. "Harlow's condition is stable, and she'll be fine. Let's see, she has a broken tibia in her right leg; it's broken in two places. One cracked rib and hairline fractures in two others. She sprained her left wrist, has a mild concussion, and a lot of bruises. Also, she lost one of her front teeth when her face smacked into the steering wheel."

"And the baby?"

"She hasn't miscarried," the doctor reassured James. "Everything seems fine, though we'll want to keep her here for a few days to monitor her condition. Your wife is in exceptional health, if a little underweight. Her athletic condition helped her survive this accident. She's lucky to be alive."

James stuttered out "Thank you" over and over again. I shuddered and turned, burying my face in Andrew's chest while James asked the doctor a few more questions.

"She's going to be okay." I straightened my shoulders and pushed a loose strand of hair out of my face. James opened his arms for a hug, and I held on for dear life. "She's okay . . . she's okay." As I stepped back, Andrew offered me his handkerchief and I mopped away my tears but they wouldn't stop coming; the exhaustion was feeding them.

The doctor looked at his watch. "She's awake." He smiled at James. "Why don't we get you back there to see her? I'll have a nurse escort you to her room." He glanced at Andrew and me. "I'm sorry, I don't want her overstimulated. You two will have to wait until tomorrow."

James decided to stay at the hospital overnight, so Andrew and I left our phone numbers as emergency contacts and headed back to my house. I stared dumbly into space while Andrew drove. What the hell were we going to do next? Exhaustion, fear, and guilt tangled my thoughts, and I kept coming back to the edge of the ravine, watching the headlights, wondering if Harlow was dead.

By the time we pulled into my driveway and stumbled into the house, the sky had clouded over. I locked the door. We dragged ourselves upstairs and settled into bed without talking. Andrew snuggled against my back, draping one arm over my shoulder as I stared at the wall. I couldn't sleep; images of the night—so alien with the sirens and crash and ice—raced through my mind, and when his arm dropped away and he started to snore, I quietly slipped out from beneath the quilt to peek through my bedroom window. A light dusting of snow was falling. The sky was illuminated from the faint hint of silver that snow clouds always bring with them. Comforted, at least for the moment, that we were safe, Harlow was safe, and the children were safe, I returned to bed and finally managed to drop off to sleep. I didn't dream at all that night.

THE SMELL OF bacon woke me up. I wandered down to the kitchen, letting my nose lead me. Andrew was busy, frying up the golden strips of pork. A fluffy three-cheese omelette and whole-grain toast were in the warming oven. My stomach rumbled, and I felt like I had a bad hangover—at least the headache part of it—as I glanced at the clock. Ten-thirty. About four hours of sleep. Murray was supposed to bring the kids back at about three, but I couldn't let that happen. After last night, I knew for sure that Mr. B & U was out for blood.

Andrew whistled as he ground the beans and tapped them into the mesh holder of the espresso machine. He leaned down and kissed me before bouncing back over to the counter to get our juice. "Good morning. How's my favorite witch?"

I groaned. "Are you sure your name isn't Twinkle Toes? That's what I'm going to call you, you know . . . Twink, for short. You are far too bright and bubbly after last night. What are you on? Some kind of uppers?"

"Oh, sure." He laughed. "Puppy-Uppers. Then I take Doggy-Downers when I reach the point where everybody wants to kill me." He slid into the chair opposite me and waited as I took a bite of the eggs. The omelette melted in my mouth, oozing with cheese and a hint, just a hint, of cayenne.

"Mmm . . . can I hire you as my personal cook? I think the kids might want to eat at home more if we ate like this every day." I bit into the bacon. Crisp, sizzling, but not so hard it hurt the teeth.

Andrew dug into his breakfast. "So, are you okay this morning?"

Was I okay? As the fog began to lift from my brain, I examined my feelings. The edge was gone from my panic but I could still feel it there, under the surface. "No, I am not okay. I feel responsible for the fact that my best friend almost lost her life last night. Now I get to wait for how long it will take both Harl and James to figure it out and dump me, and they'll have every right. When I realized that she was lying at the bottom of that ravine, I felt just like I did when I realized that I'd ignored my ex's behavior for too long. His actions were hurting my kids, and I didn't want to see it because I didn't want to face what it meant. Murray teases me about being selfish, and she's right."

"It wasn't your fault—"

"Then whose fault was it? I'm the one who got her involved in this. I'm not going to shirk my responsibility in this."

Andrew shook his head. "No. She chose to get involved, she chose to come over last night. You had nothing to do with hurting her."

I couldn't believe what I was hearing. How could he fail to see the connection? "Listen, I screw up . . . sometimes pretty bad, but I never avoid admitting my mistakes. Are you blaming Harl for this? She didn't drive off that road on purpose."

He let out an exasperated sigh. "No, I am not blaming Harlow for the accident, but you shouldn't blame yourself, either. You didn't tell the ghost to go push her off the edge. In fact, you told Harlow she had to back off. You tried to protect her. Why should you feel guilty for something somebody else did?"

I stared at my half-eaten omelette. Something about his refusal to accept that I was at least partially at fault for what had happened bothered me. Did he blow off responsibility when things went wrong because of something he did, too? He must have sensed my hesitation, because he reached over and tapped my chin.

"Emerald, I just don't want you being too hard on yourself. Blame is useless right now—our main focus should be to fix what's gone wrong. Guilt only eats up energy."

I couldn't argue with that, even though part of me still felt that something about his reasoning was off, but I was too tired to fight. After a minute, I relaxed and slumped back in my chair. "I guess we're all a little tense."

He gave a half laugh and lifted his coffee mug. "I'll drink to that."

As I picked up my fork again, the phone rang. I grabbed the receiver.

"Hey, Em . . ." Harlow's voice was shaky, but to me it had never sounded so sweet. They were keeping her for observation. She was scared, though. "Listen, I'm going to make this quick while James is off getting something to eat. So far, he thinks I just had an accident. I want to leave it that way. He doesn't believe in ghosts, he doesn't want to think about things like that. But I saw them out there on the road, and I tell you, whatever that thing is, it's dangerous . . . to you, to Susan . . . to anybody who tries to cross it. Please be careful, Em. If it tried to kill me, what's it planning on doing to you?"

"Don't worry about me." My voice broke as the tears rose back up from where they were resting. "I'm so sorry. I didn't mean for this to happen."

Harlow snorted. "You weren't the one who pushed me off the road." Her voice grew soft and she sounded phlegmy, as if she'd been crying. "But now that James knows I'm pregnant, he's so happy. He loves you, Em, but he might not take it too well if he knows what we've been up to. I won't tell him, I promise. You guys are good friends and I want you to stay that way."

My eyes misted over. "You really are an angel. Harl, you've already been a big help. Thank you for everything, but we were right—you can't get involved." I reassured her that we would keep her up-to-date on what was going on, and she reassured me that if she heard anything out of the ordinary, she'd let me know. I replaced the receiver. All I could think about was that she wasn't angry at me and she wasn't going to tell James. I'd been handed a last-minute pardon by the governor himself. I turned to Andrew.

"We're on our own, bub. Harlow's out of the picture. Thank heaven, she and the baby are going to be okay. She's not telling James about the ghost, so don't you mention it, either." I played with the rest of my eggs, no longer hungry. "We've got a real mess on our hands. I don't think I can do anything about Walter until I take care of Mr. B & U. I certainly can't bring my kids back to this house until I clear him out."

Andrew stretched. "After we take care of the dishes, we could take a drive over to Walter's. Try to talk to him."

I wrinkled my nose. "I just told you that I can't deal with him until I get rid of this spirit that's terrorizing my family and friends. And what would we talk to him about? I don't think he was too thrilled to hear that Harl and I had been down in Seattle hunting up his estranged daughter."

"I don't know," Andrew said. He sounded petulant. "I'm just trying to come up with something that might help. First you say that Susan thinks he killed her. Now we find out that he has no motive, no reason to get rid of her. Maybe we can't prove him guilty, but can we prove him innocent? Maybe Susan is all messed up because she's dead!"

I stared at him. "Maybe so, but what if she's telling the truth? What if Walter is more clever than either of us give him credit for? He can't be a stupid man, not with the career he's built for himself. I know you feel guilty about her death, but there's nothing you can do now—"

He slammed his fist down on the table. I jumped as his eyes flashed, and my stomach twisted in knots. "Why is it all right for you to get upset over Harlow's accident and accept blame for it, but I can't feel guilty over Susan's death? What's the difference?"

I hated to admit it, but what he said made sense. However, his outburst was unacceptable. "I understand what you're saying, Andrew. I really do. But don't ever raise your fist in my house again. I took that kind of anger from Roy, but I won't take it from anybody else. I refuse to be afraid in my own home."

He looked away and swallowed, pulling his hand back onto his knee. "I shouldn't have done that; I was out of line. I'm sorry."

I relented a little. There were too many other things to worry over without tackling yet another problem. "Yeah, I know. Things are a real mess, aren't they?"

Andrew shrugged one shoulder, and he gave me a wan smile. "Everything is out of kilter lately. And with Joshua's accusations, I have the feeling it's only going to get worse."

I took his hand. "Come on, let's go relax. We had a

scary night, and we're both still tired." We wandered into the living room, where I grabbed the remote. The local news was on, and we curled up on the sofa. Thank goodness it was Sunday and Cinnamon was in charge of the shop for the afternoon. As it was, I still had to call Murray to ask if she could keep the kids one more night. There was a news item about a house fire out on Steel Eye Stream; looked bad. I hoped the family had made it out safely. A quick reference to Harlow's accident flashed by, but the details were sketchy.

Andrew pressed a quick kiss onto the end of my nose. "I guess I'll spend the afternoon working. I'm starting a new book."

"New book? Good for you." I perked up. "What's the plot?"

"Wandering minstrel, midwife, evil landowner . . . another historical romance."

"Leave me one of your books." I usually didn't read romances, but I wasn't about to miss out on this opportunity.

He snickered. "I can't wait to hear what you have to say about it. Just be gentle? I'll be right back; I've got a few scattered in the car." He pulled on his shirt and dashed out into the overcast morning. More snow due this afternoon. When he returned, he was shivering. "Colder than a witch's tit out there," he said, then blushed. "Sorry."

"Andrew, I might actually admit to *being* the town witch, but I do still have a sense of humor. After all we've been through the past day or two, don't sweat it."

He dropped a book in my lap, and I picked it up and examined the cover. The woman on the cover was gorgeous, of course, with a breathless look and boobs that were ready to fall out of her elegant, yet ripped, ball gown. Behind her stood a tall, brooding man with a leer on his face, and behind both of them towered the silhouette of a mansion. *The Mistress of Peach Tree Manor.* I glanced at the author's name. Yep—Andrea Martin, like he'd first told me.

He coughed. "Women still resist buying romances

written by men. So I use a pseudonym, and by the time they figure out I'm a guy, they're hooked on my work."

Squelching a wicked desire to tease him, I bit back a few choice remarks about his subject matter. "I want to curl up and read it right now, but I'll save it for later tonight." I was flipping through the pages when a breaking news bulletin flashed on the television. I turned the sound up. The reporter was Cathy Sutton—one of Bellingham's overly bright and peppy young television personalities.

"In a surprising move, police have made an arrest in the murder of a woman found stabbed to death in her Seattle apartment on Thursday. Police announced this morning that they have taken Walter Mitchell of Chiqetaw into custody. Mitchell was married to the deceased woman's mother, author Susan Mitchell, who died last week of diabetes-related complications. Police have recovered what they believe to be the murder weapon from Mitchell's house as well as evidence from the woman's apartment."

I set Andrew's book on the table and stared at the TV. "I'll be damned."

Andrew glanced at me, uncertain. "I don't think we'll be talking to Walter anytime soon."

As I tightened the belt on my bathrobe, I couldn't shake the feeling that something didn't set right about Walter's arrest. The next headline came on, so I turned off the television. "I have to call Murray. Why don't you go ahead and do whatever you need to do."

Andrew headed for the door. "Call me later. Want to meet for dinner?"

"Maybe—let's see what happens. Pet the cats for me, would you? I miss them." He promised, and I waved as he pulled out of the driveway. The fact that Walter was behind bars felt right in so many ways but no, something was out of kilter. I sighed. Too many questions, and I had too much to do to worry about finding the answers. After a quick shower, I put in a call to Murray.

She answered on the second ring. "Hey, we were just

talking about you. When do you want me to bring the kids over?"

"Got a problem with that." I filled her in on what had happened with Harlow. "Is there any way you can come over today? Can you leave them with White Deer? I'm scared to have them back in this house."

"Hold on," she said, and I heard her talking to White Deer in the background. After a moment, she came back on the line. "White Deer will stay here another night. I'll come over and we'll plan out how we're going to exorcise Mr. B & U, but I can't actually do anything about it until tomorrow. That's when my vacation starts. I'm sorry, Em, that's the best I can do. I can't afford to miss my shift tonight."

I relaxed. "That's fine. I can hold out one more night as long as I know the kids are safe. When can you be over?"

"Give me half an hour. Meanwhile, be careful. When Harlow broke that bottle, I think the genie escaped, if you know what I mean."

As I replaced the receiver, I knew precisely what she meant. And I wasn't looking forward to trying to put the genie back in the bottle.

Nineteen

❖

MURRAY PULLED INTO the driveway as I finished making up a pot of mint mocha for us. Her breath came in little puffs as she slipped through the back door, into the kitchen. "Hey, chick." She gave me a hug as I asked how the kids were. "I left them in the middle of some top-secret projects." She winked, and I immediately had visions of being inundated with homemade potholders and birdhouses for Christmas.

I pressed a mug into her hand and handed her a plate of cookies. As she settled in at the table, I retrieved the ouroboros, which I had placed on a tray. I had fought the urge to douse it with Florida water, a Voudoun equivalent of holy water, and salt, which would neutralize some of the energy. "Don't touch it." I set the tray in front of her. "I have the awful feeling that Harlow wouldn't have been hurt if she hadn't picked this up."

Murray held her hand over the pendant, fingers a hairbreadth away from the metal. I held my breath, willing her not to slip. After a moment she pushed the plate away. "Oh, man, bad medicine. Big bad. This thing is supercharged, Em. I think you're right: Anything that comes in contact with this is a sitting duck." I had touched it. I didn't have to say anything. She knew what I was thinking. "We have to get rid of him."

I pulled out Nanna's journal. "I found an exorcism that might reverse that part of Nanna's spell. It's meant to clear out astral entities." I pushed the book over to her. "It's in German, but I can translate."

I laid out the basic text for her and she leaned back in her chair, thinking. After a few minutes, she nodded. "This should work, but it's going to be nasty going in. Think we're up to it?"

"We have to be; nobody else can do it for us." I closed the book and took another sip of my espresso. "So Walter got busted for killing Diana?"

Murray gave me a queer look. "Do you think he did it?"

Did I believe he did it? "Truthfully? I have no idea." I thought about it for another moment. "No. I can't tell you why, even though I should be the one accusing him here, considering I think he killed Susan. There's something very suspicious about this entire situation. And what the hell is up with his stepbrother? That dude has some serious issues. By the way, do you know who inherits Diana's estate?"

"Slow down—one question at a time. I'm going to attend Diana's funeral on Tuesday and see what I can find out. As far as Joshua, he's pretty much eaten up by hatred—he's so angry at Walt that it's a wonder he didn't burst in there and kill him. I'll bet he empathizes with Diana, since Walt seems to have cut them both out of the family. The inheritance thing sent him over the edge, I think." She stood up and rinsed her cup, then grabbed her jacket and zipped it up.

"Why did you decide to go to Diana's funeral?" I had thought about attending, too, but I had to work at the shop, and I'd been blowing off too many days. Cinnamon's paycheck was going to be a nice, fat one for Christmas this year.

She grinned. "I figured since Harlow's out of the picture, you need a replacement. I may not have contacts among the upper crust, but I sure as hell can find out a lot you can't. Walter won't be there—obviously. He's got money, but it will be several days before his arraignment comes up. You know, when Susan died, I was convinced it was an accident. Now that Diana's dead and it looks like Walt might be our man, I'm not so sure."

I jumped up and gave her a huge hug. "Thank you! Oh, thank you! So, we tackle Mr. B & U tomorrow evening, then?"

"We'll take him on, Em. And we'll win. I've got a meeting tomorrow afternoon, but I'll be done in plenty of time. And I'll beg another day from White Deer. By Tuesday it should be safe for the kids to come home again."

I confided to her that I was scared to go see them, considering the power the pendent seemed to have. "I don't want to draw his attention onto them. Please, tell them I love them. Tell them we're trying to clear this up. Tell them—"

She put her hand on my arm. "Quit worrying. They know you love them, and I'll make sure they know again." She paused, door half open in her hands. "Em, I don't like leaving you here alone, especially after what happened to Harlow. Are you sure you won't come home with me? Or go to a hotel where you might be safer?"

Safe? I didn't think I'd be safe anywhere. "Harlow was on the road when he got to her. If Mr. B & U wants me, he'll find me no matter where I am. I promise I'll be careful. Now go on, get out of here." As she pulled out onto the slick roads, the phone rang. It was Andrew. I asked how his work was going.

"I roughed out the outline. The beginnings of a book always scare me—I'm never sure if I can keep the momentum going."

"Can I read it as you write?" I was still amazed by the fact that he was a romance writer. Somehow it just fit— I would manage to get involved with a gorgeous man who wrote bodice rippers.

"No, you may not. I never let anybody see my work until I'm at least one draft through the book, even my writing group. So, how was your day? Any more news about Walter?"

"Not that I know of. Murray came over, and we mapped out our attack for tomorrow night." I roughly went over our plan.

"That sounds far too dangerous. Is there any other way to handle this? I don't want you to get hurt."

"There's no other choice, Andrew. Not unless I sell the house and move, and I don't think even that would do it. This thing is after me, after my family. God, I miss the kids; I can hardly wait for them to come home." The sound of splintering glass echoed down the stairway, so loud that it sounded like something had smashed through a window. "Oh, shit! I'll call you back."

I tossed the receiver on the table and took the stairs as fast as I could. The sound had come from my bedroom. Shards of my vanity mirror glittered all over the dressing table and floor, jagged edges threatening to slice anything that touched them.

Nothing was out of order except the slivers of mirror that had showered my makeup, perfume, and jewelry box. The closet was open, but no one was inside. The cats were all at Andrew's; they couldn't have been responsible for the damage. I closed the door and bounded down the steps, trying to push thoughts of vengeful spirits out of my mind. They refused to budge. In my gut, I knew this was the work of the entity trailing after Susan.

I leaned against the arch leading into the living room and tried to steady myself. What was I going to do? My nerves were shot, and I just wanted everything to be normal again. The first thing I had to do was clean up the mess. I couldn't just leave it there. Broken glass was dangerous enough by itself, but with a wayward ghost around, it could too easily turn into ammunition. Steeling my courage, I dug out the vacuum and attempted another assault on the upper story.

The bedroom was icy cold, even though the rest of the house was warm—a sure sign that a spirit had passed through. After gingerly picking up the bigger shards, I plugged in the vacuum. Propping my bedroom door open as wide as I could to give myself a head start should anything from the nether world show up, I turned on the motor and used the hose to start sucking up the slivers of glass. Thank heavens for the invention of the bagless vacuum.

I had almost finished when a tap on my shoulder jolted me into a panic. My shriek reverberated through the room as I let go of the vacuum and whirled around, hands flailing to ward off whatever might be attacking me.

Andrew grabbed me around the shoulders and pulled me into a tight embrace. "It's okay! It's okay! Em, it's just me." I began to shake, hyperventilating until he set me down on the bed and stroked my hair back from my face. "Emerald, it's okay. I'm here now. Everything's all right."

"Oh, my God, you scared me." After I caught my breath, I filled him in on the broken mirror. A spark fluttered in my heart as I realized how worried he'd been. "I can't believe you drove over here to check on me. Thank you."

"I'll clean up the rest. You stay put." He finished vacuuming the rest of the glass. Then he took a look at the wall where the mirror had been attached by heavy screws. A pensive shadow covered his face. "I can't figure out how your mirror broke. The fastenings on the wall were fine. It looks like it just jumped off all by itself. I'm not very sensitive to energy like you are. Do you think it's our ugly friend?"

"I don't know for sure, but I'd bet on it. Come on, let's go downstairs."

We settled in the kitchen with hot cocoa and cookies. With a quick look at the clock, he sighed. "I hate this. I don't want to leave you alone, but I should go home and take care of some business that I've ignored . . . contract stuff. My agent is on my back. If I don't get it done tonight, my publisher will be breathing down my neck. Would you like to come back to my place?"

I looked around. This was my home; all of my things were here. This was a haven where my children could grow up in safety, and nobody was going to run me out. My mother had left her country to follow my father across the ocean. Nanna had made the crossing alone, after

Nappa died. My father had set up his own business, risking the chance of failure. But they'd survived and prospered. How could I fly in the face of family courage and leave, my tail between my legs?

"Thanks, Andrew, but I'll stay here. We McGradys never run away from our problems, even when we marry them." I grinned at him. "As I told Murray, if Mr. B & U wants to get me, it doesn't matter where I am. I'll be careful, so you go home and work. I promise to stay out of my bedroom and keep my eyes open. Tomorrow Murray and I will blast that bad-ass out of here."

"Are you sure?" I nodded, and he gave me a long kiss. "Okay, then, but you call me if you need anything. *Anything*." I waved, tensing as the door shut behind him. The broken mirror had spooked me, and the house was quiet. Too quiet. I grabbed the remote and flipped on the TV. Christmas shows. Well, at least they were cheerful. I left the set on for background noise and picked up a copy of Victoria but soon drifted off into a nap.

Crash.

I shot straight up, blurry-eyed but most definitely awake. How long had I been asleep? The light from the streetlamps filtering through the window told me it had been at least a couple of hours. The television was going haywire—first with static and then with wild, zigzagging lines. As I rubbed the sleep from my eyes the crash was repeated by a louder one. What the hell?

The phone—where was the phone? I couldn't remember where I'd left it, and I hadn't turned on the lights before I fell asleep. I had to get to the phone in the kitchen. As I stood, a wave of vertigo raced through me. Could we be having an earthquake? I felt for a rolling under my feet, but the room itself was steady. Just then, a swirl of energy shifted and a vortex sucked me in, a dark and swirling whirlpool of chaos.

"What the hell . . ." Even as I spoke, I knew where the movement was coming from. Mr. B & U was on the prowl. I had to get out of this house. Mist had risen, blinding everything around me, and even my thoughts clouded over. Another wave hit and sent me reeling. Too dizzy to stand, I grabbed the arm of the sofa and lowered myself to my hands and knees.

Get to the kitchen . . . I had to get to the kitchen. Why? The phone, that's right. I needed to get to the phone.

More crashing from upstairs. Then, after a lull, other sounds came from my room—scratching noises—fingernails screeching on chalkboards. Footsteps raced across the ceiling as a series of knocks reverberated through the walls. What was up there? So far Mr. B & U had been nebulous, without much form, but this . . . this sounded solid. Had he managed to manifest? Was there some monster, some hobgoblin, crawling around my house, looking for me? And then, then I knew. The mirror had been a portal, and when he managed to break it, he was free to come through.

Inch by inch, I forced my way to the kitchen. The bruise on my knee burned brightly as I reeled with every movement. By the time I reached the archway, I was drenched with sweat. As I slid onto the cool kitchen tiles, something skittered loudly, racing back and forth overhead and I ducked, wondering if it would come crashing through the ceiling onto me.

Moonlight reflected into the pantry through the curtains over the kitchen sink. I debated. I could either try for the alcove or try to make it to the door. But if I went outside, I'd be barefoot, without my keys or purse. Could I make it over to Horvald's? The ice was so slick and I was so confused that I didn't know if I could manage to reach his house.

Another crash. Goddamn, couldn't anybody hear this from the street? If I heard crashes coming from a neighbor's house I'd be calling the cops.

The noises were near the stairs now, and I began to panic. How long before Mr. B & U came downstairs and found *me*? In the dim light from the window, I caught sight of the phone and grabbed the receiver, praying for a dial tone. I sat on the floor, back pressed against the wall, trying to punch in Andrew's number. I was so nervous that I had to dial twice before I got it right. Meanwhile, I kept my eye on the living room door and one ear trained on the noises coming from upstairs.

Andrew came on the line, and in hushed whispers I spilled my fear into the receiver. "Can you come over right away? There's something in the house here and I can't get to the door."

"Call the police—just do it! I don't care if you're afraid of looking psycho—dial 911. I'm out the door." The click of the receiver promised that he was on his way, but could he get here in time?

Should I call the cops? What could they do? Call in a priest? But maybe, just maybe, their presence would make it stop long enough for me to get out of here. I dialed 911. The emergency operator was so calm that her voice gave me strength. I told her that there was someone in my house. She dispatched a unit and I hung up, praying that they would get here soon.

Thump, thump, thump. The noise was on the stairs now. Shit, I had to get out of here. I eyeballed the door to the backyard, but I couldn't do it. I couldn't make myself crawl even that short distance to freedom. Confused by the kaleidoscope of energy that assailed my senses, it was all I could do to drag myself into the pantry and curl up in the corner. I wiped my nose and looked around for a weapon, but the only thing I could find were canned goods. I stacked a few cans of peaches in front of me, thinking I could throw them if nothing else.

What had Nanna taught me about psychic attack? I struggled to remember her words through the cacophony that sounded around me. Oh, yes—build a wall of energy between the attacker and me. I caught my breath, struggling to remain calm.

"Nanna, if ever I needed your help, I need it now." My whisper was lost in the rush of noise that raced through the walls, through the floor, but it must have gotten through to the other side, because I felt a gentle hand rest on my shoulder as a faint whiff of lilac perfume embraced me. The presence didn't last long—just for a few seconds—but it was enough to steady my nerves and give me the strength I needed to envision a wall of light stretching across the pantry door, a wall I hoped would keep out anything supernatural, anything that meant to harm me.

The noise was snuffling around in the living room now, coming closer.

I closed my eyes, pushing myself back into the corner as far as I could go. I had done what I could, set up a warding that might or might not keep Mr. B & U out. Grateful that my children were safe, I swallowed my tears and straightened my shoulders. Murray would take care of them. How had it come to this? How and why? I had tried to help, had tried to do what felt right. Was this going to be it? Here, on the floor of my pantry?

Damn it, I thought—no! I wasn't going out without a fight.

I struggled to my feet, leaning heavily on the shelf next to me. Maybe I could make it out, could let adrenaline push me through the haze, but if I moved now, I would draw the attention of whatever was out there in the living room. I was out of time—I couldn't make it outside before the mayhem broke into the kitchen.

The noises in the living room grew louder. A booming started up, vibrating the walls with thuds and high-pitched squeals of glee as whispers began to cascade amid the thundering. I straightened my shoulders. Mr. B & U would have to drag me screaming into the abyss if he wanted me. As the voices neared the kitchen doorway, I heard something in the background. At first I couldn't make it out through the din around me, but then it was clear and bright—a sound so sweet that I almost cried. Sirens, wailing into my driveway.

There was a sudden hush from the living room as the energy pulled back, rolling away from the kitchen like an ebb tide, away from me, away from the house. As the police broke through the back door, the lights came on in a dizzying flash and I cried out once.

I DON'T FAINT. In fact, I'd only fainted once in my life. But the sudden release of fear made my blood pressure drop. The moment I saw the officer's face peering into the pantry, I keeled over, deadweight.

By the time the medics had arrived and I managed to come around, Andrew was standing behind them, pale and drawn. When I opened my eyes and croaked out, "What happened?" he took a deep breath and slumped against the doorway.

"You'll be all right; your leg looks banged up and you cut your lip. Otherwise, I can't find anything wrong with you. Your blood pressure is a little high but not dangerous."

"What time is it?" I scooted back against one of the shelves.

Andrew checked his watch. "About 9:00 P.M."

One of the policemen knelt down beside me. "Ms. O'Brien—could you tell us what, if anything, you saw and heard?"

"Is my house completely trashed?" I wanted to help them but couldn't focus until I knew the extent of the damage.

The cop exchanged glances with Andrew, but I couldn't read what they were thinking. Then he turned back to me. "No; in fact, nothing appears to be out of place."

Andrew joined him. He reached out to take my hand. "Everything's okay, Em, not a scratch in the house, nothing broken, nothing overturned."

"That's impossible. I had heard them wrecking my house. It sounded like a freight train was rumbling through the rooms—"

The cop broke in. "We're not sure what happened, Ms. O'Brien, but we found no signs of any intruder. Maybe it was bad plumbing? That can sound pretty bad. Noises always sound louder at night." He flipped his notebook shut and I could tell that this was going to be his official explanation.

"If you could just help me into the living room . . ."

The medics shrugged and helped me up. Andrew pushed by them and lifted me in his arms, carrying me gently to the sofa. "I rather like rescuing you," he said softly.

The younger of the two paramedics grinned. "Are you sure you don't want to go to the hospital?" I shook my head. "Then please sign this form stating that we showed up and you feel okay and we're free to go."

"Don't worry," I grumbled as he handed me the pen. "You aren't going to get sued, and I'm not holding you liable for whatever happens to me because I didn't let you strap me to a stretcher." I scribbled my name across the bottom.

They gathered up their gear and followed the cops out of the house. I wondered just what the neighbors would be thinking now—cop cars and Medic One units, all with lights flashing in front of my house in the dark winter night.

Andrew saw them to the door, then returned to the living room, where I was gingerly examining my freshly purpled knee. I'd be okay, but crawling across the floor hadn't helped the bruises any. Definitely no marathons in the near future. I tried to shake off the ringing in my ears and the tingling that jolted every nerve in my body as I looked around the room.

Everything was in its place; nothing had been upset or tipped over. After what I had heard, I expected every knickknack to be on the floor, broken. But if a tornado had roared through my house, there was no sign of it now. I glanced out the window, but it was so dark that I couldn't see anything. Bad plumbing, my ass.

"You can't stay here, so don't give me any grief about it, woman. I'm taking you home with me." Andrew snagged my coat from the hallway.

"He was coming for me." I mutely accepted the coat and slid into it. "Mr. B & U was headed straight for me. He would have killed me." Andrew helped me with my boots.

"Yeah." His voice was thready. "I could hear what was going on when you called me on the phone. I was terrified that I was going to find you dead."

I couldn't help it, I began to cry, tears boiling up from the anger and fear that the evening had wrought. "I'm sick of it. I don't want to run away, I won't let that creature have control over my house! I just want whatever this is to go away."

"Ssshh . . . Murray will come over tomorrow, and then you can take care of it and the kids can come home."

I called Murray and told her where I'd be and why. Then, leaning heavily on his shoulder, I let him help me out to his car. As we pulled out of the driveway onto the glittering street, I took a last look at my house. Yeah, I was running away tonight, but Murray and I would be back, and we'd kick some ghostly ass.

Twenty

✤

THE DAY WAS more hectic than I thought possible. The only bright spot was the hour I got to spend with Miranda and Kip at the shop before White Deer picked them up to take them back to Murray's after school let out. Miranda was irritable. She wanted to come home. "Mom, when are things going to get back to normal?"

"We're doing our best. If things go right, after tonight you'll be able to come home and so will the cats." I promised that Murray and I would be careful. I only hoped that I would be able to keep my word.

I wasn't sure what to expect when I opened the door, but the house seemed relatively quiet. Murray slipped in behind me and opened her backpack. She piled an assortment of little packages on the kitchen counter. Dried lavender for peace of mind; black peppercorns to drive out evil; cedar for purification; and dragon's blood resin, which boiled like blood when dropped on hot charcoal. She added a small package of gum mastic, a resin that helped open the mind to peer into other realms; a packet of jasmine flowers; and a tiny box containing red sandalwood powder.

"I have some of these, you know." I picked up the gum mastic, staring at the pale translucent droplets, each no bigger than the end of a pencil eraser. "This stuff's insanely expensive."

"We won't need much. And I thought it was better if I brought everything just in case you were out of some of them."

"This isn't all Native American medicine. You're mixing traditions now?" I grinned at her; she'd been the one to insist that it was time to "go back to her roots" several years earlier.

She blushed. "Well, I talked it over with White Deer. She convinced me that you have to use what works, whether or not it's part of your path."

"Umm-hmm . . . good lesson."

Murray ground up dragon's blood, peppercorns, sage, and gum mastic into a fine powder. She used my coffee bean grinder to do so, and I immediately jotted a note on the dry erase board hanging on the fridge to buy a new one. She looked up from the concoction she was making. "Do you have any Florida water?"

"Yeah," I said, thinking about the stash of herbs and other oddities that I stored in a little cupboard in the pantry. Not everything fit into Nanna's trunk. I fished through the cupboard. Rose water and lavender water, there—another bottle of Florida water bought from a Santeria shop in Seattle. "Here we go. Time to lure Mr. B & U out of hiding."

"Right. Then we perform the exorcism. After we drive him out, we close the portal using the energy from this incense I'm making." She frowned, making sure that all the ingredients had been powdered to dust. She opened a small container and tapped a white powder into the incense. Saltpeter, to provide some sparks when the incense hit the charcoal burner.

"Sounds lovely . . . sounds hard. Where did you put the incantations I gave you?"

"I rewrote them on index cards and stuck them in your grandmother's journal. While I ask the spirits to bless the incense, why don't you get everything else ready? The journal is back in the trunk." She closed her eyes and began to chant in her tribal language. I couldn't understand the words, but the power behind them was chilling.

Murray had tucked two sets of cards into the journal. I had translated Nanna's ritual and adapted it for our use, making sure both the ritual and the chants were easy to remember. Basically, it was a directive to "get out and stay out." By the time I had everything ready, Murray joined me. She tapped the powdered herbs into a small jar and fixed the lid on.

I took a deep breath as she gave me the same look she used to in college when we were about to pull some incredibly stupid stunt. "Ready?"

"No, but that's never stopped us before." I tucked the book and water into a bag for easy carrying. She added the incense and draped the bag over her shoulder. The stairs looked overly steep, though I knew it was just my reluctance to attack the spirit. "Lead the way."

"Ready to rumble?" she asked, putting her foot on the first step.

My stomach burbled. "Sounds like it. Let's go." As we neared my bedroom door, I wondered just how we were going to convince Mr. B & U to show up. "It isn't quite like calling a dog . . . *Here, boy, come here, boy,*" I said.

Murray stopped a couple of yards away from my room and nodded toward the door. "I don't think you need to worry. I think he's waiting for us."

I followed her nod. A faint blue light glowed from beneath the door. "What the hell?" Torn, wanting nothing more than to turn around, go back downstairs, and get out of this house, I leaned against the wall and made sure that I'd affixed the seax dagger onto my belt. The weight hung, comforting, against the gauze of my skirt. "Let's get this show on the road. I'm tired of being afraid."

"Wait." She fumbled in the bag and pulled out the Florida water, yanking the stopper with her teeth. She handed me the bottle and picked up the bag with Nanna's book and the incense in it. When we were ready, she opened the door.

The entire room oozed with tendrils of neon-blue light.

Thick, with an oily feel that slid over the skin, the light seeped into the corners and pillowed like thick, viscous lava. Startled, I pulled back. Murray slipped past me and placed a censer on the end table near the door. She dropped the ouroboros into the brazier and then struck a match to a charcoal round, which she placed atop of the pendant. After the charcoal had lit, she sprinkled a good pinch of the incense on top.

Light emanated from behind the vanity, where it flowed out from an oval-shaped opening right where my mirror had been. Here it was at its brightest, and my eyes hurt when I looked directly at the vortex. Like a blowtorch, I thought, but I really didn't look forward to meeting the welder. A thin mist filled the room, hovering over the light. We moved forward, one step at a time, until we were standing in the middle of the room.

A line of goose bumps rose on my arms, and I shivered. The acid reflux level in my stomach warned me that I was well on my way to an ulcer. Oh, God, if I could be anywhere but right there, but I didn't have a choice. Nobody else could clear out this room, nobody else could undo the damage that Kip's spell had caused. Murray and I were on our own. I tried to push down the swelling panic—spirits, like dogs, responded to the scent of fear, and my pheromones were dripping with it. I cautiously loosened the dagger for easy access while keeping one eye on the vortex. The door slammed shut behind us, and we both jumped.

"Shit!" Murray looked over her shoulder, but I was too scared of what lay in front of us to turn around.

I hissed at her to catch her attention. "What do you see?"

She gulped. "Nothing. Nothing at all. The door just slammed by itself. I gotta tell you, Em, my respect for you just shot up 100 percent. If what you went through last night was half as scary as this, then just the fact that you actually stepped back into this house makes you a hero in my eyes." She opened the book, flipping the pages until she found the cards with the ritual I had prepared.

"By the way, what do I do with the water?" Now that

we were actually here, everything I had memorized seemed to vanish into the ozone.

"Throw it on him when he comes through the portal."

Sure thing. Nothing to it. Just throw it on the astral nasty. Florida water was used in Voudoun ceremonies, that much I knew, and Nanna had used a lot of it, but still, giving a demon a bath wasn't my idea of a good time.

We slowed, approaching the central core of light. Murray was whispering, practicing the incantation over and over under her breath. I gripped my bottle of Florida water tightly, hoping against all common sense that it would do some good when the time came. We stood less than a yard away from my vanity, staring into that brilliant mouth of light. I didn't know whether to whisper. Whatever it was obviously knew we were there. I glanced uncertainly at Murray. She took a deep breath.

"Isn't he supposed to be here before we do this?"

She gave me a long look, as if I were dense. "Uh, I think he already is. Who do you think created that portal?"

Exasperated, too tired to think clearly, I was about to make a snarky comeback when a ripping sound tore through the room, emanating from the center of the neon maw. "Great Mother, something's coming through!"

"This is it, we have to see what's beyond that light. Throw the water on it."

"Now? You said throw it on whatever moves!" I grasped the bottle, not sure what to do.

"Just throw the fucking water!"

I hesitated a moment, thinking: Demon . . . Murray. . . . Demon . . . Murray. . . . In the end, my fear of making Murray mad won out over my fear of the demon, and I splashed the water into the light, trying for as wide a dispersal area as possible. I might as well have dropped my blow dryer into the bathtub, considering the fireworks display that let loose when I set off my water bomb. Sparks shot out in a hailstorm of crackling tracers.

"Yikes, get down!" Smoke swirled around us, the scent of ozone thick. The smell nauseated me, and in an attempt to avoid losing my dinner, I twisted a hard left, promptly tripped over something hidden by the mist and went sprawling on my butt. As my tailbone landed on the floor with a painful thud, all I could think was that at least it was better than if I'd fallen on my knee again. I was immediately swallowed up by the billows of fog that now seemed to writhe and coil from the floor like a nest of serpents. The shock of the fall put an end to my queasiness.

"Are you okay?" Murray lent me her arm, and I struggled to my feet.

"Yeah." My butt ached, but I would survive.

Her gaze was fastened on the light, which flared so brightly that we had to shield our eyes. I turned my attention to the portal. As soon as I reached out to examine the energy, a cold sweat broke out over my body. "Murray . . . can you feel it? Something's moving in there." All of my courage went AWOL, and I started to panic. "Murray, I do *not* want to be here when Mr. Big & Ugly comes rampaging out of that electrical door he's created for himself. I'll just sell the goddamn house. Now let's get out of here!"

Murray's hold on the book loosened, and it slid out of her hands. "I think you might be right. He's coming . . . he's coming right through that portal . . . and we're right—" A brilliant blue light shot out from the vortex and caught her midsentence. She screamed as the ray raced through her body, sending her into a convulsion. Then—in what felt like a slow-mo instant replay—she stiffened and fell to the ground. She landed face first, inches from the corner of the footboard to my bed. Any closer and she would have cracked her skull.

"Murray!" Oh, my God, was she dead? Was she breathing? I dropped to the floor and crawled to her side. As I grabbed her wrist, I prayed for a pulse. Let her live, please let her live. There—faint and thready, she had a pulse. She was alive.

I had to get her out of there. I forced my way to my feet and started to lean over to drag her out of the room, but a sucking noise, like a caterpillar squirming out of a cocoon, stopped me. The sand had run out—the hourglass was empty. Something was coming through the vortex. No time to cry, no time to scream, no time to do anything except leave Murray where she was as I grabbed the loose pages that had scattered out of Nanna's journal. The light shifted as a dark shadow forced its way through. Hell and high water, Mr. B & U was in the building.

If he had ever been human, it was no longer apparent. The creature stood well over seven feet high and was a silhouette of black hair, matted by some unholy amniotic fluid. He was illuminated by only his brilliant eyes and by a nimbus of the neon energy that glowed like cobalt. He started toward Murray, then stopped and turned in my direction. Soft laughter echoed through the room, rising like thunder drums. I knew that laughter; I'd heard it before.

I cautiously took a step back and found myself flat against the wall. I could see Murray to my right. She moaned a little and turned, curling into a fetal position. Another person hurt because of me. Furious, so angry I felt like the brilliant white center of a candle flame, I whirled on the creature. "What the fuck are you doing in my house? Get out! Get out now!"

He laughed again, his aura flashing, and his words emanated from deep within the inky silhouette that mirrored his movements. "I was invited." The voice was sensuous. Dangerous. Mad.

"It was a mistake! Kip didn't know what he was doing."

The blue nimbus flared as he threw his head back, inhaling deeply with a satisfied sigh, almost as if he grew stronger with my outburst. And then I realized that he had. He was feeding off my anger and fear. And he'd been feeding off all the worry and pain he'd caused since Kip first opened the door and accidentally let him in. I straightened my shoulders. I had to calm down.

I took a deep breath as he cocked his head, looking at me quizzically. Unable to stop shaking, I tried to force my mind to the task before me. If I didn't banish him, both Murray and I would die—he'd feed on our essence, draining us dry, then go on to follow my children and terrorize them.

I tore my gaze away from the demon and, in a quivering voice, recited the incantation. "You demon of the dusk, begone from this house, back to the dark core of the universe from whence you came! Begone! Begone! Begone! By all the gods, by all the saints, I order you to vacate this house and never return!"

The creature snarled and lunged forward. I screamed and pulled out the dagger, holding it in front of me to keep him at bay. Again, he stopped, his eyes glowing with a preternatural anger. One step away from total panic, I bit my tongue hard, trying to bring myself out of my fear, forcing myself to remember that if I lost control, everything would be lost.

I needed help. If only I had help. Just a little nudge, a pat on the shoulder to remind me that I wasn't so totally alone. "Oh, God, Nanna, where are you? I wish you were here. Why aren't you here?" Unbidden, the plea tumbled out of my lips, words tripping over my tongue.

We squared off—the creature and I—poised, waiting. I had no doubts that he would kill me if he could. It was him or me; there were no other options. The universe consisted of this moment, this one point in time. Only the shadow-eater and I existed. My emotions began to drain away, all fear and pain and joy. This creature had no concept of what it was to be human, his only sensations those of satiety or emptiness. He took his pleasure in sucking the life from other beings. He was the essence of the void, the essence of emptiness—a chasm that would never fill.

There could be no reasoning here. He lunged again but stopped short, confused, when I held my ground against his thrust. Again, he tilted his head and craned forward to look at me; then he let out a low growl, and the rumble began to fill the room. I shook my hair away from my face, letting a blessed wave of numbness glide through me like a cool summer morning. Once again I repeated the incantation, calmly, my lips carefully forming each word, each syllable. "You demon of the dusk, begone from this house, back to the dark core of the universe whence you came! Begone! Begone! Begone! By all the gods, by all the saints, I order you to vacate this house and never return!"

As I spoke, I became aware of another presence forming in the room. Brilliant and golden, warm, and bringing the scent of lilacs and springtime with her. *Nanna.*

She stood by my side, her hand on my shoulder, and I felt her strength surge into my body. Joy raced through my veins, energy and sustenance, life and strength. Together we repeated the incantation, our voices rebounding in unison to shake the walls. "You demon of the dusk, begone from this house, back to the dark core of universe whence you came! Begone! Begone! Begone! By all the gods, by all the saints, I order you to vacate this house and never return!"

As the last word fell from my lips, I lunged to meet the creature as he sprang forward. His talons flashed as he slashed at me, but I twisted, turning hard to thrust the dagger directly into his heart. *Spark!* A jolt of current raced up my arm. I dropped the blade, doubling over from the shock. Mr. B & U let out a terrible shriek as the light began to fold in waves around him. The walls began to vibrate as the force reversed polarities, turning into a vacuum, and sucked the demon back through the vortex, the mist and fog rushing behind him. With a crackle so loud it left the hairs on my arm standing up, the neon glow shrank to a single point, then vanished with a soft "pop."

Silence blanketed the room. He was gone. Mr. B & U was actually gone.

Every part of my body hurt. As the room cleared, Murray begin to stir. Nanna patted me on the arm. I stared into her eyes, wishing she could hold me like she did when I was a little girl. My heart ached for a chance to say hello, to tell her I loved her. She mouthed the words "I know" and then faded with a flicker of pale light.

I dropped to the floor, exhausted, and reached out to help Murray crawl into a sitting position. "You okay?" I asked.

"I have no idea," she croaked. "I'm alive, that will have

to do. Look . . ." She pointed toward my vanity.

Dreading what I might see, I took a deep breath and looked. Susan Mitchell hovered near the bench, a horrified look on her face. She glided forward and stopped beside me. Slowly, with infinite care, she reached out one ghostly hand and rested it on my shoulder. Her energy rolled in gentle waves, tickling as she reached out to stroke my hair. I closed my eyes and relaxed. The demon was gone. Susan patted my shoulder again—I could feel the light pressure from her aura—and then she pulled back and moved to my vanity, where she sat on the stool.

I leaned back against the bed. The quilt was covered with a moist layer of goop. Whatever the substance was, it was slimy and dripped off my fingers in long streamers. I scraped up a handful and held it out to Murray.

She examined the slime. "Ectoplasm."

I coughed. "I thought that was a *Ghostbusters* thing."

"Nah, ectoplasm has showed up around a number of paranormal occurrences."

Wonderful. Cosmic joy-juice, spread all over my quilt. I scooted over, away from the bed, and she joined me, slumping down like a sack of potatoes. Susan, the ghostly member of our little trio, was still sitting at the vanity, patiently staring into space. I wondered what she was thinking about.

I gestured to get her attention. How did one blow off a ghost? "Uh . . . can you come back later? We're fried." She stood up and dusted off her dress. As we watched, she began to fade, and at the last moment, she gave a little wave.

Murray forced herself to her feet and retrieved the incense. The only thing left of the ouroboros was a twisted hunk of silver; whatever energy Mr. B & U had been working with had melted it to slag. While Murray smudged the room heavily, letting the clouds of incense smoke fill every corner to purify the energy surrounding us, I picked up my dagger and recited the incantations that would close the portal Kip had inadvertently opened. Half an hour later, the bedroom was clear. Wherever Mr.

Big & Ugly had come from, he had gone back via the same route.

We extinguished the charcoal in the brazier and trudged downstairs, where we dropped on the sofa, ectoplasm, smudge soot, and all.

Murray shook her head. "We're insane."

"Of course we are," I retorted.

"What do we do now?"

I considered our options. Finally, too tired to think, I held up the phone, as I had so many times during our years as college roomies together. "Pizza?"

She started to laugh. "Make it extra cheese."

Twenty-one

❖

TUESDAY MORNING, MURRAY took off for Seattle as I headed for the shop. With Mr. B & U out of the way, I was left with my original question: Had Susan been murdered? Walter was in jail for killing Diana, but had he orchestrated his wife's death, too?

When Cinnamon saw me come through the door, she raced over. "I'm glad you're here. There's so much that Lana and I couldn't take care of." She had organized piles of paperwork on my desk, and once I was settled, she brought me a cup of cranberry tea. I opened my mail, separating the invoices and bills from everything else, and then decided that I owed myself at least a brief glance at the paper.

I shook it open to find the front headline screaming out in huge block letters, "Walter Mitchell—Murderer or Scapegoat?" As I scanned the article, my heart started beating faster. Now that he had been accused of his daughter's murder, police were checking into his background and reexamining the circumstances surrounding the death of Susan Mitchell. The police were basing their inquiries on information provided by a number of sources, including two local women: Harlow Rainmark and Emerald O'Brien.

Oh, hell. We'd been fingered, probably by some stray comment made when we gave our statements. Neither of us had accused Walter of anything, but the press managed to make it sound like we'd nailed him to a cross. Now what was going to happen? Walter was being held pending bail, but when he was out, would he hunt us down? He'd had plenty of time to stew over his incarceration.

At that moment Cinnamon opened the shop, and a gaggle of customers poured through the doors. I would have to deal with this situation later. I pushed away the paperwork and went out front to help.

As I was rearranging a display, someone tapped me on the shoulder, and I turned to find myself facing the captain from the medical rescue unit. Surprised, I almost dropped the Spode creamer I was holding. After I managed to set it back on the shelf, I reached out to shake his hand.

Dressed in a turtleneck sweater and a pair of Dockers, he looked far too young to be the man who'd held my arm as I panicked about Harlow. "Remember me?" His fingers closed gently around my own. "Joe? Joe Files?"

"Of course I remember you. Thank you, again, for saving my friend."

His eyes danced over me. "Just doing my job, but I'm glad I was there and able to help. How's she doing?"

"Fine, she's doing fine." I couldn't figure out what he was doing in my shop.

He seemed to sense my puzzlement. "I'm looking for a present for my Aunt Margaret," he said.

His aunt? Of course! Margaret Files. She was a sweet old lady, a retired county clerk who came to me for tarot readings. I led him over to the wall display of jellies and cookies. "She loves biscuits and jam," I said, handing him a couple of packets.

He took them awkwardly. "Thank you. Maybe you could pick out a teapot for her, too?" As I looked around, trying to remember what patterns of china Margaret liked, he added, "Actually, I also wanted to ask if I could take you out sometime? For coffee, or something?"

As his words sank in, I began to blush. Well, bless my soul. Captain Files of the Chiqetaw Medic-Rescue Unit, who had saved Harlow, who had watched me upchuck on the side of the road, and who was probably ten years younger than me, wanted to take me out on a date. His smile was so hopeful that I found myself saying I'd think about it. "But not till after Christmas. I'm just so busy right now, Captain . . ."

"Joseph, please—just call me Joe." He blushed again, and I realized that he was as nervous as I was. His sandy hair was shot through with copper highlights, and he was tall and stocky, so obviously Scandinavian. And really cute.

I ducked my head. In the midst of all the spirits and worries over the kids, here I was feeling like a teenager again. Then guilt kicked in and I sobered. What about Andrew? But I looked into Joe's twinkling green eyes and shoved caution to the wind. "Okay, Joe. My number is in the book. Call me after New Year's and we'll meet for lunch." Satisfied, he left with more than a hundred dollars' worth of trinkets for the various women in his family.

I pushed my way through the bustle of shoppers into the back room and dropped into my chair. What was I was getting myself into? Should I tell Andrew about Joe? Was it any of his business? We hadn't talked about dating exclusively. I tried to push the whole mess out of my mind for now; we were swamped, and I needed to focus on business. As I dove back into the invoices, Cinnamon's voice rose a decibel or two. She didn't sound happy. I sighed, swigged down the last of a warm bottle of Coke, and made my way back into the fray.

She was arguing with an older woman. As I glanced over the woman's short, sturdy body, I noticed that she was swathed in what was probably top-notch designer wear. I stepped in. "What seems to be the problem?"

"How dare you slander my son? Just who do you think you are? Walter didn't hurt anybody." Her voice was shrill enough to be heard by several browsers, and I hurried to move her to one side, hoping to take us out of earshot of the rest of the shop, but there wasn't anyplace in which to have a bit of privacy.

The realization that Walter's mother had come gunning for me shook me up. Nothing worse than a bear protecting her cubs. "Mrs. Mitchell, I assure you—"

"My name is not Mrs. Mitchell. I'm Mrs. Addison. I married Bernard Addison shortly after Mr. Mitchell— Walter's father—died, and I'd thank you to at least get one thing right about our family." She sniffed and shook her blued curls at me in a dare to defy her. How was I going to get out of this one gracefully?

"Mrs. Addison, I assure you, I did not tell the police I thought Walter murdered Diana or Susan." Nope, I thought. Joshua had taken care of that. "I only told the cops that Susan had recently died and we wanted to make sure Diana knew about it." I offered her a tentative smile. She did not smile back.

"You're lying. The police questioned me—me—Walter's mother!—this morning about that awful woman and *her* daughter. I just want you to know that once we clear my Walter of these charges, you are going to find a lawsuit for slander slapped on your door. Yes, that's what you are going to find!" With that, she *harrumphed* and stomped out.

How many of my customers had heard the exchange? But most of them were studiously ignoring me, going about their business, examining teapots and china cups and bone china saucers and boxes of imported Ceylon tea. I was about to call Harl and warn that the old biddy was after us, when a new batch of customers swarmed in— the lunch crowd was here, and they were hungry. I took Cinnamon's place behind the counter so she could serve the soup and bread. The rush didn't slow down until Kip burst into the shop and I caught him in a tight embrace.

"Mom! Can we come home?" He dumped his books in the corner and shrugged out of his coat. I settled down in one of the sturdier chairs, and he leaned against me.

The door banged open again as Miranda rushed in, tears streaming down her cheeks. "I hope you're happy! I don't get to go to Space Camp now!"

Oh, God, in all the craziness, I had forgotten! Today was Miranda's scholarship test, and I hadn't even called to wish her good luck. "What happened? Did something happen during the test?" I started to give her a hug, but she shook me off.

"They wouldn't even let me *take* the test because *you* forgot to drop off the permission slip. They wouldn't let me in, and they said it was too late to call you."

Great. In one single blow, I'd just managed to destroy the progress Randa and I had made this past year. My heart cracked as I looked at her face. How could I let her down? "Oh, Miranda, I'm so sorry. There's just been no time to stop and think—"

"No kidding—you've been so busy with your ghosts and your shop and everything that matters to you that you forgot all about me! Maybe you don't care if I ever get to be an astronaut, but I do, and now I'll never get to go because we don't have enough money. You didn't even remember to call and wish me good luck!" She burst into tears and rushed into the bathroom.

Feeling like the world was spinning three steps ahead of me, I knocked on the bathroom door. "Randa, Randa, honey . . . please come out here and talk to me."

After a few minutes, she edged open the door, glaring at me as she blew her nose on a tissue. "Why do you care? Everybody else matters more than me."

I took her by the arm and eased her out of the bathroom. "Come here. You know that you and your brother mean more to me than anything else in the world. If you didn't, we wouldn't have moved here, and I wouldn't work my butt off to make sure you have a good home." I stroked her face, gently holding her chin so she had to look at me. "I love you, Miranda, and I made a horrible mistake."

Her eyes were filled with an aching disappointment, and I desperately wanted to wipe that hurt away. With a little cough, she threw her arms around my waist, sobbing into my sweater. I held her with one arm as I motioned to Cinnamon with the other. "We're closing early. Could you run the deposit across the street for me and drop it in the night box before you head home?"

Cinnamon nodded, her face grave. I handed her the envelope and watched as she made her way across the icy street and dropped it into the night deposit box. Then she turned, waved, and headed for her car.

"Come on, kids." I bundled them into their coats. "We can go home together now—Murray and I cleared out the nasty ghost. We'll talk about this after we get there."

BY THE TIME we got home, Miranda had calmed down enough to where she was just sniffling. I tried to think of something to make things better, but she shook off my overtures. Finally I repeated my apology and told the kids to wash up for dinner.

She stomped off to the bathroom. I ordered a couple of pizzas, then made a call to Andrew and asked him to come over and to bring the cats with him. At about the time that Andrew showed up, Murray returned from Seattle and pulled in the drive. The sight of the cats brought a little smile to Randa's wan complexion, and the kids ran off to play with them and to fix up the litter boxes. Andrew started to pull me in for a kiss, but I stopped him with a quick peck. There was just too much going on, and I needed some breathing space.

I gestured to the living room. "Help me take the food and drinks in there, okay?" We all gathered around the coffee table and, munching pizza, Murray and I gave a highly edited version of our fight with Mr. B & U, leaving out the superscary parts so the kids wouldn't have nightmares. I'd fill in Andrew about the rest later on.

"So he's really gone?" Miranda's eyes were still swollen from crying, but she gave me a tentative smile.

"Yes, and I don't think he'll be coming back. We booted him out of here. Susan may still be around, but she won't hurt you, honey."

Randa considered this for a moment. "White Deer explained to me how some spirits are okay and some are here to help us, and some are evil." I'd spent thirteen years trying to teach her the same thing. Par for the course, though. Kids would listen to a fence post before they listened to their parents.

Kip wiped pizza sauce off his face. "I wish I coulda been here."

"No, you don't. This was no game, Kip. Whatever you did with that witch's bottle was stupid. Harlow got hurt because of it, and Murray and I were in serious danger. We're going to have a long talk, and if you can't straighten up and fly right, then you won't be allowed to help me with charming anything again until you're eighteen."

That sobered him up real fast. After the kids had finished eating, they went upstairs to unpack. Murray and I had thoroughly cleansed and warded the house when we woke up and, though I had some residual apprehension, I knew they would be okay. Andrew finished off the last piece of pizza. Murray cleared away the plates and boxes.

"So, what happened at Diana's funeral?" I tried to shake off my worry about Randa. I had screwed up big time and would have to figure out a way to make it up to her. If only I had the extra cash sitting around, but the tuition for Space Camp was pricey and didn't include the airfare. Maybe I could ask Roy . . . but in my heart I knew he wouldn't help. He'd think it was frivolous, and in a way he was right—Randa didn't *need* to go. But she wanted it so much that I couldn't stand to see her disappointed.

"It was an odd affair. Walter wasn't there, of course, and neither was his mother." Murray pulled out a notebook and flipped through the pages. She took notes on everything.

"That's because she was standing in my shop, bitching at me about Walter. Were there *any* family members there?"

"Yeah. Joshua. I find it odd that her stepuncle, who hated his family, would be so interested in her. Doesn't set right. Anyway, he was there." Murray shrugged. "He left right after the funeral, so I didn't get a chance to speak to him. There wasn't a formal reception. Actually, it was all very sad. The minister obviously didn't know Diana; he gave the most pitiful eulogy I've ever heard. The only guests attending were a couple of people from her job; I tried to talk to them afterward, but nobody seemed to know much about her private life. From what I can make out, Diana was moody and unpredictable, a real loner."

Unstable. Several people had mentioned that now. "She obviously had emotional problems. Maybe the fact that her parents shunted her from one boarding school to another made her feel unloved. She sure didn't get along with them, at least until near the end, when she supposedly reconciled with Susan."

Or maybe, I speculated, Walter *had* molested her, and the abuse had skewed her ability to cope with the world. Her demeanor would certainly fit a young woman who'd been assaulted by her father. "I think we need to talk to Joshua. He was the last person we know of who spoke to Diana recently. He seemed to care about her. Maybe he can shed some light on what was going on."

Murray sniffed. "If you can ferret out where he's staying, go for it. I'm sure the department has already questioned him, but you never know what people are going to hold back. That's one thing I've learned being a cop: People underestimate the importance of small things—trivial incidents that can make or break a case."

Andrew headed out, he still had a snarl of paperwork to deal with, and Murray left after three assurances that we would be okay. When it came time for bed, I was nervous and so were the kids, but our bedrooms felt clear—Murray and I had done a good job on cleaning out the energy—and for the first time in days, everybody made it through the night without any problems or nightmares.

WEDNESDAY MORNING, I headed to the shop, where I called Lana and asked her to come in for a few hours during the afternoon; then I put in a call to Harlow. She was mending along nicely, but it would be a long time before she was back to normal. Eunice Addison had paid her a visit, too. Harl had skewered her like a suckling pig and browbeat her out the door, all the while keeping a smile on her face. I envied her ability to destroy people with sugar rather than vinegar.

I told her about the funeral and my speculations. "The one thing that doesn't fit is why Joshua took such an interest in Diana."

"Well, if Walter actually molested her, there's your answer. Joshua probably encouraged her to go to the cops because he saw it as a way to bring Walt to his knees. Don't underestimate the hatred between those two—Walter and Joshua were rivals from the beginning."

"How do you find out so much about everyone?"

She snorted. "That's what comes from cavorting with the social elite—I'm privy to all sorts of good gossip."

"Then tell me this—I want to talk to Joshua. Maybe I can get the scoop on what's going on. Where do you think he'd be staying up here? I can't just call all the motels and beds-and-breakfasts in town."

She thought for a moment. "Bernard died more than a year ago, and Walter's mother moved to a condominium. I know because her next-door neighbor is on the board of the Chiqetaw Players. That big old house that she and Bernard lived in has been standing empty for a year. It hasn't even been put up for sale. Why she's keeping it, I don't know. Maybe Joshua's staying there."

I could hear her shuffling papers. "Here—the address is 351 Plum Street—it's still listed under Bernard's name in the phone book." She took a deep breath and let it out slowly. "If I had anything better to do than snoop, I would. But sitting here all day watching reruns of *Three's Company* isn't my idea of fun."

I tapped my pencil on my desk. "Well, you do have a way of ferreting out information."

Harlow sighed. "Actually, yeah." She paused for a moment, as if she were trying to find the right words to tell me something. "Em, I'm closing the gym."

"What? That gym has been your dream for years! Isn't there anything you can do? Hire a manager, maybe?"

"No," she said quietly. "Truth is, we've been going

under for a while. Not enough jocks in this burg to pay its way and give me a salary, too. James told me that if I want to close up, I'd better do so before I lose everything I put into it. And with the baby, I want a job where I can work from home."

I doodled circles on the notepad, wanting to help but knowing there was nothing I could do. "Chiqetaw can exist without a gym. We have the YMCA. So, any ideas what kind of job you might be looking for?"

"I applied for one a couple of weeks ago. I think I might get it."

"Doing what?" It was hard to imagine Harlow doing something that wasn't out in the public eye. "When would you start?"

"Next month, as a research assistant. I'd be working from home, typing up notes and research on some Central American tribe a professor from WWU has been studying. The project should last six months. By the time it starts, my wrist should be out of the sling, and I'll be able to type again. I would have said something earlier, but it's just now coming together."

"Good luck, hon. I hope you get it!" I heard Cinnamon rattling around, and I glanced at the clock. "Okay, I gotta book. See you later, and give James a hug for me." As I hung up, I knew there were two things I had to do: I needed to pay a visit to the county jail to talk to Walter, if he would see me; and I needed to drive by the old Addison place. If Joshua was still in town, chances were he'd be there.

Twenty-two

✥

AFTER THE LUNCH rush, I told Cinnamon that I'd be back in an hour or so, and she waved me out. I'd never been to the Chiqetaw town jail before. Nestled beneath the city courthouse, the building was old and rose at least four stories above ground level, in red brick with a firehouse look. The jail was tucked away in the basement. There were rumors that the ghosts of men who had been sentenced to death, or who had died while in custody, haunted the courthouse. It was also common legend that Fiona Lynch, an Irishwoman who became the town's first woman law clerk, still roamed the halls, long after a massive heart attack sent her to her grave. I hoped that I wouldn't end up meeting them, considering my propensity for attracting denizens of the netherworld.

I found the elevator and punched the button for the jail. When I approached the counter, the officer behind the desk shuffled a batch of papers and then turned his attention to me.

"Officer Dowling here. What can I do for you, ma'am?"

"I'd like to talk to Walter Mitchell."

He consulted his chart and gave me a dubious look. "You his lawyer?"

"No, and I'm not family, either. I just . . . tell him Emerald O'Brien is here to see him." Most likely he'd turn me away, but I'd give it a shot. I wasn't sure what I was after, maybe just a crazy hope that he'd break down and confess to me.

Dowling was back within five minutes. His look had turned from puzzlement to caution. "He's willing to see you. I need you to leave your purse and coat with me, and empty your pockets." I passed through the metal detector and submitted to a pat-down to make sure I wasn't carrying any concealed weapons. My purse was confiscated at the door, and the cop led me to an empty table in an emptier room. He nodded to another officer, who assumed a post next to the wall, where he could keep watch on us.

"I'll be back in ten minutes," Dowling said as he left.

The door on the other side of the room opened and there, in prison blues, stood Walter Mitchell. The glare on his face might once have been enough to melt me into slag, but after what I'd been through the past few days, it barely fazed me. He sauntered over and, with one move, turned the chair and straddled it.

"So, if it isn't the nosy tea-and-china lady." He rested his elbows on the back of the chair. "Circumstances have changed since we met at my late wife's memorial. Thank you for your little part in orchestrating this event. I value your help more than you can imagine."

I winced. He was supposed to be the bad guy here, but I couldn't help but feel a little guilty. "Walter, I didn't accuse you of anything; it was your stepbrother, and you know that. I'm sorry about your trouble, but I didn't tell the cops you hurt anybody. I came here because I wanted to talk to you about Joshua."

He kept his cool, but his eyes flickered, and I realized that he hadn't been expecting that name to crop up. Point one, my favor.

"You do get around. I suppose you read tea leaves as well as fortunes? So read for me. Tell me what good old

Josh has been up to lately. Throwing temper tantrums and beating up girlfriends again? Losing control and ending up in the loony bin again?" He cocked his head and tipped his chair so it rested against the edge of the table. "He made a big mistake by coming back to town. We made it clear years ago that he was persona non grata in our family."

Irritated by his machismo, but keeping track of everything he said, I shook my head. "Come on, Walter. You won, you know. You inherited his share of your stepfather's money."

His reaction surprised me. He dropped the tough-guy routine and leaned toward me, expression grim. "What did you say? You think I beat out my stepbrother in some sort of sick family contest? You're as crazy as Josh, then. Let me tell you something: Joshua Addison is certifiably dangerous. He's out to get me any way he can. Susan and I should have moved out of state years ago, but no, we thought everything was under control. Now it's too late. Too late for Susan, and probably too late for me." A faint glimmer of remorse flooded his eyes. "I didn't think he'd try anything, not after all this time."

"You're saying that you're being framed?"

Walter let out a sharp breath and rubbed the bridge between his eyebrows. When he looked up, his face was set in an impenetrable expression. "I have no idea how that knife got into my house, nor do I know how a cufflink matching the one found in Diana's apartment got into my bathroom. They found a letter, you know. In it, she accused me of molesting her, but it's not true. I didn't kill Diana, and I didn't do anything to Susan."

Mesmerized by the sincerity I heard below the bluster, I stared at him. "Walter, if I ask you something, will you tell me the truth?"

He snorted. "That all depends on what you ask."

"Did you beat Susan? Did you hit her? I know you cheated on her."

He snorted. "Beat her? Hit her? So that's what she was telling people. No wonder Diana was prone to lying. Like mother, like daughter." He probed me with his gaze, and

I felt a chill rush over me, as if I were naked. "Well, now, we all have our secrets, don't we? Frankly, sweetheart, I don't give a damn whether you or anybody else thinks I beat her up. None of that matters anymore, and maybe it never did. Some mistakes haunt you from the beginning; by the end, you just want out, you just want to get away from the past."

Cryptic, but what should I have expected? I started to get up, but he pointed to my chair. "Sit. Do yourself a favor and pay attention to me. If you never listen to me again, listen to me now. Be very careful around Joshua; he bites. I'm a cold bastard and proud of it, it's made me a successful businessman, but I'm not nearly as nasty as my dear stepbrother, so watch your step."

The evidence was damning, but something in his demeanor told me Walter was telling the truth. I digested what he said, reading between the lines. "Are you saying Joshua might have had something to do with Diana's death?"

He framed his words carefully. "I'm saying that Joshua has a history of violence. He's battled with insanity all his life and never should have been let loose. From day one, Josh was up to no good. Never turn your back on a wounded animal. They'll rip out your throat."

As I contemplated his unwavering stare, I realized that I believed Walter. He hadn't killed Diana. Feeling a perverse need to reassure him, I blurted out, "I don't think you murdered her. I believe you."

He held my gaze for a moment. I didn't look away. Then, slowly, he eased the chair back down on all four legs and pulled back. "If you'll excuse me now, I need to speak to my lawyer. We've got a lot of ground to cover before my arraignment tomorrow." He stood up, indicating the interview was over. As the waiting cop led him to the door, Walter paused and turned back to face me. "Watch your step, Emerald O'Brien. Insanity and strength are a dangerous combination. I would hate to see such a pretty lady as yourself get mixed up in a world built on the love of pain."

I gratefully accepted my purse and hurried out of the

building. On my way back to the shop, I thought over the strange interview. He *never should have been let loose.* Let loose from what? Jail? The military?

Walter had inherited the money that would have gone to Joshua. Joshua hated Walter. Just how far would either of them go to get revenge? With these and other questions whirling in my mind, I drove back to the store.

"DAMN, IT'S COLD out there. The sky is so clear that the stars almost blinded me." Andrew shook off the snow as I let him in. Murray had volunteered to take the kids out to get the Christmas tree. I wanted to go along, but I was so tired that all I could do was lean back in the recliner and rest. With the promise that tomorrow night we'd decorate the house, they were more than willing to let Murray lead the expedition. Randa still wasn't speaking to me, and I still hadn't figured out what to do about it.

I tried to find the words to ease into the subject, but it wasn't easy. Finally I opted for my usual: blunt honesty. "I talked to Walter today."

Andrew looked at me as if I'd just grown another head. "Excuse me? You went to the jail, alone?" He rubbed his forehead and let out an exasperated sigh. "I can't believe you. Do you like putting yourself in danger?"

I glared. "I wasn't in danger. There were cops everywhere. Don't exaggerate."

"And I suppose he told you he didn't do it?"

Just what I needed to help me think clearer, sarcasm on the half shell. I gave him a stony look. "Of course he did. The damn thing is, I believe him." I flipped on the television. *It's a Wonderful Life* was on, and I settled back in the chair and sipped at my tea, waiting for the blowup.

Andrew stood up and began to pace. "You went to the jail to visit a man accused of murdering his daughter, who *you* also think murdered his wife, and all of a sudden you believe him? What happened to 'Susan needs me'? Is it his money? His suave sophistication? Did he promise to fund your shop if you switch sides?"

"What? What are you talking about?" I'd expected a protest, but he was totally off base, so much so that I had no idea what he was talking about.

"He obviously got to you. You waiting for him to get out now?"

"You think that I'm interested in Walter? You really think that?" I stared at him, aghast. How could he believe that I'd get involved with someone like that?

"I can't believe that you're standing up for a scumball who beat his wife and molested his daughter." He turned to me, eyes blazing.

"You're jealous." I could see it in his look, his stance. "You think that I want Walter? Thanks a lot for your confidence in me—I truly don't think he did it. We had an interesting talk, but I think I'll keep that to myself, since you're being such an ass."

"Well, you certainly haven't been giving me much attention lately. What do you expect me to a think?"

"I expect you to think with the head on top of your neck. As to giving you attention, don't you remember that I told you that once the kids were home, we were going to have to adjust our relationship?"

"I know!" His eyes flashed, then he leaned back and said more softly, "I know. I'm just . . . how long do you think it will take? How can I prove that I'm worthy so you'll let me stand up and tell the world you're my lover, my girlfriend?"

I shook my head. How could I make him understand? I had to be sure, had to know that this was more than a dalliance, more than a simple liaison. Ten days or so of ghost-hunting together wasn't enough to prove anything. The excitement alone was enough to make some guys hang around to see what came next.

"Can't you understand? It's not a matter of you proving that you're worthy. I wouldn't be with you if I thought you were a jerk. All I'm asking is that we go slow for a while. I have to keep the kids from getting their hopes up too high. If you sleep in my bed, they're going to think that you've become a permanent addition to the family. What happens if you change your mind in a month?

They're the ones who get hurt, because right now they cling to any adult who shows them the affection their father withholds. I'm sorry if this stings your ego. If I could change it, I would."

"So where does that leave us? Holding hands like schoolkids?"

I didn't like the sneer in his voice. "If that's what it takes, yes. If casual dating isn't enough, then maybe I'm not the right woman for you. I'm not saying that we have to be celibate, but you can't sleep in my bed when the kids are here. Not yet."

I could tell he was angry, but there was no way he could argue—he knew I was right about this. "Damn it, I need to think. I'm going home."

"Should I tell the kids good-bye for you?"

"That's not fair!"

Tired of the argument, I lost my temper. "No, it isn't fair. And it wouldn't be fair for them to think you're going to be a part of the family and then have you walk away because you decide you aren't ready for the commitment this family requires. They come first, until they walk out that door to lead their own lives. Got it?"

As he slipped his coat on, the kids came trudging in. They were helping Murray carry a huge blue spruce. As soon as they set it in the corner, Kip ran over to Andrew. "You're leaving already? Aww . . . we just got back with the tree and were going to have hot cocoa!"

To his credit, Andrew gave Kip a smile. "Yeah, got to, kiddo, I've got work to do tonight."

Kip threw his arm around Andrew's waist. "Bye! Don't forget, you promised to challenge me to a Mario Brothers marathon." I wanted to call my son back, tell him to leave Andrew alone, but that would have triggered off too many questions. Instead, I waited to see what Andrew had to say.

"I won't forget. Tell you what: Maybe this weekend, before I have to leave for Christmas, we can get together and have that game?"

"Yeah!" Kip jumped up and down. He missed Sly, I

could tell that already, and was trying to fill the gap any way he could.

Tentatively, I gave Andrew a smile and mouthed the word "Thanks" to him. He stared back at me, then shrugged and ducked out into the snowstorm. If I'd been alone, I might have called him up, ranted about how he was being a butthead, but it wouldn't do any good. Andrew was as stubborn as I was.

I backtracked to the kitchen. Kip wandered in and pulled out the cat food. He was being good about remembering his chores. "Mom, what's Randa gonna do? She's really upset."

I gave him a long look. "I don't know just yet. I'll think of something."

He nodded, head down. "You can take my Christmas presents back and use the money to send Miranda to camp—I don't mind. It means a lot to her, and I messed up things bad by using Nanna's book." Through his mumbling, I could sense his fear that I might take him up on it, but still, he had made the offer.

I wanted to laugh and cry at the same time. I settled for ruffling his hair. "Don't you worry about it, hon. Listen, that was a very noble offer and I'll remember you made it. Don't fret. I'll figure something out."

After he fed the cats and returned to the living room, I settled down at the counter, thinking. Kip had made a gesture directly from his heart. He had been willing to give up something of his own to ensure the happiness of his sister. Even if I'd been heartless enough to take him up on it, his presents wouldn't have covered more than the cost of a couple of days' tuition. There had to be something I could do . . . and then, then I knew. I knew what I could do to raise the money for the tuition.

I dug out my phone book and thumbed through the "T's." Bette Thompson had asked me to sell her a piece from my private collection last year—the Waterford globe. I'd said no at the time, but now, maybe it was time to let go.

I punched in a number and waited. "Bette? This is Emerald O'Brien. Are you still interested in my Waterford globe that you asked me about last year? I've decided that I'm willing to sell. My asking price is a firm $1,500, half the retail cost. You are? Why don't I drop over tomorrow morning, then? It will be early, though. . . . No, everything is fine. . . . I just realized that holding on to old memories isn't always as important as creating new ones."

The Waterford globe was the one really gorgeous gift Roy had given me. I knew without a doubt it had come from his heart, out of love. I'd carried the treasure as a beacon through both rough times and good. He'd brought it home to me the day after I told him I was pregnant with Randa, and I'd kept it as a tribute to the existence of love. Now it would fund her dreams. It seemed so ironic, and so perfectly right.

EARLY NEXT MORNING, I woke up the kids and told them I had errands to run. "I want both of you to meet me at the store after school. Have cereal for breakfast and don't forget to feed the cats."

On my way out, I unlocked the étagère in the living room and retrieved the crystal globe. I turned it over in my hands, feeling the familiar weight that had journeyed with me through the maze of anger and worry and pain. Time to let go, time to say good-bye to the past. Resolutely, I slipped it into a box and packed it carefully so it wouldn't break on the ride across town. Twenty minutes later, Bette Thompson wrote me a check for $1,500.

I gave her a quick hug. "Thanks, Bette. This will go to good use."

"Is your shop having problems?" Her eyes darted quickly, and I knew if I didn't squash the rumor, by tomorrow it would be all over town that I was destitute.

"Nope, business is brisk. I just want to make Christmas extra special for my kids this year." She nodded, smiling. I could tell she was thinking I spoiled them. But what did I care? I had the money, she had the globe, and Miranda was going to Space Camp.

Still a good hour before I had to be at the shop. Time to talk to Joshua. Walter had warned me that Josh was dangerous, so I hunted around the back of the car and found the hatchet I kept in the back. It wouldn't fit in my purse, but it was small enough to slip through my belt. I set it in the front seat next to me. Probably an over-reaction, but hey, I'd rather look like an idiot than make a deadly mistake. The address Harl had given me for the old Addison house said it was on Plum Street. I knew where the street was, but little more about that area of town. The neighborhood was old and run down; few people lived there anymore. I slipped the key in the ignition. Time to rumble, as Murray would say.

Twenty-three

✤

AS I TURNED onto Plum, a flash of sunlight broke through the clouds and glistened on the mounds of snow that covered everything in sight. Finally, a break in the gloom. I rounded the bend and parked behind a row of hydrangea bushes.

I sat in the car for a moment, staring up at the old Addison house.

"Mausoleum" would have been a better word—or "monstrosity." The house was set up on a hill. Retro Norman Bates or *The Munsters;* 1313 Mockingbird Lane had found a final resting place in Chiqetaw. Three stories high, the Addison house was a tribute to a designer's nightmare. The weathered paint peeled off in gray flakes, and broken windows let both rain and sunlight in. No wonder Walter's mother had vamoosed as soon as the old man died. Sprawled across the acre lot, it nestled behind a double row of oak trees. They were sparse, black, and bare against the backdrop of winter.

After slipping the hatchet through my belt, I cautiously ascended the steep stone steps that led to the path. As I caught a glimpse of someone standing by the front door, I stopped, cold in my tracks. Joshua? Squinting, I tried to

make out who it was. Susan! Susan Mitchell was standing
near the front door. Another flash of light beamed down
from the unusually bright day, and in the glare, I saw her
waving frantically. Yep—I was on the right track, all
right. As I hurried to the bottom of the steps leading up
to the house itself, she disappeared.

The snow had been trampled in several areas. Someone
had been here recently, someone corporeal. I took hold of
the railing and, cautiously watching for rotten boards,
made my way up to the front porch. A squeak made me
jump, but it was just the screen door, twisted half off the
hinges and blowing in the wind. I gingerly opened it,
wincing at the muffled creaks.

The front door seemed to be intact. I steeled myself
and knocked . . . once, twice, a third time. Nobody answered. I tried the knob. Unlocked. Maybe Joshua wasn't
home. If he was staying here, then he must not be too
worried about burglars. Should I go in?

Trespassing wasn't high on my list of to-do-before-I-
die activities, but if I didn't stay long, didn't touch anything . . .

I kept telling myself that Nancy Drew would have
charged in without fear, but then again, Nancy had been
a teenager who probably thought she was invulnerable,
and more important—she wasn't real. I wasn't a teenager
anymore and I knew I could get hurt. I weighed my options and then grabbed the knob. I had come this far, I
might as well go a little farther. More importantly, Susan
had given me the go-ahead. Maybe the secrets hidden
within these walls would help her spirit find peace. With
no cars on the street, no neighbors peeking out their windows whom I could see, I poked my head through the
front door into the musty hallway.

The hallway was old, with faded pictures still hanging
on the walls. There were none of Walter or his mother,
but there were pictures of an older man, probably Bernard.
In one photograph he was standing with Joshua. I could
see the resemblance between the two, but there was a
queer glint behind Joshua's gaze that was missing from
Bernard's stern, ice-blue eyes.

A cabbage rose paper ran the length of the hall, under which paneling took hold—scratched and chipped in a number of places. A series of doors lined either side, broken by an archway leading into what I assumed would be the main living room. I took a deep breath and decided to start there. I quietly slid along the wall, then inched my head around the archway to peek in.

The room was grand, or had been at one time. Huge, lovely, filled with dusty antiques. Why had Walter's mother left all this to rot? Even at this distance, I could tell the furnishings were worth a great deal. So far the weather hadn't found its way into this room, but it was only a matter of time before the cracks in the windows let in the rain and snow. Other than a handful of icky-looking spiders, the only signs of life were a couple of take-out boxes from Teriyaki's Take-Home, and an empty pizza box. The dust on one sofa had been disturbed, but nothing else seemed out of place.

Back in the hall, I listened for a long time at the next door before I gathered the courage to push it open. The hinges protested with a tiny squeak but then swung open, and I found myself in the formal dining room. A thin layer of mold covered everything. A broken window had let the outdoors creep through; dormant ivy vines were trailing around the edges of the ceiling along with the rot and mildew.

The table could seat at least sixteen, if not more. The more I poked around, the more perplexed I became. When Walter's mother left, she hadn't taken anything. Not the silver, not the china, not even the knickknacks. Why would she leave such expensive items here? Why wouldn't she renovate the house and at least rent it out, if she didn't want to stay here herself? Thousands of dollars of antiques sat there, bounty for any thief who had the mind to come get them. So far, Walter's mother had been lucky, but her luck couldn't hold forever.

With a nervous glance behind me, I pushed through the swinging doors into the kitchen. As ancient and clunky as the rest of the house, the room was a mess, but at least it told me somebody had made himself at home.

Dirty plates filled the sink. The garbage bin was packed with take-out boxes and half-empty booze bottles. A pile of soot-covered rags sat on the counter next to the stove, a big old gas model.

A quick search led to a utility room and a back porch. I leaned over the railing but pulled back sharply as the rail began to teeter. As I brushed the snow away, I saw that the wood was rotten all the way through. That nixed any idea I had of taking a walk down into the backyard. The snow on the steps hadn't been disturbed, and I was reasonably sure that Joshua came and went through the front door, unless there was some side entrance I didn't know about.

I cautiously peeked back over the edge, holding myself away from the railing. Directly below the balcony, a rusted iron gate—one of those old-fashioned ones with spiked railings that looked like minarets—opened into a series of gardens. The snow covering the lawn was un-disturbed as well.

Back in the hall, I was left with one door I hadn't examined. The "room" was actually a small, windowless alcove with two sets of stairs—one leading up, one leading down. I dug my flashlight out of my bag. If I had to leave in a hurry, going down would be faster than going up. I looked up the uninviting passage. Was all this worth it? And then I remembered the image of Diana, cut down so young, and Susan—possibly murdered as well. Nope, I didn't have a choice. I had to find out whatever I could to help both of them. I began my ascent, turning at the landing with apprehension, but there was no one there.

Once safely in the second-story hallway, I chose a room at random. Bingo! Someone—my guess was Joshua—had nested here. The bed had been stripped of old covers and a sleeping bag was spread across it, along with a couple of new pillows. Two suitcases rested atop one dresser, both open, and a kerosene lamp sat on an-other. The curtains had been opened as far as they would go. I closed the door behind me and examined the open luggage. The tag on the handle had two initials: J. A. Joshua Addison. It had to be.

Should I look? I valued privacy. I'd never once thought of reading Miranda's diary, even though I knew exactly where she hid it. But considering the circumstances, considering that both Diana and Susan were now keeping time with the worms, I decided to make an exception. I took a deep breath and began a quick search of the first suitcase. Men's clothing, a razor kit, a couple of porn mags, and a carton of cigarettes. The second, though, was filled to the brim with files, papers, and notebooks.

I bit my lip, then decided to go for broke. With trembling hands, I opened the first folder. A marriage license. Was Joshua married? Nobody had ever said anything about that. I adjusted the flashlight so I could read.

Joshua Reed Addison and Susan Virginia Walker.

Susan! Good God, he'd been married to Susan! I calculated the dates in my head. They had gotten married in Seattle when Susan was barely seventeen. It must have been shortly after Joshua ran off. A sudden chill raced down my back. *"I was murdered by my husband but nobody knows. . . ."* Could Joshua be the husband Susan's spirit was talking about? I worked quickly; the feeling that I was in danger loomed heavily, and I knew that I'd better be done and out of there before he showed up. I shuffled through the rest of the bag.

A sheaf of papers from Western State Hospital caught my eye, and I flipped through them. Photocopies of psychiatric records, including a commitment order for Joshua signed by Susan and Bernard. A release order . . . dated a decade later. Violent behavior, psychosis . . . lovely. There was a note attached to one of the papers—a copy of an official decree granting Susan Addison a legal annulment, along with a notarized document certifying her name change back to Walker. They had been married less than a year.

And then I found it: an authorization signed by Joshua at the same time he'd been committed, releasing any parental rights he might have to the child Susan was carrying. Susan had been pregnant when she returned to marry Walter, but it hadn't been his child. Diana was Joshua's daughter.

Flabbergasted, I sat down on the bed. The hatchet poked into my side, so I slid it out of my belt and set it on the nightstand next to me. All this time, everyone assumed Diana was Walter's daughter, but all along, she'd belonged to his stepbrother. Joshua knew, Susan knew, Bernard had to know, Walter knew. And nobody said a word. And if Joshua was so off-kilter, maybe that's why Diana was so unstable. Maybe it was in her genes.

I dropped the order and quickly rifled through the rest of the suitcase. Bank statements, all in Diana's name, and letters. Under the pictures I found a crumpled Father's Day card from Diana to Joshua, and then another sheaf of letters.

So she'd found out; somehow she found out that Joshua was her father. Had he looked her up, told her he was her real father and not Walter? Had that been what caused the fights between Diana and her parents?

A note scribbled on floral stationery stood out among the rumpled papers—something seemed familiar in the handwriting, and then, I knew. Those looping letters were all too recognizable.

> *I can't believe that you actually dared to contact me. Walter will kill you if he knows you're back in town. So you've been snooping around, have you? I got your package and burned it, but I suppose you have more where that came from. Get your ass up here next Thursday. I'll make sure the house is clear. We'll talk, but I warn you—I'm not a good person to make an enemy of. You'd better have the goods if you expect me to pay the price you're asking. Susan*

The letter was dated a few days before the date of Susan's death. Clipped to the letter was a picture of Susan. She was kissing some man, but it wasn't Walter. They were going at it pretty hot and heavy, by the looks of it. I flipped the photo over. Someone had jotted down two names on the back: Susan M. and Ned Cantrell. I studied the picture. Where had I seen this man before? Cantrell

. . . Cantrell . . . Now I remembered! He'd played the lead in *Obsidian*.

Was he the man she'd hinted at in her argument with Andrew? News like this could disrupt her position as the "Dragon Lady of Romance," that was for sure. Her happily married readers might not look too fondly on their inspiration if they knew what was going on in her private life, with the abuse, affairs, and counteraffairs. Drop in a child fathered by a madman and it worked out to the makings for a *Victim of the Week* movie.

Next to where the letter had been thrust rested a bottle of Valium. I picked it up. The pills were prescribed for Joshua Addison. Confused, but positive I was on to something, I scrambled in my pocket for my cell phone and punched up Harlow's number. Joshua had been married to Susan. And just what had happened during their meeting? Had Joshua blackmailed Susan, then killed her when something went wrong? Had murder been the plan all along and blackmail a ruse? Did Diana find out what had gone on? Was that why she'd been killed?

Harlow answered on the third ring. "Harl, listen to me. I think I've found proof that Joshua killed Susan. He was married to her, Harl . . . married to her! She was supposed to meet with him on the day she died."

She was all ears. "Oh, my God! Where are you right now? What should I do?"

"We've got to call the police, get them over here. I'm in Joshua's bedroom on the second floor of the old Addison place. Man, it's creepy. I need to get out of here before he comes back and finds me. Walter's right: The dude is dangerous, very dangerous. Susan and Bernard committed him to a mental hospital for violent behavior—" I paused as a creak sounded in the hallway. "Hold on."

I held my breath as I tiptoed over to crack the door and peered out. Nothing—nobody there. I let out a deep sigh and leaned against the wall. God, I longed for the security and safety of my little shop, of my home. I wasn't cut out for sneaking around. I stuffed the letter from Susan in the pocket of my skirt along with the picture and returned to peek out the window, trying to see if there was a car anywhere on the grounds.

"Harl, I better—"

Another creak made me start, and as I headed for the door, it flew open. Joshua Addison stood there, his eyes glimmering with an icy light. He was wearing a black duster and a hat that made me think of Crocodile Dundee. But no good-natured smile creased his face, and that big old knife he was carrying wasn't nearly as sexy as the one Paul Hogan had waved around.

"Put the phone down. Turn it off and drop it." He held up the knife. Every finger sported a thick silver ring. I turned off the phone and tossed it on the bed as he demanded, "Who are you? What do you want?"

Maybe I still had a chance. Maybe I could get out of here with my skin intact. I cleared my throat. "I've always liked this house. I wanted to see what the inside was like."

"Just like that, huh? You broke in to see what it looked like? No thoughts about the police catching you? No thoughts that maybe somebody lived here?" He took another step closer, and a wave of Calvin Klein's Obsession overwhelmed me.

I nodded. "Yeah . . . stupid, I know. But I thought that the house was abandoned. It's not like I was going to take anything." He had to know I was lying. I couldn't pull off an innocent ingenue act if my life depended on it, and right now, it did.

Joshua reached my side and glanced down at my bag. He pulled it off my shoulder, and I didn't object with that wannabe machete waving in my face. I leaned against the window, praying that Harlow had heard something of the exchange.

He dumped the contents of my purse onto the bed and thumbed through them. With a glance at my driver's license, he stopped short and stared at me again. "Emerald O'Brien, eh? So you're one of the pretty ladies who found my daughter, so cold and pale and dead."

His eyes shifted from gray to blue, and the temperature in the room dropped a good ten degrees. My blood froze into a river of ice as the hairs on my arms began to stand at attention. Something was very wrong. Shivering, I tried to edge toward the nightstand where I'd left the hatchet.

Joshua was quicker than I could hope to be. He leaped between me and the hatchet, shaking his finger at me as if he were scolding a child. "Don't even think of it. You don't need that nasty old hatchet; not where you're going." He picked up the file I'd been leafing through. "Why are you nosing around in my business?" He tossed the documents back in his suitcase.

I debated whether to speak, and decided it might buy me some time. "Susan told me her husband killed her. She asked for my help. I just didn't realize it was you and not Walter."

He jerked his head up. "What are you talking about?"

"Her ghost. She came to me the night after she died and told me she'd been murdered and asked me to prove it, since everyone thought she took an overdose. I assumed that Walter had killed her. I was wrong."

"You're asking me to believe that Susan's ghost appeared in your house and asked you to help her? You're crazier than I am. Those quacks at the hospital should have a go at you. They'd have a real field day." He held up the knife as he circled me warily, smiling—a lion gauging the fight left in his quarry.

I turned with him, never letting him leave my line of sight. "You were married to her. You were going to meet her on the day she died. Tell me about it."

Without warning, he lunged, grabbing my arm. Startled, I shouted as he threw me onto the bed. I gasped as I hit the mattress and, before I could twist away, he straddled my chest, gently waving the knife in my face. "I bet you were one of Walter's pretty Pollys. One of his conquests? I have to tell you, he'd be an extremely bad choice for a husband." He leaned closer and whispered, "Did you know that he's never been faithful a day in his life? Even when he first married Susan, he was still playing the field."

I shifted, trying to avoid the blade that hovered so close to my throat. I had to be prepared, ready to take advantage of any mistake he might make. Forcing myself to remain calm, I said, "Walter wasn't my lover. And I know he was unfaithful. Susan knew about it. That's why she cut him out of her will and assigned all her money to her daughter. She stayed with him too long. She made a lot of mistakes."

Joshua brought the knife down hard, and I screamed as it whistled past my ear and plunged into the mattress. Before I realized what he was doing, he had both my wrists over my head, pinning me to the bed by brute force. He leaned close and nuzzled my neck, his nose and lips cold against my skin. I thrashed, trying to avoid his touch. His energy enveloped me, a dangerous combination of leather and blades and glistening insanity.

"Oh, I wouldn't call it a mistake, not from where I'm sitting. Diana's money goes to me. Since we didn't want questions, we made it simple. She left a will, naming me as her beneficiary. I encouraged her to make nice to Mama, you know, told her it wasn't fair to lose her rightful inheritance just because Mama and Daddy never told her she had a different father, just because they bounced her from school to school like a dodge ball. Susan and Walt played right into my hands."

Cold sweat dripped from every pore in my body. "How'd you get Diana to make a will without her being suspicious?"

"Nothing to it. We made our wills at the same time, and like a good father and daughter should, named each other as beneficiary. My sweet little idiot was what you might call gullible. Too bad she was so stupid; she might still be alive. But then again, I'm not the paternal type. Now, to matters at hand." He leaned close and forced his lips over mine.

Panicking, I fought, trying to throw him off. He reared back and, crazy strong, his smile never wavering, back-handed me. Startled by the force of his blow, the slash along my cheek burned where his rings grazed the flesh, leaving a trickle of blood to wend its way down toward my ear.

He gave me a smug grin. "You know, you're not my type, but I find myself strangely attracted to you. I'm going to enjoy this." He laughed and ground his pelvis against mine. Even through the layers of clothing, I could tell he was aroused. "Oh, yes, you're the icing on the cake. I'm a very rich man, thanks to my dearest Diana, and I got my revenge on both Susan and Walter after all these years, and now I get a bit of fun on the side."

Abruptly, he grabbed the knife as he stood, dragging me along with him. He whipped me around and slammed me up against one of the dressers, knocking the wind out of me. My stomach felt like it had been hit with a sledge-hammer as I doubled over the chest of drawers.

Joshua slashed the back of my parka and said, "Take off that coat."

I struggled to keep calm as I slowly unzipped my parka and tossed it on the bed. I could tell that he'd reached the end of his interest in talking. I had to do something. I whirled, heading for the door. Joshua sprang over the footboard. I tried to push him away, but he was terribly quick. In one swift move, he grabbed me by the throat and held the knife to my jugular.

"Planning on going somewhere, my pretty beryl? I don't think so. I think the only place you're headed is to the basement with me." He paused for a moment and thrust his nose against my neck. I could feel his breath on my skin. "You smell delicious. Did you know that? Take it nice and slow. We're going to move this party to your new home. But I'm afraid it's also going to be your *last* home."

Twenty-four

HE SHIFTED SO his arm was around my waist and the knife pointed at my back. I could feel the tip pressing through the weave of my sweater. Trickles of sweat dripped down my face, cold and clammy. As we neared the stairs, I moaned and started to sink to the floor.

"What the fuck are you doing? Get up, bitch."

"My knee, I hurt my knee," I stammered, trying to buy time. Anything to buy a few more minutes. "I tore it up last week, and it hurts to walk."

He yanked me up by the elbow. "You'll jolly well do anything I tell you to if you don't want me to make this any worse than it has to be." He leaned close to my ear. "Believe me when I tell you that I know how to make you hurt. Pain is the butter on my bread, and when we're down in the basement, no one will hear you scream. Now get down those stairs!" He shoved me toward the stairwell. If I wanted to escape, it had to be now. So what if I broke my neck? I'd be dead anyway, if I waited much longer.

I dove for the stairwell and went rolling down to the landing, covering my head as I fell. A loud curse echoed above me. I tried to shut out his voice, tried to shut out the blinding pain that arced through my knee into the rest of my body as I forced myself to my feet. One more flight to go.

He was on my heels as I rounded the landing. No more time, no more choices—either I let him kill me, or I embraced the fire. I coiled back for the spring and, screaming as loudly as I could, took the flight of stairs in one leap. As I hit the bottom, the abrupt stop jarred me to the bone, but I couldn't let the pain stop me. Still screaming, I hurled myself back into the hallway. As I cleared the door, I could feel a breeze as Joshua slashed at the air behind me, the tip of his knife almost catching my blouse.

How long could I keep this up? Not long enough to make it to my car, not down those icy steps. Without a clear plan, thinking only to get away, I raced into the dining room and grabbed one of the candelabras, turning to throw it at him as hard as I could. The brass holder bounced off his arm and he dropped the knife, swearing as he stopped to recover it. Time enough to get to the kitchen, where there should be something I could use as a weapon. There, on the counter, the knife block! I grabbed the biggest, meanest knife I could find with one hand, and a cleaver with the other.

He entered the room, wary but with blade raised. If he'd had a gun, he would have used it by now, so the worst he could do was stab me, choke me, or beat me to death. I raised my weapons and we stood, frozen, waiting. A trickle of blood flowed down my nose to puddle on my lip. I gasped, trying to catch my breath. The adrenaline rush down the stairs had kept me going, but now I could feel fear working at me, slowing me down.

Joshua cocked an eyebrow, and a slow smile spread across his face. "I'm having fun, babe. How about you? You're hot, even if you are crazy." His words were smooth; his pupils dilated, and I knew that he was psycho enough to risk that I might stab him.

"Stay away. I'm not going to let you hurt me." I tried to bolster my courage.

Joshua snorted. "I've already hurt you, and I'm going to hurt you a lot more." He leaped forward. I stumbled back against the range, dropping the cleaver as I screamed. He laughed. "Good one, girl. Good one. Okay, it's time to get down to business. I can make this easy or I can make this hard. Your choice. Put down the knife."

He stood between me and the door. What to do? Try to lunge, try to stab him? In the core of my heart, I knew that I couldn't do it—he was stronger than me, he was psychotic, he was winning this battle, and I would go down in flames. Flames . . . that was it! I held him at bay with the butcher knife while, with my other hand, I grabbed the pile of rags on the counter and dumped them on one of the burners. Then one quick twist to the knob and a quick prayer that the range still worked. *Light, please light, please don't be one of those stoves that requires a match.*

Whoosh . . . the rags flared to life, burning with a thick black smoke. They must have had some kind of solvent on them, because they raged a brilliant orange against the dim shadows of the kitchen. Coughing, I used the tip of the knife to catch one of the flaming rags and tossed it at Joshua. He jumped out of the way, giving me the opening I needed to barrel past him. I burst through the door and onto the precarious balcony.

A low roar came from the kitchen; the flames had touched off the pile of garbage. Smoke billowed out the door, and I could see through the grimy window that the room was ablaze. Joshua stumbled out, wiping his eyes. I'd managed to singe his hair with my impromptu fireball. I held the knife in front of me, but my hands were shaking.

"You've done it now, girl. Set the place to crackling. Good riddance, anyway. Saves me the trouble of destroying the evidence. Put down the knife, and I promise I'll make this easy." His eyes were compelling, glittering as they mirrored the snow and icicles hanging around us.

I thought I could hear sirens in the distance. I had to distract him. "Before I do, answer me one thing."

"What?" His voice was flat now, and he seemed to have sunk into some kind of trance. I recognized the look from long ago, from one awful night when I'd been attacked during college—it was the look of a predator who felt nothing for his prey. I'd gotten away then . . . would I be as lucky this time?

"Why did you come back to Chiqetaw? You hated them all, you killed Diana and her mother and set up Walter to take the fall. Why come back here?" My stomach churned.

Joshua shifted and shrugged. "To watch Walter crumble. Why else? Can't paint a masterpiece and not want to look at it. And it would have all gone together just right if you hadn't been so damned nosy. That knife was the crowning jewel in my plan, and it was so easy to plant in his house before I showed up at the memorial." He gave me a slow smile. "I just wish I'd thought to have one last go with Susan while she was out cold. She always did have a fine ass."

My stomach roiled. "What kind of pervert are you?"

He ran his blade over one thumb, and I saw a drop of blood weal up before he answered me softly. "The best kind—successful." With a shift, he readied himself to lunge. I had only one hope, only one chance. Smoke raged out of the door in a thick cloud and if he didn't kill me, the fire would. I swallowed and dropped my knife.

"Good girl. We have to finish this quicker than I like. Those sirens are getting close, and I have to disappear." Joshua held up the dagger and I steeled myself, waiting, counting fractions of seconds. As he swung the blade toward my chest, I threw myself against the side of the burning building.

With nothing for the blade to encounter, the motion unbalanced him, and he lurched forward. At that moment I felt a familiar presence and looked up to see Susan standing beside me. Joshua scrabbled to his feet, incredulous. As she stepped forward, he screamed. "You're dead—I killed you. You can't be here!"

She ignored his cries and glided toward him. He raised his knife to fend her off, but the blade sliced through her like smoke. With one last shout, he backed up against the railing, and a rending sound split the air as the rotten wood splintered. For a brief second our eyes locked and

I could see the whirl of chaos that raged within him, the flare of surprise.

Susan stepped aside and I watched as he teetered on the edge, flailing for support. The railing cracked, and Joshua went hurtling over the edge. He screamed all the way down, and I heard a nasty thud. I gathered up my courage and cautiously crept to the edge. Joshua Addison lay crumpled on the glittering snow below.

I took a deep breath as Susan frantically pointed to the kitchen, then vanished. I wasn't out of danger yet—the fire had spread and was tonguing the doorway leading to my precarious perch. The jump to the ground below was too far; I'd never make it without major damage. It was either chance the porch steps or become a crispy critter. Having just survived a madman's attack, I wasn't ready to lose my life as the treat on the end of a marshmallow stick. I edged my way over to the steps, laid on my stomach, and, feet first, began to inch my way down. Testing the wood with my toes for strength, I thought though it felt soggy, it might support me. As I held onto the rungs for extra balance, I slithered onto the steps.

The sirens were shrieking now. It sounded like they were in the front yard and I began to scream for help, my voice raw from the smoke and overuse. I was about a third of the way down the stairs when an explosion rattled the kitchen. A fireball raced out of the door and billowed into the air, hovering over the backyard. The flames must have reached the discarded bottles of liquor. I grabbed hold of the step above me and hid my face as the staircase first rocked, then began to crumble away.

I was hanging only by my fingertips, dangling in mid-air, unable to see what was down below. More iron spikes? Gardens covered with snow?

The fire spread to the stilts supporting the back porch; it was about to go down and take me with it. As I clung to my shaking world, someone began yelling at me from below. "Emerald! Emerald! Let go! We'll catch you!"

I couldn't see who was there, but I could place the voice—Joe Files, captain of the Medic Rescue Unit. Time

had run out. I had to have faith, to trust. I took a deep
breath and let myself fall.

THE POLICE FINISHED taking my statement as
the medics worked me up to go to the hospital. The fire
crews were busy extinguishing the flames. It looked as
though they might save most of the house—a surprise,
since I'd expected the mansion to go up like a tinderbox.
The heavy snowfalls had saturated the roof and some of
the walls with moisture, so most of the wood was safe
except for the kitchen, which had been packed with garbage.

The cops puzzled over my accounts of Susan's ghost,
but they recovered Joshua's suitcases. I only hoped there
would be enough evidence there to piece things together.
I pulled the letter and photograph out of my pocket,
enough in themselves to tell part of the tale. Murray was
on the scene; she would see to it that they paid attention
to what I told them.

"How did you find me?"

She patted me on the shoulder as Joe held an oxygen
mask up to my face. "Harlow called the station, and the
station called me. By the time we got here, a neighbor
had seen the smoke and already notified the fire department. You were near enough to the swimming pool that
you could have broken your neck if you had dropped
without the boys below to catch you."

I leaned back and found myself snuggling against Joe.
I started to pull away but then thought, what the hell, and
rested my head on his shoulder. He felt strong—safe and
secure. Whatever happened, I would never forget that he
saved my life. When the paramedics insisted on taking me
to the hospital, I didn't put up a fuss. Every place on my
body hurt, and I was ready for a good rest.

Andrew was waiting at the hospital, and Joe backed
away when he saw him. I felt a momentary stab of guilt
but then pushed it aside. Andrew kissed me on the forehead and held my hand as they wheeled me into the ER.

"Didn't we do this with Harlow last week? What is this? Some new chick trend?"

I laughed and he squeezed my hand, and then the nurse chased him out. When they cut away my soot-stained skirt, the doctor shook his head. "You have a grudge against that knee of yours? I'm afraid this is a little more serious than a bruise. I can already tell that you've probably got a fracture in your leg, and you'll be lucky if you didn't shatter your kneecap. You're going to be in a cast for a month or two. What do you have to say to that?"

I gave him a big smile. "It sounds absolutely wonderful."

Twenty-five

✢

HOURS LATER, ANDREW carried me up the
porch steps and into the house while Murray brought
in my crutches. The nurse at the hospital had given me a
bath since I was covered with soot, so at least I felt clean,
but the gown was atrocious, and I longed for a little lipstick.

Andrew set me in the recliner and then parked himself
on the sofa. "That fire guy? Files? He said he'd come
over tomorrow and help me build a nonskid ramp for you
so you can get in and out of the house. Those stairs are
far too icy and dangerous for crutches. That way you can
get down to your shop."

Joe? Joe and Andrew were going to build a ramp together? That should prove interesting. "Thank you, both."
I gave him a bright smile and then flashed a look of panic
at Murray, who stifled a laugh.

She peeked out the window. "Harlow and James are
here." James had been at the hospital to pick up Harl when
the ambulance brought me in. The two insisted on following us back to my house. Andrew went to help James
carry Harlow's chair up the stairs, and then they wheeled
her into the living room.

Harlow shook her head. "Woman, you take the cake. Burning down a house? Nailing a psycho? What's next?"

Murray's cell phone went off, and she stepped into the kitchen to answer it. When she returned, she settled herself in the rocker. "Looks like we have what we'll need to prove that Joshua was behind both deaths, at least circumstantially. Valium, credit card receipts from a gas station here in town that match up with the date of Susan's death, a key to the Mitchell house—probably a copy of Susan's. We also found his car. He told police in Seattle that it had been stolen, but we found it out in back of the Addison place in the garage. There's a bloody handprint on the driver's side—the forensics guys are checking, but I'll bet you anything it turns out to be Diana's blood."

"And Walter?" I prayed that Walt wasn't guilty of molesting Diana. After experiencing the sadistic side of Joshua, I didn't think I could handle another pervert.

"Walter's off the hook. We have your statement that Joshua confessed to planting the knife in his house, and this morning detectives found a trucker who remembers seeing Walter and his car in the parking lot on Thursday. Guy drives a regular route and always stops at the Restover Truck Stop on his way in and out of town. There aren't too many black Porsches around Chiqetaw, so it stuck in his mind. We're still going over the suitcases, but it's my guess that Susan was telling the truth. Her husband killed her. Her ex-husband. And then he killed Diana."

Harlow shook her head, a look of wonder crossing her face. "I'll be damned." She looked over at me, wincing gingerly as she turned. "Do you realize you just proved a man's innocence?"

I shivered. I might have proved Walter's innocence, but I couldn't stop thinking of how Joshua plunged to his death. Images of those final moments darted through my thoughts with blinding clarity—the flash of his knife, the crackle of flames, the stairway groaning as it gave way. His death was the only key to my survival. Susan had saved me by frightening him over the edge. I was glad he died—if he'd been caught alive, I'd always be afraid that he'd escape and come back to finish what he'd started.

Harlow broke into my thoughts. "What was Walt's alibi, anyway?"

Murray answered her. "He got a call Wednesday night from a man claiming to have proof that one of Walt's affairs had been with a minor. That alone could destroy his reputation. The guy said he would sell the proof to the newspapers unless Walt came up with some money. Walter panicked and agreed to meet him. He waited alone at the Restover for hours Thursday morning—during which time, Joshua murdered Diana. Then Joshua planted the knife in Walter's house on Saturday night while everybody was at the memorial and showed up to make his accusations."

I closed my eyes, and Joshua's piercing gaze once again shattered my composure. I began to shake. "What about Diana's letter to the cops accusing Walter of molesting her?" For some reason, that thought bothered me more than almost anything else in this whole damned mess.

Murray knelt in front of me and took my hands. She brushed the hair back from my face, and as I looked into her eyes, I knew that I would be calling on her friendship more than ever during the coming weeks as I dealt with the aftermath. "Joshua, again. We found the original. Diana thought Walter killed her mother—she wrote a letter to the cops, asking them to look into it. Joshua probably panicked, thinking it would stir up trouble. I suppose that's when he decided to kill her and frame Walter by forging the letter about the abuse," she said. "We combed through her diaries. There's no indication Walter ever laid a hand on the girl."

"Joshua was a cruel man and he enjoyed the pain he inflicted on others." I hung my head and cleared my throat, still in shock. I was grateful for the numbness. I wasn't ready to face what had happened to me.

Andrew rested his hand on my shoulder lightly, as if he were afraid he might startle me. "What about Susan? Why on earth did she agree to see him?"

Murray shrugged. "Blackmail, or at least that's what he used to gain entrance. We're still trying to sort everything out. Mrs. Addison says there's an aunt on his father's side who always favored Joshua. Maybe he kept contact with her to find out what was going on in the family. We do know that he was released from the institution thanks to a reduction in operating funds. Since they thought he could function on his own, they let him out."

I didn't say anything, but I could see exactly what had happened; it played out as clearly as if I were watching a show on TV. Joshua had come to visit Susan. They had a drink, and he spiked her wine with Valium. Eager to get the meeting over with, she hadn't suspected that he actually meant to kill her. After the drug took effect, he gave her a hefty shot of insulin.

Nobody was there to see him come and go. He waited until she slipped into a seizure, and then left, knowing it would be hours before the maid came home. Susan would have ensured their privacy, not wanting a scene with Walter. Joshua went back to Seattle, and a week later he killed Diana. The whole plan had been so coldhearted, so methodical and brilliant, that it made me sick. Yes, evil existed, both in this world and in the spirit world, and I had come face-to-face with it on both levels, battled it, and survived. But I would never be the same.

The doorbell rang, and Andrew went to answer. He returned, a cautionary look on his face. Following behind him, Walter Mitchell strode into my living room with a dozen red roses. He came over and gently placed them in my lap.

"Emerald O'Brien . . . our paths seem meant to cross." He knelt beside me, ignoring everybody else. "I can never apologize enough for what my stepbrother did to you. There's nothing I can say that probably hasn't already gone through your mind. I'm just grateful you're going to be okay. You proved my innocence. I'm in your debt." He stood and offered his hand. I'd thought he'd been imposing enough at the memorial. Now I felt completely dwarfed. I gingerly accepted his gesture. He squeezed a little too tightly, and I pulled away.

"Actually, I prefer to think that I helped *Susan* find

some sort of peace." His eyes twinkled. I knew he heard my subtext. "How's your mother?"

He cocked one eyebrow. "My mother is feeling much better, now that I'm out of jail. She wanted me to apologize to you. She's not a woman who says 'I'm sorry' easily, so please accept it as it is meant."

I nodded in silence, then curiosity got the better of me. "May I ask you something?"

"Of course. What is it?"

I glanced around the room. Everyone was waiting, poised to see what I'd say. I cleared my throat, feeling conspicuous. "Why doesn't your mother do something with that house and its contents? There are some lovely pieces of furniture in there, and I'd think she would want to preserve them."

Walter laughed. "Ever the shopkeeper, aren't you? I'll tell you why—the house belonged to Joshua. My stepfather willed the money to me, but he left the house and everything in it to Joshua on the stipulation that he not be told about it until Joshua asked about his own inheritance. When he heard I'd inherited the money, he took off. It was a game of power, if you will, between a stubborn man and his even more stubborn son."

The irony made my head spin. "So here was Joshua, angry at you because he thought you had inherited everything, when in reality he could have been a wealthy man if he'd swallowed his pride enough to ask."

"Yes, something like that. I followed my stepfather's wishes and kept quiet about it. Since Joshua is dead, the property automatically reverts to my mother and me. She wants to donate the china from it to your shop—you may sell it or keep it as you like. Consider it our way of saying thank you."

I gasped. There was thousands of dollars' worth of beautiful china in that house. Visions of table settings began to dance in my head.

"Please accept. We want you to have it."

Even though Walter was a rat, even though for a time I had really believed he was guilty, even though his mother was a fruitcake . . . I couldn't resist such a fortuitous gift. And besides' I'd earned it. "Thank you, I accept."

"Fine, I'll have it shipped over to you when we take inventory of the house and appraise what's there. It might be several months, but you have my word. And now, good-bye." He bobbed his head, even to Harlow, and Andrew showed him out.

"You realize you've just been bought off," Harlow said. "His way of asking you to keep quiet about his family's dirty laundry."

I gave her a smile. "It doesn't matter whether I say a word; the press will get wind of it by tomorrow, if they haven't already. And he really didn't kill Susan."

Harlow and James made their farewells. As they pulled out of the driveway, there was a squeal of laughter from the back door as Kip and Miranda raced into the room. They crowded around me, Kip chanting "Mommy! Mommy!" as Miranda dropped to the floor by my side and grabbed my hand.

"Cinnamon took us over to Ida's." Randa squeezed my fingers so tightly I thought she was going to bruise them.

"What happened? What's going on? Why are you in a cast?" Kip darted from one side of my chair to the other in a frenzy of motion. He grabbed me around the neck and planted a big kiss on my cheek.

As I stared at my children, it hit me just what I would have lost if Joshua had won. I could be sleeping forever in the basement of that old house. Shivering, I brushed my hand across my eyes, glad that I was sitting down. There had been too much death recently, I'd seen too many twisted sides to the soul—both in body and in spirit. I pulled Kip and Miranda close, smelling their hair, holding them safe.

"Mom? Mom, what's wrong?" Kip looked at me, worry creasing his forehead. I wanted to speak, to tell him how much I loved him, but I couldn't find the words. I buried my face in their hair and kissed the top of their heads. Overwhelmed, I cast a glance at Murray. She nodded, reading my expression, and motioned for them to come over to her. "How about if we decorate the tree so your mother has something pretty to look at? She's had a rough day."

They cheered as Andrew helped her carry in the blue spruce. I told Murray where to find the decorations, and she brought them out. They strung the lights first, then the sparkling garlands of beads, and after that the kids took over. As they chattered away, their moods lifted with each glimmering orb they hung on the tree. Andrew retreated to the kitchen and returned carrying a tray of hot cocoa and sugar cookies.

Murray poured the cocoa. By the time everyone held a cup, I had managed to get my emotions under control. I lifted my mug in salute. "I propose a toast. May all our spirits—and all the spirits—be joyful this Christmas." I nodded to Kip. "Turn on the lights, hon." As he plugged them in, the tree lit up in a shimmering rainbow of colors. The silver and gold globes reflected the dazzling array. I drew in a slow breath.

Randa ran over to kneel beside my chair, her head resting on my lap. "Thank you, thank you, Mom. It's so pretty."

Murray rested her hands on Kip's shoulders as he stared up at the glittering tree. "This is prettier than any tree we ever had," he said, his whisper hushed and reverent.

He was right. The tree *was* the prettiest one we ever had. Andrew and Murray excused themselves to make dinner, taking the kids with them. I leaned back in the chair, watching the lights twinkle. Samantha jumped into my lap, nesting in a circle before she curled up to purr. I thought about calling Randa in to tell her that she was going to Space Camp, but decided to put it off until after dinner. She would be okay not knowing for another thirty minutes, and I needed the time to sort out the whirlwind of feelings racing through my heart.

Snow was falling again, illuminated by the soft glow of the streetlights. I leaned back in the recliner, clinging to the peace that had descended on the house, when I got the sensation that I was being watched. A glance around the room found Susan peeking out from behind the Christmas tree. Behind her stood the pale shade of another woman. It was Diana, with the shyest of smiles.

Susan's eyes sparkled, reflecting the lights. We looked at one another—I in my world and she in her shadowy realm—and a tremendous wave of relief washed over me. She would find her peace, and so would her daughter, and I was responsible for helping light their way. Susan held up her hand and they faded from sight.

Just then, Miranda came racing in from the kitchen. "Mom, this was on the kitchen table—it's got your name on it." She handed me a gift-wrapped package. I frowned, wondering who it was from as I unwrapped it. The paper fell away to reveal a thick volume—a copy of Susan's last novel. I opened the volume. Blinking back tears, I stared at the title page. In bold, looping letters, it read:

To Emerald O'Brien,
a woman who sparkles brighter than jewels,
Yours in eternal gratitude,
Susan Mitchell.

Mystic Moon Protection Charm

※

6-inch circle of purple satin or felt
1 yard of green satin ribbon
2 drops of lavender essential oil
½ cup of dried rose petals
½ teaspoon of each (dried):
    Sage
    Lavender
    Black peppercorns
    Spearmint

If edges of material are ragged, you might want to hem them using a very small seam allowance. Mix the dried herbs and rose petals; mound in the center of the satin or felt. Add the drops of lavender oil on top of the herbs. Bring the sides of the satin or felt together to enclose the herbs; then wind the ribbon around the neck of the sachet nine times while you focus on the energy of protection surrounding your home or car (depending on where you want to keep the charm). Tie the ribbon together with three firm knots and keep in your bedroom or your car. And always remember: Use your common sense. Lock your doors and keep an eye on your purse, because all the magic in the world won't do any good if you haven't taken practical measures first.